"No matter what happens between you and me, I think you should find the wife who's meant for you."

"Does that mean you prefer Micah over me?" Neziah asked.

"I didn't say that."

He felt his heart swell with…hope. "So I'm still in the running?"

She turned to him, and in the darkness he could feel her more than he could see her. "Now you sound like Micah. This is not a contest." She rose. "I should get home."

He jumped up. "I guess we need to talk about what happened with us. When we ended our courtship. Do you want to talk about that, Ellen?"

To his surprise, she gave a laugh. "I think we've had enough serious discussion for one night, don't you?"

He smiled and fell in step beside her. "Can I hold your hand?" he whispered.

She laughed again and gave him a little push. And then he felt her small, warm hand slip into his and he grinned all the way to her farmhouse steps.

Emma Miller lives quietly in her old farmhouse in rural Delaware. Fortunate enough to be born into a family of strong faith, she grew up on a dairy farm, surrounded by loving parents, siblings, grandparents, aunts, uncles and cousins. Emma was educated in local schools and once taught in an Amish schoolhouse. When she's not caring for her large family, reading and writing are her favorite pastimes.

Books by Emma Miller

Love Inspired

Lancaster Courtships

The Amish Bride

The Amish Matchmaker

A Match for Addy

Hannah's Daughters

Courting Ruth
Miriam's Heart
Anna's Gift
Leah's Choice
Redeeming Grace
Johanna's Bridegroom
Rebecca's Christmas Gift
Hannah's Courtship

Visit the Author Profile page at Harlequin.com for more titles.

The Amish Bride

Emma Miller

Recycling programs for this product may not exist in your area.

ISBN-13: 978-0-373-81859-4

The Amish Bride

This edition published by arrangement with Love Inspired Books.

www.Harlequin.com

Printed in U.S.A.

A friend loves at all times…
—*Proverbs* 17:17

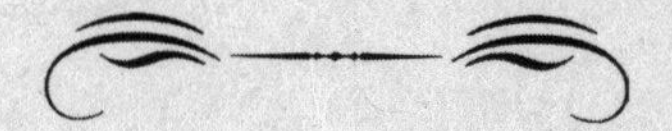

Chapter One

Lancaster County, Pennsylvania

It was half-past nine when Ellen Beachey halted her push scooter at the top of the steep driveway that ran from her parents' white farmhouse down to the public road. Normally, she would be at the craft shop by nine, but this had been one of her mother's bad days when her everyday tasks seemed a lot more difficult. Her *mam* was in her midseventies, so it wasn't surprising to Ellen that she was losing some of her vim and vigor. After milking the cow and feeding the chickens before breakfast, Ellen had remained after they'd eaten to tidy up the kitchen, finish a load of wash and pin the sheets on the line.

She didn't mind. She was devoted to her *mutter*, and it was a gorgeous day to hang laundry. There wasn't a cloud in the sky, the sticky heat of August had eased and there was a breeze, sweet with the aroma of ripening grapes and apples from the orchard. But with her *dat*'s arthritis acting up, and her *mam* not at her best, Ellen felt the full weight of responsibility for the shop and the household. The craft store was her family's main source of income, and it was up to her to see that it made a profit.

This had been a good week at Beachey's Craft Shop. School would soon be starting, and many English families were taking advantage of the last few days of summer vacation to visit Lancaster County. Ellen had seen a steady stream of tourists all week, and the old brass cash register had hardly stopped ringing. It meant good news for Lizzie Fisher, in particular. Her king-size *Center Diamond* quilt, meticulously stitched with red, blue and moss-green cotton, had finally sold for the full asking price. Lizzie had worked on the piece for more than a year, and she could certainly use the money. Ellen couldn't wait to tell her the good news. One of the best things about running the shop was being able to handle so many beautifully handcrafted Amish items every day and to provide a market for the Plain craftspeople who made them.

A flash of brilliant blue caught Ellen's attention, and she glimpsed an indigo bunting flash by before the small bird vanished into the hedgerow that divided her father's farmstead from that of their neighbors', the Shetlers. Seeing the indigo bunting, still in his full summer plumage, made her smile. All her life, she'd been fascinated by birds, and this particular species was much rarer than the blue grosbeak or the common bluebird. Ellen wondered if the indigo bunting had a mate and had built a nest in the hedgerow, or was just passing through in an early migration. She scrutinized the foliage, hoping to see the bird again, but it remained hidden in the leaves of a wild cherry tree. She could hear the bird's distinctive *chrrp*, but it didn't reappear.

And, Ellen reminded herself, the longer she stood there watching for the bird, the later she'd be for work. She needed to be on her way. She shifted her gaze to the steep driveway ahead of her.

Maybe this was the morning to be sensible and act like the adult she was. She could just walk her scooter to the bottom of the lane and then hop on once she reached the road.

But the temptation was too great. She scanned the pavement in both directions as far as she could see for traffic. Nothing. Not a vehicle in sight. Taking pleasure in each movement, Ellen stepped onto the scooter, gripped the handles and gave a strong push with her left foot. With a cry of delight, she flew down the hill, laughing with excitement, bonnet strings flying behind her.

Ellen waited until the last possible moment before squeezing the handbrakes and leaning hard to one side, whipping the scooter around the mailbox, onto the public road. A cloud of dust flew up behind her, and pebbles scattered as she hit the pavement. The scooter fishtailed and she continued to brake, bringing it to a stop.

One of these days, Ellen thought. *One of these days, you're going to come down that hill so fast that you can't stop and land smack-dab on top of the bishop's buggy.* But not today.

As she stepped off the scooter, her heart still pounded. Her knees were weak, and her prayer *kapp* was hanging off her head from a single bobby pin. She was definitely too old to be doing this. What would the community say if they saw John Beachey's spinster daughter, a fully baptized member of the church and long past her *rumspringa* years, sailing down her father's driveway on her lime-green push scooter? Although most Plain people were accepting of small eccentricities within the community, it would almost certainly be cause for a scandal. The deacon would be calling on her father out of concern for her mental, spiritual and physical health.

Chuckling at the thought, Ellen pinned up her *kapp* and shook the dust off her apron. She moved to the crown of the road and began to make her way toward the village of Honeysuckle. However, she'd no sooner rounded the first wooded bend when she saw a familiar gray-bearded figure sitting on the side of the road.

"Simeon!" she called, pushing the scooter faster. "*Vas is?* Are you all right?" Simeon Shetler, a widower and a member of her church district, lived next door with his two grown sons and two grandsons. Ellen had known him since she was a child.

"Hallo!" He waved one of his metal crutches. "*Jah*, I am fine." He gestured with the other crutch. "It's Butterscotch who's in trouble."

Ellen glanced at the far side of the road to see Simeon's pony nibbling grass fifty feet away. The pony was hitched to the two-wheeled cart that her one-legged neighbor used for transportation. "What happened?" she asked as she hurried to help Simeon to his feet. "Did you fall out of the cart?"

"*Nay*, I'm not so foolish as that. I may be getting old, but I'm not dotty-headed." They spoke, as most Amish did when they were among their own kind, in *Deitsch*, a dialect that the English called *Pennsylvania Dutch*. "But I will admit, seeing your pretty face coming down the road was a welcome sight."

"Have you been like this long?" she asked, taking no offense at his compliment, which might have seemed out of place coming from most Amish men. Simeon was known as something of a flirt, and he always had a pleasant word for the women, young or old. But he was a kind man, a devout member of the community and would never cross any lines of propriety.

"Long enough, I can tell you. It took me ten minutes to climb back out of that ditch."

As a young man, Simeon had had a leg amputated just below the knee. Although he had a prosthetic leg and had gone to physical therapy to learn how to walk with it, he never wore it. For as long as Ellen could remember, the molded plastic and titanium prosthetic had hung on a peg on his kitchen wall. Usually, Simeon made out fine with his crutches, which extended from his forearms to the ground, but when he fell, he wasn't able to get back on his feet without a steady object like a fence post, or the aid of a friendly hand.

Simeon grinned. "Some fool *Englisher* threw a bag of trash from one of those *food-fast* places into the ditch. I thought I could pick it up if I got down out of the cart. I would have been able to, but I slipped in the grass, fell and slid into the ditch. And then by the time I crawled back out, that beast—" he shook his crutch again at the grazing pony "—trotted away." He chuckled and shrugged. "So, as you can see, I was stuck here until a Good Samaritan came along to rescue me."

"Are you sure you're all right?" she asked, looking him over.

"I'm fine. Catch the pony before he takes off for town," Simeon urged. "Then we need to have a talk, you and me. I think maybe it was God's plan this happened this morning. I have something important to discuss with you."

"With me?" Ellen looked at him quizzically. Simeon was an elder in their church, but she couldn't think of anything that she'd done wrong that would cause concern. And if she *was* in trouble for some transgression, it should have been the deacon who'd come to speak to her and her parents to remind her of her duties to the faith community.

Unless…

Was it possible that Simeon or one of his sons had recently seen her antics on the push scooter? She didn't think so. She was careful about when and where she gave in to her weakness for thrilling downhill rides. And Bishop Harvey had approved the bright color of her push scooter, once she'd explained that she'd gotten it secondhand as a trade for a wooden baby cradle.

The unusually bright, lime-green push scooter was an expensive one from a respected manufacturer in Intercourse. She could have had it repainted, but that would cost money and time, even if she did it herself. Bishop Harvey was a wise leader and a practical man. He understood that, with Ellen's father owning only one horse, she needed a dependable way to get back and forth to the craft shop without leaving her parents stranded. And if the fluorescent color on the push scooter was brighter than what was customarily acceptable, the safety factor made up for the fancy paint.

"See, there he goes." Simeon pointed as the pony moved forward, taking the cart with him. "Headed for Honeysuckle, trying to make a bigger fool of me than I already am. We'll be lucky if you catch him."

"Oh, I'll catch him, all right." Ellen reached for the lunch box tied securely in her scooter basket on the steering column. She unfastened it, removed a red apple and walked down the road toward the pony. "Look what I have!" she called. "Come here, boy."

Butterscotch raised his head and peered at her from under a thick forelock. His ears went up and then twitched.

Ellen whistled softly. "Nice pony."

He pawed the dirt with one small hoof, took a few steps and the cart rolled forward, away from her.

"Easy," Ellen coaxed. "Look what I have." She held up the apple. "Whoa, easy, now."

The pony wrinkled his nose and snorted, side-stepping in the harness, making the cart shift one way and then the other. Ellen walked around in front of him and took a bite out of the apple before she offered it again. Butterscotch sniffed the air and stared at the apple.

"*Goot* boy," she crooned, knowing he was anything but a good boy.

The palomino was a legend in the neighborhood. For all his beauty, he was not the obedient pony a man like Simeon needed. This was not the first time Butterscotch had left his owner stranded. And Butterscotch didn't stay put in his pasture, either. He was a master of escape: opening locked gates, squeezing through gaps in fences and jumping ditches to wander off into someone's orchard or garden to feast on forbidden fruit. He'd been known to nip and kick at other horses, and more than once he'd run away while hitched, overturning the cart. Ellen couldn't imagine why the Shetlers kept him. He certainly wasn't safe for Simeon's grandsons to ride or drive. A clever pony like him was a handful for anyone to manage, let alone a one-legged man in his sixties.

Cautiously, Ellen took a few steps closer to the pony. Butterscotch tossed his head and moved six feet farther down the road. "So that's the way it will be," she said. The sound of a vehicle alerted her to an approaching car. The driver, coming from the direction of Honeysuckle, slowed. The pony stood and watched as the sedan passed. He wasn't traffic shy, which was the one good thing that Ellen could say about him.

When the car had disappeared behind her, Ellen took another bite of the apple, turned her back on Butterscotch and retraced her steps toward Simeon. She heard the creak of the harness and the rattle of wheels behind her, but she kept walking. She kept going until she was almost even with Simeon, then stopped and waited. It wasn't long before she felt the nudge of a soft nose on her arm. Without making eye contact, she held out the remainder of the apple. Butterscotch sunk his teeth into the piece of fruit, sending rivulets of juice dripping down Ellen's arm. Swiftly, she reached back and took hold of the pony's bridle.

"Gotcha," she murmured in triumph.

Once Simeon was safely on the seat of the cart, reins in hand, with the cart turned toward Honeysuckle again, he waved to her scooter. "Why don't you put that in the back? Ride with me. We can talk on the way."

Curious and a little apprehensive, Ellen lifted her scooter into the back. He offered his hand. She put a foot into the iron bracket and stepped up into the cart. "Have I done something wrong?" she asked.

She couldn't imagine what. She hadn't been

roller skating at the local rink in months, and she took care to always dress modestly in public, even if she did wear a safety helmet when she used her scooter in high-traffic areas.

"Of course not." Simeon shook the reins. "Walk on." Butterscotch moved forward and the cart rolled along. "You're an excellent example for our younger girls, Ellen," he said, turning to favor her with a smile. "You're devout and hardworking."

Now he *really* had her attention. The familiar sound of horse's hooves alerted her to a horse and buggy coming up behind them. Ellen glanced over her shoulder; the driver was Joseph Lapp. She and Simeon waved as Joseph swung around, passing the pony cart. He waved back and quickly moved on ahead of them.

"Wonder if we'll start tongues clucking, riding together," Simeon remarked.

Ellen looked at him, hoping he was joking. Simeon wasn't going to ask if he could come courting, was he? It seemed like once a month he was asking *someone* permission to court—a matter that kept the women of the community, from age eighteen to eighty, chuckling. But the twinkle in his faded blue eyes told her that he was teasing, and she relaxed a little.

"I want to discuss with you a problem that's been worrying me in my household." He tugged at his full gray beard thoughtfully. "As you know, ours is a bachelor house—one grandfather, two grown sons and two small boys. And we're sorely in need of a woman's hand. Oh, we cook and clean and try to keep things in order, but everyone knows a good woman is the heart of any home."

Unconsciously, she clasped her hands together and tried to think of what she would say if he asked to walk out with her. A few months ago, he'd asked her twenty-nine-year-old widowed friend, Ruthie.

"You're what, Ellen? Two and thirty?"

"Thirty-three," she said softly.

"*Jah*, thirty-three. Almost three years younger than my Neziah." He fixed her with a level gaze. "You should have married long ago, girl. You should be a mother with a home of your own."

"My parents..." she mumbled. "They've needed help, and—"

"Your devotion to your mother and father is admirable," he interrupted. "But in time, they'll both be gathered to the Lord, and you'll be left alone. And if you wait too long, you'll have no children to care for you in your old age."

Her mouth went dry. What Simeon was saying was true. A truth she tried not to think about. It wasn't that she hadn't once dreamed of having a husband and children, simply that the time had never been right and the right man had never asked her. She'd had her courting days once, but her father had gotten ill and then there was the fire…and the years had simply gotten away from her. She believed that God had a plan for her, but her life seemed whole and happy as it was. If she never married, would it be such a tragedy?

"I've long prayed over my own sons' dilemma," Simeon confided as he loosened the reins and flicked them over Butterscotch's back to urge him on faster. "Neither one is married now, and both would be the happier if they were. So I've prayed and waited for an answer, and it seems to me that the Lord has made clear to me what must be done."

Ellen turned to him. "He has?"

Simeon turned the full force of his winning smile on her. "You should marry one of them." He didn't wait for her to respond. "It makes perfect sense. My land and your father's are side by side. Most of his is wooded with fine old hardwood, and we make our living by the lumber mill. I've known you since you were a babe in arms, and there's no young woman I'd more willingly welcome into our family."

She, who never was at a loss for words, was almost speechless. "I..." She stopped and started again. She couldn't help but stare at Simeon. "You think I should marry Neziah or Micah?"

"Not only think it, but am certain of it. I already told them both at breakfast this morning." He narrowed his gaze. "Now I expect you to be honest with me, Ellen. Do you have any objection to either of them for reason of character or religious faith?"

She shook her head as the images of handsome, young, blond Micah and serious, dark-haired Neziah rose in her mind's eye. "*Nay*, of course not. They're both men of solid faith, but—"

"Goot," he pronounced, "because I don't know which the Lord intends for you. I've told both of my sons that I expect each of them to pay court to you and make a match as soon as may be decently arranged. The choice between them will be yours, Ellen. Steady Neziah and his children or my rascally, young

Micah." He gazed out over the pony with a sly smile. "And I care not which one you take."

It was an hour later at the craft store when Ellen was finally able to share her morning adventure with Dinah Plank, the widow who helped in the shop and lived in the apartment upstairs. Dinah, a plump, five-foot-nothing whirlwind of gray-haired energy, was a dear friend, and Ellen valued her opinion.

"So, Simeon came right out and told you that you should marry one of his sons?" Dinah paused in rearranging the display of organic cotton baby clothing and looked at her intently through wire-framed eyeglasses. "Acting as his sons' go-between, is he?"

"So it seems." Ellen stood with an empty cardboard box under each arm. She had two orders to pack for mailing, and she wanted to get them ready for UPS.

"What did you tell him?" The older woman shook out a tiny white infant's cap and carefully brushed the wrinkles out of it. Light poured in through the nine-paned windows, laying patterns of sunlight across the wide-plank floor of the display room and bouncing off the whitewashed plaster walls.

"Nothing, really. I was so surprised, I didn't

know what to say." She put the mailing boxes on the counter and reached underneath for a couple of pieces of brown-paper wrapping. "I didn't want to hurt his feelings. They've been such *goot* neighbors, and of course, my *dat* and Simeon are fast friends."

"You think Simeon has already said something to your father?"

"I can't imagine he did." She lined the first cardboard box with two pieces of brown paper. "*Dat* would have certainly said something."

Dinah propped up a cloth Amish doll, sewn in the old-fashioned way, without facial features. The doll was dressed for Sunday services with a black bonnet and cape, long black stockings and conservative leather shoes. "Well, you're not averse to marrying, are you?"

"*Nay.* Of course not." She reached for the stack of patchwork-quilt-style placemats she was shipping. "I'm just waiting for the man God wants for me."

"And you'll know him how?" She rested one hand on her hip. "Will this man knock on your door?"

Ellen frowned and added another layer of

brown paper to the box before adding eight cloth napkins.

"My marriage to Mose was arranged by my uncle, and it worked out well for both of us." Dinah tilted her head to one side in a way she had about her when she was trying to convey some meaning that she didn't want to state outright. "We each had a few burrs that needed rubbing off by time and trial and error, but we started with respect and a common need. I wanted a home and marriage with a man of my faith, and Mose needed sons to help on his farm."

Ellen nodded. She'd heard this story more than once, how Dinah and Mose had married after only meeting twice, and how she'd left Ohio to come to Lancaster County with him. The marriage had lasted thirty-four years, and Dinah had given him four sons and three daughters. Most lived nearby, and any of her children would have welcomed Dinah into their home. But she liked her independence and chose to live alone here in the apartment in Honeysuckle, and earn a living helping with the craft shop.

"I was an orphan without land or dowry," Dinah continued, fiddling with the doll's black bonnet. "And few ever called me fair of face. But I was strong, and God had given me health and ambition. I knew that I could learn to love the man I married. Mose was no looker, either, but he owned fifty acres of rich ground and was a respected farrier. Together, with the help of neighbors, we built a house with our own hands and backs."

"And were you happy?"

Dinah smiled, a little sadly. "*Jah*, we *were* very happy together. Mose was an able provider and he worked hard. Respect became friendship and then partnership, and…somewhere along the way, we fell in love." She tapped the shelf with her hand. "So my point of this long story is that Mose didn't come knocking on my door. Our marriage was more or less arranged."

Ellen sighed and smoothed the denim blue napkins. "But it sounds so much like a business transaction—Simeon deciding that his sons need wives and then telling them who they should court. Me living next door, so I'm the nearest solution. If one of them wanted to walk out with me, why didn't he say so, instead of waiting for their father to make the suggestion?"

Ellen sank onto a three-legged wooden stool carved and painted with a pattern of intertwined hearts and vines. She glanced around the room, thinking as she always did, how much she loved this old building. It had started life nearly two hundred years earlier as a private home and had been in turn a tavern, a general store, a bakery and now Beachey's Craft Shop.

"Maybe you should have married when you had the chance."

"I wasn't ready," she said. "And you know there were other reasons, things we couldn't work out."

"With Neziah, you mean?" Dinah passed.

Ellen nodded. She was as shocked by Simeon's idea that she should consider Neziah again, as she was by the whole idea that he should tell her or his boys who they should marry.

"That was years ago, girl. You were hardly out of your teens, and as hardheaded as Neziah. Are you certain you're not looking for someone that you've dreamed up in your head, a make-believe man instead of a flesh-and-blood one?" The sleigh bells over the front door jingled, indicating a visitor.

Ellen rose.

Dinah waved her away. "I'll see to her. You finish up packaging those orders. Then you might put the kettle on. If it's pondering you need, there's nothing like a cup of tea to make the studying on it easier."

"Maybe," Ellen conceded.

Dinah shrugged. "One thing you can be glad of."

"What's that?"

"That old goat Simeon wasn't asking to court you himself." She rolled her eyes. "Thirty-odd years difference between you or not, he wouldn't be the first old man looking for a fine young wife."

"Dinah!" she admonished. "How could you say such a thing?"

Dinah chuckled. "I said it, but you can't tell me you weren't thinking it."

"I suppose Simeon *is* a good catch, though a little too old for me." Ellen glanced up, smiling mischievously. "Maybe *you're* the one who should think about courting one of the Shetler bachelors."

Dinah laughed as she walked away. "Maybe I should."

Chapter Two

That afternoon Ellen walked her scooter up the steep driveway to her house. "Start each day as you mean to go," her father always said. And today surely proved that wisdom. She hadn't reached the craft shop until past her usual hour that morning, and now she was late arriving home. She left the scooter in the shed in a place where the chickens wouldn't roost on it, and hurried toward the kitchen door.

Ellen had left chicken potpie for supper. On Tuesdays and Wednesdays, the days that she closed the store at five, she and her parents usually had their main meal together when she got home. It was after six now, though. She hoped they hadn't waited for her.

Ellen had been delayed because of a mix-up with the customer orders that Dinah had packed and mailed a week earlier. The reproduction spinning wheel that had been intended for Mrs. McIver in Maine had gone instead to Mrs. Chou in New Jersey. And the baby quilt in the log cabin pattern and an Amish baby doll Mrs. Chou had been expecting had gone to Mrs. McIver. Mrs. Chou had taken the mistake with good humor when Ellen had called her from the store's phone. Mrs. McIver hadn't been so understanding, but Ellen had been able to calm her by promising to have the spinning wheel shipped overnight as soon as she received it back from Mrs. Chou.

Dinah felt terrible about the mix-up; unfortunately, it wasn't the first time she'd made a mistake shipping an order. Dinah was a lovely woman, but other than her charming way with tourists who came into the shop, her shopkeeper's skills were not the best. After two years behind the counter, she still struggled running credit cards, the cash register continually gave her a fit and Ellen had given up trying to get her to make the bank deposits. But Dinah needed the income, and since the fire, it had been comforting to have someone living in the apartment upstairs. So, in spite of the disadvantages of having Dinah as an employee, Ellen and her father agreed to keep her as long as she was willing to work for them.

As Ellen climbed the back steps to her parents' house, voices drifted through the screen door, alerting her that they had visitors. And since they were speaking in Deitsch, they had to be Amish. *But who would be stopping by at suppertime?*

Ellen walked into the kitchen to find Simeon Shetler, his two sons and his two grandsons seated around the big table. The evening meal was about to be served.

Ellen covered her surprise with a smile. "Simeon. Micah. Neziah. How nice to see you." The table was set for eight, so clearly the Shetlers had been expected. Had her mother invited them for supper and forgotten to mention it? It was entirely possible; there were many things that slipped Mary Beachey's mind these days.

Of course, there was the distinct possibility that plans to have dinner together had been made *after* her conversation with Simeon this morning. Ellen's cheeks grew warm. Surely Micah and Neziah weren't here to—

The brothers got to their feet as Ellen entered the kitchen, and she saw that they were both wearing white shirts and black vests and trousers, their go-to-worship attire—which meant that the visit was a formal one. For them, not their father. Simeon wore his customary blue work shirt and blue denim trousers.

It appeared that the two younger Shetler men had come courting.

She opened her mouth to say something, anything, but nothing clever came to her, so she looked at her father. Surely there had been a misunderstanding or miscommunication with the Shetlers. Surely her father would have wanted to talk in private with Ellen about Simeon's proposition before inviting them all to sit down together to talk about it.

John Beachey met his daughter's gaze and nodded. He knew her all too well. He knew just what she was thinking. "*Jah*, Ellen. We've talked, Simeon and I."

"You have?" she managed.

"We have, and we're in agreement. It's time you were married, and who better than one of the fine sons of our good neighbor. A neighbor, who," he reminded pointedly, "helped us out so much when we had the fire."

The fire, Ellen thought. *That weighty debt: rarely mentioned but always remembered.*

How many years ago had it been now?

Seven or eight? The suspicious fire, probably caused by teenaged mischief makers, had started at the back of the store and quickly spread through the old kitchen and up through the ceiling into the second floor. Quick-thinking neighbors had smelled smoke and seen flames, and the valiant efforts of a local fire company had prevented the whole building from being a loss. But smoke and water had destroyed all of the contents of the shop, leaving them with no means of support and no money to rebuild. Simeon had showed up early the next day with a volunteer work force from the community to help. He'd provided cash from his own pocket for expenses, lumber from his mill and his sons' services to provide the skilled carpentry to restore the shop. Over the years, her father had been able to repay Simeon's interest-free loan, but they owed the Shetlers more than words could ever express.

"Sit, please." She waved a hand to the men and boys.

Having Simeon's sons standing there grinning at her was unnerving. Or at least, handsome, blond-haired Micah was grinning at her. Neziah, always the most serious of the three Shetler men, had the expression of one with a painful tooth, about to see the dentist. He nodded and settled solidly in his chair.

The room positively crackled with awkwardness, and Ellen wished she were anywhere but there. She wished she could run outside, jump on her push scooter and escape down the drive. Everyone was looking at her, seeming to be waiting for her to say something.

Neziah's son Joel, age five, came to her rescue. "Can we eat now, *Dat*? I'm hungry."

"*Jah*, I'm hungry, too," the four-year-old, Asa, echoed.

The boys did not look hungry, although boys always were, Ellen supposed. Joel, especially, appeared as if he'd just rolled away from a harvest table. His chubby face was as round as a donut under a mop of unruly butter-yellow hair, hair the same color as his uncle Micah's. Asa, with dark hair and a complexion like his father's, was tall for his age and sturdy. Someone had made an effort to subdue their ragged bowl cuts and scrub their hands and faces, but they retained the look of plump little banty roosters who'd just lost a barnyard squabble and were missing a few feathers. Still, the boys had changed the focus from her and the looming courtship question back to ground she was far steadier on—the evening meal.

"We waited supper for you," Ellen's mother explained. "Come, *Dochter*, sit here across from Micah and Neziah."

Ellen surveyed the table. There would be enough of a main dish for their company because she'd made the two potpies. She also saw that her mother had fried up a platter of crispy brown scrapple and brought out the remnants of a roasted turkey. "Let me open a jar of applesauce and some of those delicious beets you made this summer, *Mam*," she suggested. As she turned toward the cupboard, she took off her good apron, which she wore at the shop, and grabbed a black work apron from a peg on the wall. "I'll only be a moment," she said. "I'm sure the boys like applesauce." Tying the apron on, she retrieved the jar and carried it to the table.

"Do you have pie?" Joel called after her. "*Grossdaddi* promised we would have pie. He said you always got pie."

"And cake," Asa chimed in.

"Boys," Neziah chided. "Mind your manners."

"But *Grossdaddi* said," Joel insisted.

Ellen went to the stove and scooped biscuits

from a baking sheet and dropped them into a wooden bowl that had been passed down from a great-grandmother. They were still warm, so they must have just come from the oven.

Her mother rose to seek out a pint of chow-chow, and a quart of sweet pickles that they'd put up just a week ago. In no time, they were all seated, and Ellen's father bowed his head for the silent prayer.

When Ellen looked up once prayer was over, Micah met her gaze, grinning. He seemed to be enjoying the whole uncomfortable situation. But as she started to pass the platters and bowls of food, she found herself smiling, as well. Having friends at the table was always a blessing. She might not have expected to find the Shetlers here this evening, but here they were, and she'd make the best of it. So what if they were there to talk about a possible courtship between her and one of the Shetler men? No one was going to *make* her marry anyone.

Shared meals were one of the joys of a Plain life, and it was impossible not to enjoy Simeon and Micah's teasing banter. The children concentrated on devouring their supper, eating far more than Ellen would suppose small boys could consume. Unlike Micah, Neziah ate in silence, adding only an occasional *Jah* and a grunt or nod of agreement to the general conversation. Neziah had always been the quiet one, even as a child. How he could have such noisy and mischievous children, Ellen couldn't imagine.

Simeon launched into a lengthy joke about a lost English tourist who stopped to ask an Amish farmer for directions to Lancaster. The story had bounced around the community for several years, but Simeon had a way of making each tall tale his own, and Ellen didn't mind. At least when he was talking, she didn't have to think of something to say to either of her would-be *suitors*.

Joel looked up from his plate, waved his fork and asked, "Now can we have pie?"

"Rooich," Micah cautioned, raising a finger to his lips. *Quiet.* He then pointed his finger in warning to keep Asa from chiming in.

Ellen glanced at Neziah to see his reaction to his brother chastising his boys, but Neziah's mouth was full of potpie and he seemed to be paying no mind. It was his third helping. She was glad she'd made two large pies, because the first dish was empty and the second held only a single slice.

Neziah suddenly began to cough and Micah

slapped him on the back. Neziah reddened and turned away from the table. His brother handed him a glass of milk, and Neziah downed half of it before clearing his throat and wiping his mouth with a napkin. "Sorry," he gasped, turning back to the table. "Chicken bone."

Ellen blushed with embarrassment. "I'm sorry," she said hastily. She'd been so certain that she'd gotten all the bones out of the chicken before adding it to the other ingredients.

"I may be a dumb country pig farmer," Simeon said, delivering the punch line of his story, "but I'm not the one who's lost." He looked around, waiting for the reaction to his joke and wasn't disappointed.

Her *mam* and *dat* laughed loudly.

"Jah," her mother agreed. "He wasn't, was he? It was the fancy *Englisher* with the big car who was lost."

Simeon slapped both hands on the table and roared with delight. "Told him, didn't he?" Tears ran down his cheeks. "Lot of truth in that story, isn't there?"

Ellen's father nodded. "Lot of truth. Not many weeks pass that some tourist doesn't stop in the craft shop to ask how to find Lancaster. And I say, you're standing in it."

"Course he means the town," Ellen's *mam* clarified. "Lancaster County's one thing, the town is another."

"Town of Lancaster's got too many traffic lights and shopping centers for me." Simeon wiped his cheeks with his napkin. "But I do love to laugh at them *Englishers*."

Joel wiggled in his chair and whined. "I want my pie. *Grossdaddi*, you promised there'd be pie for dessert."

Ellen eyed the two little boys. Asa and Joel were unusually demanding for Amish children; some might even say they were spoiled. And, to her way of thinking, Joel's father allowed him perhaps too many sweets. He was a nice boy when he wasn't whining, but if he got any chubbier, he'd never be able to keep up with the other kids when they ran and played. If he were her child, he'd eat more apples and fewer sugary treats. But, as her *mam* liked to say, people without kids always had the most opinions on how to raise them.

"Enough, boys!" Neziah said, clearly embarrassed by their behavior. "You'll have to forgive my children. Living rough with us three men, they're lacking in table manners."

Micah chuckled.

Since he was still unmarried, he didn't have a beard. The dimple on his chin made him even more attractive when he laughed. Ellen couldn't imagine what he would want with her when half the girls in Lancaster County wished he'd ask to drive them home from a Sunday night singing.

"It's more than table manners, I'd say," Micah teased. "These boys are wild as rabbits and just as hard to herd when it comes time for bath or bed."

"Which is why they need a mother's hand," Simeon pronounced. "And why we came to ask for your daughter in marriage, John."

"To one of us," Micah added. "Your choice, Ellen." He chuckled again and punched his brother's shoulder playfully. "Although, if she has her pick, Neziah's starting this race a good furlong behind."

Ellen glanced at Micah. Self-pride wasn't an attribute prized by the Plain folk. Everyone knew that Micah was full of himself, but still, with his likeable manner, he seemed to be able to get away with it.

And to prove it, he winked at her and grinned. "Tell the bishop I said that, and he'll have me on the boards in front of the church asking for forgiveness for my brash talk."

"Micah! What will the John Beacheys think of you with your nonsense?" Simeon asked. "Be serious for once. Your brother is as good a candidate for marriage as you. And Ellen would be a good wife for him, as well." He shrugged. "Either way, we'll have a woman in the house to set it right and put my grandsons' feet on the narrow path."

Ellen frowned, not liking the sound of that. Did the Shetlers want her, or just some woman to wash, cook and look after the children? Maybe it was true that she was getting too old to be picky, but she wouldn't allow herself to be taken advantage of.

She glanced at the plate of food she'd barely touched. She couldn't believe they were all sitting there seriously talking about her marrying one of the Shetlers.

The kitchen felt unusually warm, even for a late-August evening, and Ellen ran a finger under the neckline of her dress to ease the tightness against her skin. What could she say? Her parents and the Shetlers were all looking expectantly at her again.

Folding his arms over his chest, Neziah spoke with slow deliberation. "You're telling

Ellen that she should choose between us, but I've not heard her say that she'll have either of us. This is your idea, *Vadder*. Maybe it's not to Ellen's liking."

"Not just *my* idea," Simeon corrected. "*Nay*. I say plainly that I believe it's God's plan. And John's in agreement with me. Think about it. I don't know why we didn't see it before. Here I sit with two unwed sons, one with motherless children he struggles to care for and the other sashaying back and forth across the county from one singing to another in a rigged-out buggy with red-and-blue flashing lights." His brow furrowed as he stared hard at Micah. "And don't mention *rumspringa*, because it's time you put that behind you and came into the church."

"Listen to your father." Ellen's *dat* nodded. "He's speaking truth, Micah. He wants what's best for you. He always has."

"Jah," Simeon said. "I've held my tongue far too long, waiting for the two of you to stop sitting on the fence and court some young woman. Neziah's mourned the boys' mother long enough, and Micah's near to being thought too flighty for any good family to want him. It's time."

Micah toyed with his fork. "I'm not yet

thirty, *Vadder*. It's not as if no girl would have me."

"I'll fetch the coffee and apple pie," Ellen offered. She began clearing away the plates while Simeon wagged a finger at Micah.

"You know I'm but speaking what's true. Deny it if you can. Neither of you have been putting your minds to finding a good wife. And you must marry. It's not decent that you don't. I've talked to you until I'm blue in the face, and I've prayed on it. What came to me was that we didn't have to look far to find the answer to at least one of our problems."

"Jah." Ellen's mother leaned forward on her elbows and pushed back her plate. "And you've worried about your sons no more than I've lost sleep over our girl. She should have been a wife years ago, should have filled our house with grandchildren. She's a good daughter, a blessing to us in our old age. But it's time she found a husband, and none better than one of your boys."

"I agree," Ellen's father said. "I've known Neziah and Micah since they were born. I could ask no more for her than she wed such a good man as either of them." He smiled and nodded his approval. "The pity is, we didn't think of this solution sooner."

"No solution if Ellen's not willing," Neziah pronounced. His serious gaze met hers and held it. "Are you in favor of this plan or are you just afraid to speak up and turn us out the door with our hats in hand?"

Everyone looked at her again, including the two children, and Ellen felt a familiar sinking feeling. What *did* she want? She didn't know. She stood in the center of the kitchen feeling foolish and clutching the pie like a drowning woman with a lifeline. "I… Well…"

"Is the thought of marrying one of us distasteful to you?" Neziah asked when she couldn't answer.

He had none of the showy looks of his brother. Neziah's face was too planed, his brow too pronounced, and his mouth too thin to be called handsome. Not that he was ugly; he wasn't that. But there was always something unnerving about his dark, penetrating gaze.

Neziah was only three years older than she was, but he looked closer to ten. Hints of gray were beginning to tint his walnut-brown hair. The sudden loss of his wife and mother in the same accident three years ago had struck him hard. Maybe it was the responsibility of being both father and mother to two young children that stamped him with an air of heaviness.

"We're all friends here," Neziah continued. "No one will think less of you if this isn't something you want to consider."

Micah relaxed in his chair. "I say we've thrown this at her too fast. I wouldn't blame her for balking." He met Ellen's gaze. "Give yourself a few days to think it over, Ellen. What do you say?"

"Jah," Ellen's mother urged, rising to take the pie from her hands. "Say you will think about it, daughter."

"You know your mother and I wouldn't even consider the idea if we thought it was wrong for you." Her father beamed, and Ellen's resistance melted.

What could be wrong with thinking it over? As Simeon and her *dat* had said, either of the Shetler brothers would make a respectable husband. She would be a wife, a woman with her own home to manage, possibly children. She took a deep breath, feeling as if she were about to take a plunge off the edge of a rock quarry into deep water far below. She actually felt a little lightheaded. "I will," she said. "I'll think on the whole idea, and I will pray about it. Surely, if it is the Lord's plan for me,

He'll ease my mind." She held up her finger. "But my agreement is to *think* on the whole idea. Nothing more."

Simeon smacked his hands together. "*Goot.* It is for the best. You will come to realize this. And whichever one you pick, I will consider you the daughter I never had."

Ellen turned toward Simeon, intent on making it clear to her neighbor that she hadn't agreed to walk out with either of his sons when the little boys kicked up a commotion.

"Me!" Asa and Joel both reached for the pie in the center of the table. "Me!" they cried in unison.

"Me first!" Joel insisted.

"*Nay!* Me!" Asa bellowed.

"I knew you'd see it our way, Ellen," Micah said above the voices of his nephews. He rose from his chair. "I was so sure you'd agree that I brought fishing poles. You always used to like fishing. Maybe you and me could wander down to the creek and see if we could catch a fish or two before dark."

Ellen looked at Micah, then the table of seated guests, flustered. "Go fishing? Now?"

"Oh, go on, Ellen," her father urged. "We can get our own pie and I'll help your mother clean up the dishes." He glanced at Micah.

"Smart thinking. Best strike while the iron is hot, boy. Get the jump on Neziah and put your claim in first."

Mischief gleamed in Micah's blue eyes. "It'll get you out of here." He motioned toward the back door. "Come on, Ellen. You know you want to. I'll even bait the hook for you."

She cut her eyes at him. "As if I need the help. If I remember correctly, it was me who taught you how to tickle trout."

"She did," Micah conceded to the others, then he returned his attention to her. "But I've learned a few things about fishing since then. You don't stand a chance of catching the first fish or the most."

"Don't I?" Ellen retorted. "Talk's cheap but it never put fish on the table." Still bantering with him, she took off her *kapp*, tied on her scarf and followed him out of the house.

Fifteen minutes later, Micah stepped out on a big willow that had fallen into the creek. The leaves had long since withered, but the trunk was strong. Barring a flood, the willow would provide a sturdy seat for fishermen for years. And the eddy in the curve of the bank was the best place to catch fish.

He turned and offered Ellen his hand.

"Don't worry," he said, "it's safe enough." He had both fishing poles in his free hand, while Ellen carried the can with the bait.

The rocky stream was wide, the current gentle but steady as the water snaked through a wooded hollow that divided his father's farm from her *dat*'s. When they were children, he, Neziah and Ellen had come here to fish often. Now, he sometimes brought his nephews, Joel and Asa, but Neziah didn't have the time. Sometimes the fishing was good, and sometimes he went home with nothing more than an easy heart, but it didn't matter. Micah thought there was often more of God's peace to be found here in the quiet of wind and water and swaying trees than in the bishop's sermons.

"Thanks for asking me to come fishing, Micah," Ellen said as she followed him cautiously out onto the wide trunk. "I needed to get out of there, and I couldn't think of a way to make a clean getaway without offending anyone."

"Jah," Micah agreed. "I wanted to get away, too. Not from supper. That was great. But my *dat*. When he takes a crazy notion, he's hard to rein in."

"So you think that's what it is? His idea

that you and Neziah should both court me, and that I would choose between you? It's a *crazy notion*?"

The hairs on the back of Micah's neck prickled, warning him that he'd almost made a big misstep, and not the kind that would land him in the creek. "*Nay*, I didn't mean it like that. It's a good idea, one I should have come up with a long time ago. Me and you walking out together, I mean, not you picking one of us. I don't know why I didn't think of it. My *vadder* is right that I've been *rumspringa* too long. I didn't want to discuss it back there, but I've been talking to the bishop about getting baptized. I'm ready to settle down, and a good woman is just what I need."

Ellen sat down on the log and dangled her legs over the edge. She was barefooted, and he couldn't help noticing her slender, high-arched feet. "I'm nearly four years older than you," she said.

He grinned at her. "That hasn't mattered since I left school and started doing a man's work. I've always thought you were one of the prettiest girls around, and we've always gotten along." Maybe not the prettiest, he thought, being honest with himself, but Ellen was nearly as tall as he was and very attractive. She'd always been fun to be with, and she was exactly the kind of woman he'd always expected to marry when he settled down. Ellen never made a fellow feel like less than he was, always better. Being with her always made him content…sort of like this creek, he decided.

"And our fathers' lands run together, of course." She took the pole he offered and bent over her line, carefully threading a night crawler onto the hook. "Handy for pasturing livestock."

He studied her to see if she was serious or testing him, but she kept her eyes averted, and he couldn't tell. He decided to play it safe. "We've been friends since we were kids. We share a faith and a community. Maybe that's a good start for a marriage."

"Maybe." She cast her line out, and the current caught her blue-and-white bobber and whisked it merrily along.

"*Dat* says all the best marriages start with friendship," he added.

"And it doesn't bother you that I'm thirty-three and not twenty-three?"

"Would I be here if it did?" Now she did raise her head and meet his gaze, and he smiled at her. "It was my *vadder*'s idea, but

I wouldn't have agreed if I didn't think it was something I wanted to do. You're a hard worker. I hope you think the same of me. I've got a good trade, and I own thirty acres of cleared farmland in my own name. And the two of us have a lot in common."

"Such as?"

"I like to eat and you're a good cook." He laughed.

She smiled.

"Seriously, Ellen. You get my jokes. We both like to laugh and have a good time. You know it's true. There's a big difference between me and Neziah."

"He has always been serious in nature."

"And more so since the accident. He doesn't take the joy in life that he should. Bad things happen. I didn't lose a wife, I know, but I lost my mother in that accident. You have to go on living. Otherwise, we waste what the Lord has given us."

She nodded, but she didn't speak, and he remembered that he'd always liked that about her. Ellen was a good listener, someone you could share important thoughts with.

"Sometimes I think my brother's meant to be a preacher, or maybe a deacon. He's way too settled for a man his age. Just look at his driving animal. I always thought you could tell a man's nature by his favorite driving animal."

"Neziah drives a good mule," she suggested.

"Exactly. Steady in traffic. Strong and levelheaded, even docile. An old woman's horse." It was no secret that he was different than Neziah. He liked spirited horses and was given to racing other buggies on the way to Sunday worship, not something that the elders smiled on.

"Don't be so hard on your brother," Ellen defended. "He has his children's safety to think about. You know how some of these *Englishers* drive. They don't think about how dangerous it is to pass our buggies on these narrow roads."

"*Jah*, I know, but I'm careful about when and where I race. I don't mean to criticize Neziah. He's a good man, and I'd not stand to hear anyone criticize him. But he's too staid for you. Remember that time we all went to Hershey Park? You and me, we liked the fast rides. Neziah, he got sick to his stomach. We're better suited, and if you'll give me a chance, I'll prove it to you."

"I think I—" She sounded excited for a second then sighed. "I had a bite but I think the fish is playing with me." She reeled in her line and checked the bait. Half of her worm was missing. "Look at that. Now I'll have to put on fresh bait."

He steadied himself against a branch and watched her, wondering why it had taken his father's lecture to stir him into action. For years he'd been going to all the young people's frolics, flirting with this girl and that, when all the time he'd hardly noticed Ellen. He had seen her, of course, gone to church with her, worked on community projects with her, eaten at her father's table and welcomed her to his own home. But he hadn't thought of her in the way he suddenly did now, as a special woman whom he might want to make his wife. The thought warmed him and made him smile. "You don't think I'm too young for you, do you?" he asked.

"Nay," she said, taking her time to answer. "I suppose not. But it's a new idea for me, that I marry a friend, rather than someone I was in love with."

Micah felt a rush of pleasure. "How do we know we won't discover love for each other if we don't give ourselves the chance?"

Her dark eyes grew luminous. Her bobber jerked and then dove beneath the surface of the creek, but Ellen didn't seem to notice the tension on her fishing pole. "You think that could happen?"

He grinned. "I think that there's a very good possibility that that's *exactly* what might happen."

Chapter Three

They walked back to her lane just as twilight was falling over the farm fields. "*Danki*, Micah," Ellen said. "The fishing was fun. I'd forgotten how much I liked it."

Her first moments alone with him, when they'd left the house, had been awkward. But then they'd fallen back into the easy rhythm of their younger days with none of the clumsiness of the situation that she'd feared. Being so comfortable with Micah made her wonder if maybe they could be happy together. What if Micah *was* whom God had intended for her all along?

"You should take these," he said, holding a string of three perch.

"You caught two of them. Don't you want to take them home to fry for breakfast?"

He still held them out. "Three measly fish for the five of us? Not worth the trouble of cleaning and cooking them. No, you'd best take them."

"*Danki* for the fish, too, then. *Dat* loves fried fish for breakfast."

"You're welcome. And you *are* going to think about walking out with me," Micah reminded. "Right?" He stood there, fishing poles in hand, smiling at her and completely at ease.

"*Jah*, I will." She smiled at him. "God give you a restful sleep."

"And you, Ellen." He used no courting endearments, but she liked the way he said her name, and she felt a warm glow inside as she savored it. She didn't want to spoil the feeling and was afraid that he might linger, might want to sit with her on the porch or stay on after her parents had gone to bed. Instead, he bestowed a final grin and strode off whistling in the direction of his own home.

Ellen walked slowly up the driveway and through her father's barnyard, inhaling deep of the scent of her mother's climbing roses and the honeysuckle that grew wild along the edge of the hedgerow. She drank in the peace of the coming night. Crickets and frogs called their familiar sounds, and evening shadows draped over the barnyard, easing her feelings of indecision. How wonderful life is, she thought. You expect each day to be like the one before, but the wonder of God's grace was that you never really knew from one hour to another what would come next.

A single propane lamp glowed through the kitchen window, but the house was quiet. Simeon, Neziah and the boys had left. The only sign of movement was a calico cat nursing kittens near the back door. But the light meant that her parents were still up. Her father was too fearful of fire to retire and leave a lamp burning. Ellen stepped inside, the string of fish dangling from her finger. *"Mam?"* she called softly. *"Dat?"*

"Out here." Her father's voice came from the front of the house.

Their home was small as Amish homes went, but comfortable. When her father and his neighbors had built it, he and her mother were already past the age when they expected to be blessed with children. A big kitchen, a pantry, a living room, bath and two bedrooms comprised the entire downstairs. Her room was upstairs in an oversize, cheerful chamber with two dormer windows and a casement window that opened wide to let in fresh breezes from the west. She also had a small bath all to herself, a privacy that few Amish girls had. Growing up, her girlfriends, most from large families, had admired the luxury, but she would have gladly traded the cheerful room with its yellow trim, clean white claw-foot tub, fixtures and tiny shuttered window for a bevy of noisy sisters crowded head to foot in her bedroom.

The double door near the staircase stood open, and her father called again to her from the front porch. “Come, join us. And bring another bowl for beans.”

Butter beans, Ellen thought. The family often sat on the porch in the evenings this time of year and shelled butter beans. She and her mother canned bushels of beans for winter. Quarts of the beans already stood in neat rows in the pantry beside those of squash, English peas, string beans, corn, tomatoes and pickles. She wrapped the fish in some parchment paper and put it in the propane-run refrigerator. They'd keep until morning when she or her father would clean them. She washed her hands, found a bowl and carried it out to the porch. Her parents sat side by side in wooden rocking chairs, baskets of lima bean hulls and bowls of shelled beans around them.

"Catch any fish?" her father asked.

"In the fridge. If you clean them, I'll fry them up for our breakfast." Ellen took the chair on the other side of him. Her chair. Her mother sat still, her chin resting on her chest; she was snoring lightly. Her mother often drifted off to sleep in the afternoon and early evening. She didn't have the vigor that Ellen was used to, and she worried about her. "Has she been asleep long?"

"Just a little while. Company wore her out." He dumped butter beans still in their shells into Ellen's bowl. "Course, you know how she loves to have people come. And she adores children, even those rascals of Neziah's. Nothing makes her happier than stuffing a child with food, unless it's singing in church. Your mother always had the sweetest voice. It was what drew me to her when we were young."

Ellen nodded and smiled. She knew what her father was up to. They were so close that she was familiar with all his tricks. He was deliberately being sentimental about her mother to keep Ellen from talking about what she'd sought him out for. He knew that she was unhappy with the ambush that had happened at supper, and he wanted to avoid the consequences. But she suspected that he'd be disappointed if she let him get away with it, so she went straight to the heart of the pudding.

"You shouldn't have asked the Shetlers here for supper to talk about this courting business without talking to me first," she admonished gently. "I can't believe you didn't wait to see whether I was in favor of this or not."

"*Ach...ach*, I was afraid you'd be vexed with me. I told your mother you would." He gestured with his hand. "But it is such a good solution to Simeon's problem and ours. And how could I refuse him? He came to me at midday, told me what was on his mind and said that he'd already approached you with the idea and you were in favor. Then he invited himself and his sons to supper." He shrugged as if to say, *what could I do?* "He's a good neighbor and an old friend."

"Friends or not, I'm your daughter, and who I will or won't marry is a serious matter. If you knew I wouldn't approve, you shouldn't have done it," she said, unwilling to surrender so easily to being manipulated.

She had the greatest respect for her father's judgment, but he'd always fostered independence in her. Even at a young age, he'd treated her more as another adult in the home than as a child. Maybe it was because her mother had always been an uncomplicated and basic person, content to allow her husband and the elders of the church to make decisions for her, while his was a keener mind that sought in-depth conversation. Or perhaps it was because she'd been the only child and he doted on her.

In any case, the Bible said "Honor thy father and mother," and she hoped she hadn't taken advantage of his leniency. She'd taken care not to be forward in front of others, especially with the more conservative of the community. But here, in their own home, with none but him to hear, how could she do less than protest his high-handedness?

"What was I to say to Simeon?" he went on. "'*Nay*, old friend, you can't come to share bread with us until I see if my daughter wants to marry either one of your boys?'" He found a withered lima bean and cast it to the brown-and-white rat terrier sitting at his feet. Gilly caught the bean in the air and chomped it joyfully.

"It was a shock to see Micah and Neziah all dressed in their best, here at the table." Ellen glanced at her mother, but she snored on, her hands loose in her lap, her bowl of unshelled beans hardly started. "She was good tonight, don't you think?" she said, waffling by talking of something easier. "Her morning started bad, so I worried..."

Her father's face was lost in shadow now, but Ellen knew he was smiling. He had such fondness for her mother, his love seemingly growing stronger with his wife's slow mental decline. "She perked up when I told her that the children were coming. Buzzed around the kitchen like she was forty. Her biscuits were light enough to float, don't you think? And she was sharp as a needle at supper." Her father continued to hull limas, his fingers moving unconsciously without pause. Fat beans dropped by ones, twos and threes into the wide basket in his lap.

"Jah," Ellen agreed. "No lapses in memory." And her mother's biscuits *had* been good tonight. She'd not forgotten the rising or the salt as she did sometimes. And she hadn't let them stay in the oven until the bottoms began to burn. Once, not long ago, Ellen had come in from the garden to find the kitchen full of smoke and her mother standing motionless in the center of the room, staring at the stove and coughing. Ellen had had to get the biscuits out of the oven and shoo her mother outside where

she could breathe. It was those lapses in judgment that made Ellen apprehensive about her mother's health.

"So, *Dochter*, did you enjoy yourself on your outing with young Micah?"

"I did have a good time," she admitted. "But you know I would have put the Shetlers off if I'd had the choice. This isn't something that I can decide in a few hours."

"But you *are* open to being courted by Micah or his brother?" When she didn't answer right away, her father pressed on. "You have to marry, Ellen. You know that, don't you? What will you do when your mother and I go to our reward? We're not young, either of us. You're a healthy young woman. You need a family of your own. And it would fill our hearts with joy if you could give us a grandchild before we die."

She swallowed. Her throat felt tight, as if an invisible hand was squeezing it. It was all perfectly logical, of course, but what about her heart? Her parents had married for love, and she had hoped for the same.

"I'm not asking you to marry either of Simeon's boys," he father went on. "I'm only asking that you give them a chance."

Her gaze met his, but she still didn't speak.

"Just…just a month. That's all I ask of you. Give them a month." He smiled the smile he knew she could never resist. "Is that too much for an old man to ask of his daughter?"

He said it so sweetly that she sighed and looked at the lima bean in her hand. "No, I suppose it's not too much to ask, so I will walk out with them," she said softly. "But I'll tell you now—" she pointed with the empty hull at him "—I'll only truly consider Micah, not Neziah."

"Don't be foolish. You cared for Neziah once. You came close to marrying him."

She tightened her mouth. "That was a long time ago," she said. "Marrying Neziah would have been a mistake. We were—*are*—too different. He isn't the husband for me, and I'm certainly not the wife for him." Memories she hadn't stirred up in years came back to her, and she felt her heart trip. Things had been so complicated with Neziah, and she had been so young. "I'd feel trapped in a marriage with him."

"Then you're wise to refuse him." He leaned closer to her. "But you *are* open to being courted by Micah?"

She nodded. "*Jah.* If you think I should do that, I will."

"And you don't think it's being unfair to Neziah to allow him to believe you're considering his suit?"

"Honestly, *Dat*, I think he went along with Simeon's idea just to please his father. I bet he's trying to figure out at this very moment how to get out of this."

"Then we will put this all in God's hands," her father said. "He's never failed to be there when we need Him. It pleases me that you are willing to walk out with the Shetler boys, and I will place my hopes and prayers on the best solution for all of us."

She nodded, her heart suddenly lighter. "I'll put my trust in Him," she agreed. And for the first time in years, she allowed herself to think of a different life than she had thought hers would be...one that included a husband, a baby and new possibilities.

"I'm hungry," Joel said in Deitsch as Neziah lifted him out of the bathtub and wrapped him in an oversize white towel.

"*Jah*, me, too," Asa agreed in Deitsch. "I want milk and cookies. Can we have milk and cookies, *Dat*?"

"English," Neziah reminded them. "Bath time is English. Remember? Soon Joel will go to school, and the other children will speak English. You wouldn't want them to call him a woodenhead, would you?" Asa wriggled out of his grasp and retreated to the far end of the claw-footed porcelain tub. "Come back here, you pollywog." He captured the escapee and stood him beside his brother. It always surprised him how close they were in size, even though Asa was nearly two years younger. Neziah wrapped his younger son in a clean blue towel and sat him on the closed toilet seat.

The bathroom was large and plain with a white tile floor, white fixtures and white walls and window shutters. Neziah wondered if his boys ever realized how lucky they were not to have to use an outhouse as he had for much of his childhood. He hadn't minded the spiders and the occasional mouse or bat as much as he had the cold on winter nights. He smiled. This modern bathroom with its deep sink, corner shower and propane heater was a great improvement. The Amish elders might be slow to change, but they did make some concessions to the twenty-first century, and bathrooms, in his opinion, were at the top of the list.

"My tummy hurts," Joel said in English, sticking out his lower lip. "I have hungry."

"After the big dinner and all the pie you ate at the Beacheys?" Neziah chuckled. "I don't think so. You'll have to wait for breakfast."

Joel's face contorted into a full-blown pout, and Asa chimed in. "Me hungry, too."

"Bed and prayers." Neziah whisked off the towels and tugged cotton nightshirts over two bobbing heads. "Brush your teeth now, and maybe we'll have time for a little *Family Life* before lights out." *Family Life* was one of the few publications that came to the house, and Neziah made a practice of reading short stories or poems that he thought his sons might like at bedtime.

"But we're hungry," Joel whined, retreating to the Deitsch dialect. "My belly hurts a lot."

"Then cookies and milk will only make it worse," Neziah pronounced. He scooped up Asa and draped him laughing over his shoulder and took Joel's hand. "Bed. Now." Joel allowed himself to be tugged along reluctantly to the bedroom and the double bed the boys shared. Neziah deposited Asa between the sheets then reached down for Joel.

"Read," Asa reminded. He pulled the sheet up to his chin and dug his stuffed dog out from under his pillow while Joel wormed his way over his brother and curled up on top of the light cotton blanket and sheet.

A breeze blew through the curtainless windows on the north side of the bedroom. Like the bathroom, this was a sparse chamber: the bed, a bookcase, a table and two chairs. There were no dressers. The boys' clothing was all hung inside the single, small closet. Neziah pulled up a chair, lit the propane lamp and together they shared a short prayer. Then he took the latest copy of *Family Life* magazine from the table. He'd read to Joel and Asa every night since their mother had died. It was something she'd always done with the children, and although he wasn't as much at ease with reading aloud as Betty had been, he felt it was the right thing to do.

Strangely, the practice, which he'd begun out of a sense of duty, had become the highlight of his day. No matter how tired he was, spending a few moments quietly with his sons brought him deep contentment. Asa, in particular, seemed to enjoy the poetry as much as Neziah did. It wasn't something that Neziah would have willingly admitted to anyone, but he found the sounds of the rhyming words pleasing. Joel preferred the stories, the longer the better, but Neziah suspected that it was simply a way of delaying bedtime.

Tonight, Neziah chose a short and funny poem about a squirrel that stored up nuts for winter and when he had finished it he said, "Sleep well," as he bent to rest a hand lightly on each small head. Joel's hair was light and feathery; Asa's thick and curly. "God keep you both," he murmured.

"Dat?"

"*Jah*, Joel, what is it? No more about cookies tonight."

"*Nay, Dat.* I was wondering. Is Ellen going to be our new *mutter*?"

Neziah was surprised by the question; he had wondered how much his sons had understood from the conversations he and Micah had had with their father and later at the Beacheys' table. Apparently, they'd caught the gist of it. "I don't know," he answered honestly. He made it a point never to be dishonest with his children, not even for their own good. "Maybe. Would you like that?"

"*Grossdaddi* said she might marry you," Joel said, avoiding the question.

"*Jah*, and…and Uncle Micah, too," Asa supplied.

Neziah chuckled. "A woman can only marry

one man, and a man only one woman. Ellen might marry me or your uncle Micah, or she might not marry either of us." Neziah slid the chair back under the table and retrieved a crayon from the floor. It was almost too dark to see, and he wouldn't have noticed it if he hadn't stepped on it. "Good night, boys."

"But will she?" Joel persisted.

He stopped in the doorway and turned back to his boys. "We'll have to wait and see. If she marries your uncle Micah, she'll be your aunt."

Joel wrinkled his little nose. "Is that like a *mutter*?"

A lump rose in Neziah's throat. Joel had been so small when his mother died, and Asa only an infant. Neither of them could remember what it was like to have a mother. Neziah felt a faint wave of guilt. Had he been selfish in waiting so long to remarry? His sons deserved a mother; everyone in Honeysuckle thought so. But would Ellen be right for them? For *him*?

"Ellen makes good pie," Joel said.

Asa yawned. "I like pie."

"Ellen *does* make good pie," Neziah conceded. "Now, no more talking. Time for sleep." Pretending not to hear the muted whispers behind him, Neziah made his way out of the boys' room and down the stairs. He didn't need a light. He knew the way by heart.

He continued on through the house, past the closed door to the parlor, where a thin crack of light told him that his father was still awake reading the Bible or working on correspondence as part of his duties as a church elder. He walked through the kitchen and outside, making his way to the old brick well that stood near the back porch. The windmill and a series of gears, pipes and a holding tank delivered water to the house and bathroom, but the coldest water came from the deep well. Neziah unlatched the hook and slid aside the wooden cover. With some effort, an overhead pulley, a rope and a wooden bucket rewarded him with an icy drink of water scooped out with an aluminum cup that was fastened to the iron frame.

Neziah leaned against the old brick and savored the water. This was another habit of his. Every night, if it wasn't raining, sleeting or snowing, he'd come out to the well and draw up fresh water. He liked the sensation of the liquid, the rough texture of the bricks and the familiar curves of the bucket and cup. He'd always loved the well. It was a good place to think.

He was still standing there, one hand steadying the bucket, when he heard the rhythmic sound of a stone skipping across water. Instantly, he knew what it was. He finished his water, hung the cup back on the hook and walked across the yard, past the grapevines. At the edge of the small pond in the side yard, he spotted the outline of a figure. The figure tossed something just so and again Neziah heard the familiar splash, splash, splash of a rock skipping across water.

"Only three. Can't you do better than that?" he called, walking toward his brother.

"It's not about how many hops. I'm practicing my technique," Micah explained.

"Ah." By the light of the rising moon, Neziah picked up a stone from the water's edge and slid it back and forth over his fingertips, judging its shape and weight. A good rock had to be flat and oval and just the right weight. "Your spin's still not right."

"My spin is fine." Micah picked up another rock, crouched and threw it.

Four skips.

"You should try standing up to start…like this." Neziah lifted his hand above his head, his wrist cocked, and then swung down and out in one smooth movement. The stone hit the water and skipped one, two, three, four, five times before disappearing beneath the surface.

"Okay, that was just practice. Best two out of three tries," Micah challenged, picking up another rock.

Neziah smiled. The two of them had been competitive for as long as he could remember, mostly because of Micah, he liked to think. To Micah, everything was a game. But the truth be told, though, Neziah had a small competitive streak himself. Or maybe it just bugged him that his little brother was so good at everything. Nothing ever came hard to Micah.

"Best score of three," Neziah agreed. He leaned over to find three perfect rocks. "How was fishing with Ellen?"

"Great."

Neziah could just make out Micah's face; he was grinning ear to ear. "And Ellen really is agreeable to marrying one of us?"

Neziah saw Micah shrug in the darkness as he picked up a stone, ran his fingers over it and rejected it. "It makes sense, and she's a sensible woman. Or haven't you noticed that?"

"You're not usually so quick to seize on

one of *Vadder*'s ideas." Finding a near-perfect stone, Neziah passed it to his left hand for safekeeping.

"He's right. It's past time I married. I look at you with your two boys and..." Micah turned to Neziah, casually tossing a stone into the air and catching it. "You know what I think of them. Scamps or not, it's time I had a few of my own. And for that I need a wife. Why not Ellen?"

"She's older than you."

Micah laughed. "That's what she said. Wasn't our *mutter* older than our *vadder*?"

"A year, I think, but there's more than that between you and Ellen."

"If it doesn't bother me, it shouldn't bother you, brother." Micah stared at Neziah for a moment. The grin came again. "Not having second thoughts, are you? Wishing you hadn't called things off when you did?"

"Of course not," Neziah said a little too quickly. "We walked out together, that's true, but there were differences that we couldn't seem to..." He sighed and stood at the edge of the water. "Your turn."

Micah squatted down. "If my courting Ellen is a problem for you, now's the time to speak up. I like her, but I won't let a woman come between us. Not even Ellen." He let go of his first stone. "Yes!" he cheered when it hopped five times.

"*Dat*'s idea is that she choose between us. I agreed to it, same as you." Neziah tossed his stone and it skipped five times. "I just don't want you to hurt her, Micah. Don't make promises you can't keep."

Micah tossed his next stone. Three skips. He didn't cheer. "Sounds like you've made up your mind to step aside."

Neziah skipped his second stone. Five again. "I didn't say that." He didn't like it when people put words in his mouth.

Micah prepared to toss his final stone, taking his time to glance at the water and get himself into position. "So you do still have feelings for her?" He let the stone fly…five skips.

Neziah thought about it for a minute and realized that as much as he would like to deny it, he couldn't. He raised his hand high over his head, the rock just right between his fingers. "We didn't break up because we didn't care for each other. It was because we weren't sure that we were suited to be the best partners. Marriage is for life, and some differences can loom large as years pass." He let the rock go, spinning it just right…six skips. "I win," he declared.

Micah turned to Neziah, his tone teasing. "So what you're saying, brother, is that you're in?"

"I'm in," Neziah admitted.

"And no hard feelings if she picks me?" Micah opened his arms wide. "Because you know I'm hard for the girls to resist."

"Why would there be any hard feelings?" Neziah asked and then glanced away. He loved his brother, always had, but he wondered, as the words came out of his mouth, how he would feel seeing Ellen marry him. "It's her choice."

"*Goot.* Contest on. And may the best Shetler bring home the bride!" Micah snatched up another stone. "Now come on. One more time. Best out of five stones."

Chapter Four

Ellen pushed her scooter into the yard and scanned the road below. Immediately, she caught sight of a horse and buggy coming from the direction of town. It was Micah. He reined in the gelding and waited. Suspecting that she'd been ambushed, Ellen smiled and walked down the hill toward him.

As she approached the buggy, she saw Micah grinning at her. She knew the expression. He hadn't changed much since he was a mischievous boy. He knew that she hadn't been expecting him to be here this morning, and he looked delighted to have surprised her. "You're right on time today," he called.

"Good morning, Micah." She wasn't sure if the tingling she felt in her chest was pleasure or aggravation. She felt as though everyone around her was trying to manage her, and she liked to make her own decisions. Was this how it was going to be—Micah popping up everywhere, grinning?

"Good morning."

"Did you come to see my *dat*?" she asked, pretending innocence, but certain Micah had come to see her, probably to offer to drive her to the shop. "He's in his workshop." She stood there a few yards from the buggy. "We had the fish for breakfast this morning. Delicious. Thanks for letting me keep them."

"Wish I'd been here to have some with you." Blue eyes twinkling, Micah swung down lightly out of the buggy. He wasn't a small man. He was muscular, with broad shoulders and long legs, but Ellen had always thought Micah moved easily, like a fine-blooded horse. Maybe it was because he liked playing ball. He'd always been more athletic than his brother, Neziah.

"Maybe not. I burned the last batch."

"I doubt that," he said laughing. "I've come to drive you into Honeysuckle."

Unconsciously, she folded her arms, tightening her mouth into a thin line. If only he wasn't so cute, she thought. It was so hard not to be flattered by Micah's attention, but he got his way far too often because he was hard to resist. "No need to put yourself out. I've got my scooter." She offered a half smile. "I'm sure you've got a lot of work to do today at the sawmill."

He spread his hands in an endearing gesture. "No trouble at all. *Dat* needs turnip seeds. He's a mind to put in a fall crop where we tore down the old shed. So I've got to drive right past your shop. It would be foolish for you to take the scooter when you could ride."

She nodded. "I can see your point. But you can't convince me that you'd drive all the way into town for turnip seeds so early on a workday."

Micah chuckled and reached for her scooter. "I'll put this in the back of the buggy so you'll have a way home after work."

She wasn't letting Micah off so easily. "Tell the truth. This is all part of some scheme of yours, isn't it?"

His smile broadened, showing even white teeth. One thing about the Shetler brothers, Ellen thought. They'd been fortunate enough to inherit their mother's beautiful teeth. Neither Neziah nor Micah had ever had a cavity, while she had made regular trips to the dentist. If she did marry one of them, maybe their children would have good teeth. She almost laughed out loud at the thought. Was she really considering marriage prospects based on dentistry?

"Just giving a neighbor a lift into town." Micah tucked her scooter under his arm. "But that brother of mine will be wishing he thought to come this morning. He can be slow at the start, but he likes a good competition as much as I do. He just doesn't like to admit it." Behind him, the black gelding shook his head and shifted impatiently. Like his owner, the spirited horse was happier when in motion.

"I'm not sure I like being part of a *competition*. And I haven't said I'd ride in with you, have I?" she asked.

It was flattering to have Micah show up bright and early this morning, and she'd enjoyed herself on their fishing expedition the previous evening, but her quiet life was suddenly moving way too fast. Simeon had only mentioned this scheme to her the previous morning, and this would be the second time she and Micah had been alone together in less than twenty-four hours. And riding to town in his buggy would set tongues to wagging. This was a close community, and by nightfall people would be wondering if she and Micah were walking out together.

"Come on, won't you ride into Honeysuckle with me?" Micah asked. "I'm already here. You might as well." And for the first time this morning, behind the teasing, Ellen could see that it was important to him. He'd be hurt if she refused.

"I suppose you're right," she replied. "It's going to be a warm day for September. Better I arrive looking fresh for my customers."

"You look fine to me," he said as he loaded the scooter into the back of the vehicle. "Is that a new dress you're wearing? I like green on you. It makes your eyes green."

"My eyes are just hazel," she said as she climbed onto the front seat. "I wasn't looking for you to give me compliments, but *danki* for saying so."

"Didn't suppose you were." He slid onto the seat beside her and picked up the reins. "It's one of the things I've always admired about you, Ellen. Your eyes aren't always the same color. They change."

"Change how?" She averted her gaze and brushed at the wrinkles in her apron. Was this what it would be like to court Micah, all compliments and blushing? Was this what she wanted, a woman of her age?

"Just, whatever color dress you wear, your eyes look different. It's one of the things I remember about you from school. Thanks to your eyes, I ate Henry Chupp's whoopie pies four days in a row."

Puzzled, she stared at him. "How and why did you eat Henry's dessert?"

"I bet him that he couldn't guess the color of your eyes each day before you arrived and I could." He grinned at her. "Your eyes were always the color of your dress, and you always wore the same color dress on the same day—green on Monday, blue on Tuesday, then the green again and then the blue. On Friday it was supposed to be a lavender dress, but that week you wore brown instead and ruined the whole thing." He shrugged. "I told Henry your eyes were going to turn purple and I lost."

Her eyes widened. Gambling was forbidden by the *Ordnung*, the rules most Amish communities lived by. "That was very wrong of you. We don't bet on things, not horse races or what color a girl's eyes will be."

Micah grimaced. "I know. Neziah found out and threatened to tell *Dat* if I didn't make it up to Henry. I had to give him my Little Debbie cakes for a whole week. My favorites. The ones with the sticky cream inside."

"Served you right."

"I guess. Neziah was tough. I didn't think he would tell *Vadder* because Neziah wasn't a tattletale, but he had ways of making me toe the line. It was enough to make me give up gambling for life." He sighed dramatically. "My mother didn't buy us store cakes often. Usually we had the ones she made. Those Little Debbie cakes were a big deal."

"I suppose children do make mistakes. How old were you?"

"Let me see. Neziah was out of school and working in the sawmill. I must have been eleven. Teacher used to have you give us spelling tests, and you always gave us more than one chance to spell the word correctly."

"You didn't need an extra chance. You were the best speller in your grade." It was strange to think that the rosy-cheeked boy in suspenders and bare feet she'd once known might now become her beau. Micah had always been a handful, never a bad kid, but always full of mischief. She'd always suspected that Micah had been the one who'd put a frog in her lunchbox when she was in the eighth grade.

"But I always liked you, Ellen. Even though

the teacher called on you to be her helper, you never took advantage of it. You weren't silly like most of the other girls. You don't play games with people."

She chuckled. "Don't I? And who used to strike you out when we played softball at school?"

"Not those kinds of games," he said as he maneuvered the horse to turn the buggy around. "You know what I mean. You always went out of your way to include the shy girls in your group. You were popular with the teacher and the other kids, but it didn't make you stuck up."

"I hope not."

"*Nay*, you weren't. If you had been, I'd have noticed." He glanced at her. "You didn't have any brothers or sisters. That's unusual. A lot of people expected you to be spoiled, but you weren't. It was something my *vadder* used to talk about, how much he admired your parents for being sensible raising you."

"I was blessed with good parents," she said softly. "And I think you were, too."

"*Jah*, but I wish..." He trailed off and Ellen suspected that he was thinking of his mother, who'd died so tragically in that van accident, the same accident that had claimed the life of Neziah's wife, Betty.

"That you hadn't lost your mother."

"True enough," he said. "*Dat* never says much, but I know he still grieves for her."

"We have to believe that she's safe in the Lord's hands."

"We do," Micah agreed. "I pity those who have no faith to hold them up in hard times. It must be bitter...not to know that." His brow furrowed. "Easier by far for me, a man grown, to lose a mother than Neziah's two boys. They need a mother's hand, and if you pick one of us, I hope you'll give them what they're lacking."

"I'd do my best," she promised.

"And that's all anyone can do, I suppose. Do your best." He eased his horse to a halt at the end of the driveway. A car approached, and Micah held the lines firmly. "Easy. Good boy." When the car passed, he said, "Walk on." He flicked the leathers over the gelding's back, and the horse started forward, first at a walk and then at a pace.

"You've done well with him," she said as the buggy rolled swiftly along the blacktop. She had to admit to herself that she liked fast horses almost as much as Micah did. And it was plain to her that he'd taken a roughly broken saddle horse and worked with him until the animal showed amazing promise as a driving horse. When Micah had come home from the auction with the three-year-old last fall, his father and her own had expressed doubt that the gelding would ever make a reliable driver.

"He was bred to be a racehorse," Ellen's father had explained more than once. "Lots of standardbreds turn out to make good driving horses, but that animal was left a stallion too long. I wouldn't trust him."

As usual, her mother had echoed her father's warning, but Ellen had kept her opinion to herself. Micah was known for having patience and a soft hand with horses. She'd secretly hoped that the dire predictions would turn out to be groundless. Flashy the black might be, but the horse Micah called Samson had intelligent eyes, and she'd seen no evidence of meanness around other animals. This was the first time she'd ridden in a buggy behind Samson, and it was too soon to pass judgment, but she thought the gelding seemed well suited to his owner.

"He has a sweet mouth," Micah said. "Still a little nervous around motorcycles, but he's young yet. I think he'll be fine."

"Worth a lot more than you paid for him," she agreed. "If you wanted to sell him."

"Which I don't. I'm not fickle. When I commit to something or someone, I stick with it."

Ellen didn't answer. She felt safer when the conversation was confined to the horse or to other ordinary subjects, but she felt that Micah was straying from the shore into deeper water. She slid over on the seat a little, widening the distance between them so that she could brace her hand on the buggy frame. "Thanks for thinking of driving me in this morning," she said. "It was kind of you."

He raised his shoulders and let them fall. "I'm giving my good neighbor a ride to town. It isn't as if we're crying the banns for our wedding."

He was right, and she felt a little foolish for making so much of his showing up in her lane this morning. Slowly, she nodded. "It's just that it takes some getting used to, thinking of you as a..."

"A suitor?" He smiled and clicked to the horse. Samson quickened his pace. "I thought we'd settled that last night."

"Did we, Micah?"

"I thought so."

She tightened her grip on the edge of the

seat. "But it doesn't bother you that this was all your father's idea?"

"*Dat* said that he thought that it came as an answer to his prayers. And maybe it did. We can't say for sure how God tells us what He wants us to do, can we?"

She shook her head. "I guess not."

"Maybe it was me who needed the nudge to see what was right in front of my eyes for years. I like you, Ellen. If it's meant to be and we give it a chance, maybe..."

"Jah." She sighed. "Maybe." A bubble of happiness tickled her insides. Maybe Micah was right. Maybe he'd been right in front of her and she'd never really looked at him. The possibilities were intriguing.

"It *is* just a ride to town," he reminded her. "No strings attached...unless you decide you want them."

They exchanged a smile, and she closed her eyes and savored the sensation of the wind on her face. This was certainly cooler than she would have been pushing her scooter along the road. She found herself relaxing and enjoying the ride.

Micah, never at a loss for words, began to tell her about a pig that had escaped from Roland Yoder's wagon. Roland, a butcher, was taking the animal to his brother's place to be fattened for autumn, but as he was crossing the highway near Bird-In-Hand, a dog ran out at the buggy. The barking frightened the pig that then jumped over the rails and landed in the center of the road. Cars braked and horns honked. The pig ran back and forth causing a traffic jam.

Ellen smiled and waited for the punch line. Like his father, Simeon, Micah's stories were usually funny, sometimes hilarious. But Micah abruptly broke off in midsentence and reined in the horse.

"Did you see that turtle?" he asked.

She glanced over her shoulder. "Turtle?"

"*Jah*, a box turtle. Just a little one, smaller than your fist." He guided Samson onto the shoulder of the road. "Sit tight," he said. "I'll be right back." Micah handed her the reins, climbed down off the seat and hurried back along the road. About thirty feet behind them, Ellen saw him cross to the center of the blacktop and pick up a round object. "Got him!" he proclaimed, holding the creature up for her to see. He carried the turtle to the far side of the road and put him down safely at the edge of the woods.

"That was a small one," she agreed as Micah got back into the buggy. "You don't usually see them on the roads by the first of September." This wasn't the first time Micah had shown compassion for a small animal. She remembered him catching a six-inch black snake in the school cloakroom. Some of the other boys had wanted him to snap its neck against the shed wall, but he'd faced down two sixth graders and marched the snake to a hedgerow where he released it in the brush.

"I always liked box turtles," Micah said. "When we were young, Neziah and I always wanted to keep them as pets and train them to do tricks, but *Dat* wouldn't let us. He always made us put them back exactly where we found them. He said they have their own territory, and if you move them out of it, they won't rest until they get back to where they belong. A lot of them are run over by cars on the roads. I feel sorry for them, so I always take them across when I see one." He arched an eyebrow. "You probably think it's dumb."

"Nay." She shook her head. "I think it's a decent thing to help any of God's creatures." She smiled in approval. "And I think you are a *goot* person, Micah Shetler, one any woman would be proud to have court her."

* * *

The day at the shop was spotty, customer-wise. No one would come in for an hour, and then two or three cars would stop. Once, Ellen was ringing up an English woman, Dinah was showing quilts to another and two more people were waiting in line. At midday, she and Dinah took advantage of a lull in business to take their lunches out onto the porch where they could eat and watch the tourists and her Amish neighbors drive by.

"I'm so excited about the new watercolors that arrived today," Ellen told Dinah as she took another bite of her ham salad sandwich. There were four watercolors of Amish scenes painted by an ex-Amish woman in another area of the state. Each one showed a different season of the year. Her favorite, summer, was a scene of a mother hanging clothes on a line. Two daughters helped while a baby played on a blanket. All of the figures were shown from the back so that none of the faces could be seen, a concept that fit perfectly with the Plain way of living. The artist had signed her work simply as Rachel. Ellen thought the paintings were beautiful. The colors were soft blues and greens, and the frames were handcrafted of cherry. She expected them to sell quickly because Amish art was a favorite with her out-of-state customers.

"They're fine paintings," Dinah agreed, sipping from a pop can. She cocked her head toward the shop. "Did you hear something?"

"I don't think so." Ellen shook her head. "What do you mean?"

"It's nothing." Dinah adjusted her glasses. "Been hearing things all week. Yesterday morning I was sure I heard someone on the back porch in the middle of the night. Silly."

"Do you think someone was trying to break in?" Ellen asked, immediately concerned. They had a very low crime rate in Honeysuckle, but she wasn't so naive as to think nothing bad could ever happen.

"No, nothing like that," Dinah pshawed. "I should probably have my hearing checked next time I see that doctor." She returned her full attention to Ellen. "What do you think you want to do with the watercolors?"

"I was thinking that we have enough stock to open the other front parlor." Pushing the last corner of bread into her mouth, Ellen carefully folded the waxed paper and tucked it into her lunch box to use again. "I think pottery and the two Windsor chairs would go nicely in there with the paintings and the carvings.

Then we'd have more room in the main area for jams and the display of baby clothing."

"Jah," Dinah agreed. Since she lived upstairs in the apartment, the older woman could easily have gone up to have her lunch, but eating on the porch was one of the highlights of their day. "Remember, I'm leaving early today. Right after lunch. I've got to help Naomi get ready for tomorrow night's haystack supper."

"That's fine, we can do it later in the week. I'd like to hang these paintings on the wall by the fireplace." That section of the old house hadn't been damaged in the fire, and the woodwork and floor were lovely in there. "I'll have Carl make another of those oak benches and put it in there for customers to sit on." Ellen removed a peach from her lunch box. It smelled heavenly. She took a bite, and juice ran down her chin. She quickly wiped it with a napkin. "How is the Blauch baby? Do the doctors know when he can come home?" She knew that the widows' group's upcoming supper was to raise money for Mary's little Raymond. The baby had been born several months early and had been rushed to the children's hospital in Philadelphia.

"Nay," Dinah said. "He has to be five pounds. He's gaining, but he still has some

other issues that have to be taken care of. It's a blessing that Mary and David didn't lose him, like the last two."

"But the doctors are hopeful?"

"*Jah.* Little Raymond is a fighter. My daughter says the doctors expect him to be just fine." She shook her head. "But the hospital bills are awful. The widows' group can help, but I think the whole community will have to pitch in."

Ellen nodded. Their faith didn't hold with insurance, but whenever tragedy struck a member of the church, other families were quick to offer help. There had already been a livestock auction for the Blauch baby, and the youth group was planning a pancake and sausage breakfast. The bishop had asked for donations, and she knew her parents had contributed. It was one of the things that made life in Honeysuckle, and in all Amish communities, fulfilling. There were many families, but they came together as one when someone needed help.

As Ellen finished her peach, a tour bus pulled into the restaurant down the street, and dozens of people got out. Some went into the Mennonite restaurant, but others made their way toward the businesses along the street. A group of three women crossed over and came in Ellen's direction.

"Maybe I should stay," Dinah said. "You might need the help."

"*Nay*, you go on. I'll manage," Ellen said. "Naomi and the others need you."

"Are you coming to the supper?"

"I wouldn't miss it. And I'll bring that tray of brownies I promised you. Folks love their desserts."

Dinah took her leave, and Ellen welcomed her potential customers. One of the three purchased an Amish rag doll and complete set of clothing for it. They were just making their way out when two more women entered. By 2:00 p.m., she'd surpassed the previous day's total. Before the afternoon was over, Ellen had made two more substantial sales and several smaller ones. And in the midst of the confusion, two acquaintances arrived to add and remove food from the large freezers on her enclosed back porch.

Since electricity had been approved by the bishop for use in the shop, Ellen had convinced her parents that it would be worthwhile to buy several commercial freezers. Members of the Amish community paid a fee to rent space in the freezers, so there was constant coming and going. Often friends would come in to chat or drop off crafts for her to sell. It added to her enjoyment in managing the shop.

Just before closing, Lizzie Fisher stopped by to pick up her money from the sale of her quilt. Since there were no other customers in the store, Ellen made tea and the two sat and exchanged neighborhood news. Ellen reached over and clasped Lizzie's hand. She was a petite girl of nineteen who appeared much younger. Far too young to be a widow and a mother of so many, Ellen thought. When her husband suddenly died recently, she was left with seven stepchildren, ranging in ages from three to thirteen. "How are you doing?"

"All right." She nodded. "Everyone has been so kind. Selling that quilt was a big help to me." Lizzie sighed. "The kids have taken the loss of their father very hard. Between trying to help them through this and managing the garden and the children, I don't know when I'll find time to return to my quilting. I keep telling myself that I should be working in the evenings after they go to bed, but…" She shrugged. "The days just keep getting shorter." She finished her tea. "I better run. The kids are with family, but I don't want to be gone too long."

"I understand." Ellen couldn't imagine how full Lizzie's day must be. "If there's anything I can do to help, please let me know."

Lizzie tucked a loose strand of dark auburn hair under her *kapp*. "Are you coming to the haystack supper tomorrow night?"

"Absolutely. My *vadder* and *mutter*, too. They're looking forward to it."

"The kids are, too." She offered a slight smile.

Ellen walked to the door with her. Lizzie limped slightly due to a birth defect, but it had never slowed her down. "You're in my prayers, Lizzie. Please remember that."

"*Jah*, I do. I think prayer is what will get us through this bad time. See you tomorrow night at the supper."

Ellen was clearing away the teacups, the sugar and the milk when the sleigh bells on the front door jingled. To her surprise, it was Neziah who walked into the store, his wide shoulders filling the open doorway.

"Neziah." She laughed, flustered, not sure why.

His two boys peeked around him into the shop.

"Stay where you are," he warned them.

"It's all right. They can come in." Ellen walked toward them, drying her hands on her apron.

"Not unless you want half the things in your shop broken. A store is no place for them. Where they go, trouble follows."

Ellen wasn't sure how to respond; his observation was accurate. Instead, she just smiled.

"You close early on Wednesdays," he said.

"*Jah.* I do."

"And it's past closing time. I was wondering—"

"Ice cream!" Asa blurted.

"We're going for ice cream cones, and Asa and Joel and I thought maybe you'd like to come along," Neziah explained. "Have one with us. I'd like to talk with you."

Ellen knew immediately what he wanted to talk about. He wanted to talk about the fact that he wasn't interested in courting her. He probably just wanted to discuss how they would handle their parents. To her surprise, she was disappointed. Just a little, though why, she had no idea. "Ice cream?"

"Don't you like ice cream?" Asa demanded. "*Dat* said you did."

Ellen smiled at Asa. "*Jah*, I do. Very much." She couldn't believe that he remembered she loved ice cream.

"I think they have strawberry," Neziah said. "I'm buying."

And he remembered her favorite flavor. She sighed to herself. If this conversation had to take place, she thought this was as good a way as any. With the boys with them, it wouldn't get too personal. Ellen's smile widened at the boys. "How could I say no to strawberry ice cream?"

Chapter Five

Neziah and the children waited on the front porch while Ellen went through her routine to close the shop for the day. She locked the side door that Dinah would use when she returned, and the inner back doors. She left the outer doors leading to the enclosed porch unlocked for those who might want access to the freezers. She counted out the cash drawer and locked the contents in an old safe that had come with the property. Then she turned off the lights. As she went out the front door she reversed the wooden sign in a window that read Open to reveal the other side, which declared: Closed, Please Come Again.

"Almost ready," Ellen said as she joined them on the front porch. "My push scooter is around back."

"We can pick it up after we have our ice cream." Neziah lifted his gaze to meet hers for just a second. "We thought maybe you'd ride home with us in the buggy."

"Danki," she replied softly, following him down the steps. She was apprehensive about having this talk with Neziah, but she admired him for coming to her. Maybe he would have some idea about how to deal with their parents concerning the matter. Of course, she would have to make it clear to Neziah that just because they wouldn't consider each other, that didn't mean she was just going to agree to court Micah. Agreeing to court a man, at her age, was a serious matter. It meant she was considering marrying the man, barring any serious issues. Issues like the ones she and Neziah had encountered when they were courting.

Ellen smiled down at Asa as he trudged down the sidewalk, holding his father's hand, and peering back at her with curiosity on his face. The boy spoke well for a four-year-old, although most of what he said was an echo of his brother. He was an attractive child, but like his father, appeared to be serious in nature.

Several cars passed as the four of them walked along the street, but Honeysuckle was only a small village, so traffic was light. The historic village, consisting of old stone-and-frame buildings, a few stores and a tiny post office in what used to be a bank, had been there since the early nineteenth century. Large trees shaded the homes and sidewalks, their gnarled roots pushing up through the concrete to make the path uneven, but the residents had long grown accustomed to the irregularities. Porches were lined with rocking chairs, window boxes of flowers and friendly neighbors who smiled and waved as Ellen, Neziah and the children passed.

"Afternoon, Ellen." A gray-haired man looked up from his flower bed and raised a garden trowel in greeting. "Nice weather today."

"Not too humid. Fall's in the air," she replied. "Your roses are wonderful."

George beamed. He was a retired high-school principal and an avid gardener who had, several years ago, rescued a neglected Queen Anne–style house on Main Street and restored it.

Although most of the residents of the actual town of Honeysuckle were English, no one stared rudely or pointed fingers at the Amish in their quaint dress. Those *Englishers* who lived and worked there had long come to accept their Amish neighbors and were often on a first-name basis with them. It was a friendly village, a place where Ellen always felt at ease, unlike busy Lancaster or the larger towns that were overwhelmingly worldly.

McCann's Grocery occupied the site of a 1920s schoolhouse, and the parking lot had once been the play yard. Several pickup trucks, a few cars and two gray Amish buggies stood outside the brick store. Baskets of fresh vegetables were displayed on wide tables on either side of the peaked entranceway. Jason, a teenage stock boy, stopped stacking watermelons to greet them.

"Hey, Ellen."

"Hi, Jason," Ellen said. "We've come for ice cream. What's the flavor of the day?"

Jason, a freckle-faced redhead with a flattop buzz, grinned. "Peach. And it's great!"

"I want a double dip!" Joel cried. "*Dat*, can I have a double dip?"

Ellen chuckled, looking down at the boy. "I think a single dip is plenty of ice cream, even for a big man like your *vadder*. You couldn't eat a double if you tried."

"I could!" Joel protested.

"Jah." Asa nodded vigorously. "I could."

Neziah pushed open the door, and the boys rushed past him, dodged around the two checkout lanes and ran toward the ice cream counter, where another Amish family was waiting for their order.

Neziah held the door for Ellen. Their gazes met, and she felt her cheeks grow warm. "*Ach*, sorry," she said quickly. "I didn't mean to interfere." Why couldn't she control her tongue? What Neziah did with his sons was none of her affair.

To her surprise, his expression was more relieved than defensive. He offered a lopsided grin that was similar to his brother's. "You weren't interfering. I agree with you. The servings of ice cream here are huge. One dip should be enough, but..." He shrugged. "It's not easy knowing how strict to be with Asa and Joel when it comes to food." He followed her in. "My *vadder* says that Joel is just healthy, a boy with a *goot* appetite and that his weight will even out over time. But Joel doesn't run around like other boys his age. He always seems out of breath. I think he eats too much, but how do you refuse your child food when he tells you he's hungry?"

"It must be hard for you, being both mother and father." She reached into the pocket of her apron for her change purse, but Neziah stopped her with a wave of his hand.

"I told you this is my treat. I invited you."

"Danki."

The expression in his eyes warmed. "You know how it is, living with parents," he said quietly. "My *vadder* is a wise man, and he has raised children to adults, and it's not my wish to argue with him in his home, but..." He lifted a broad shoulder and let it fall.

"Sometimes it's difficult for our parents to see us as grown-ups," she offered. They reached the ice cream counter where Joel was bouncing eagerly.

"Two scoops," Joel begged.

Neziah laid a hand on his shoulder. "Four cones," he told the teenaged Amish girl behind the counter. "One dip each." He glanced at her. "Strawberry?" She nodded, and he went on. "Two chocolate, one strawberry and a butter pecan."

When they had all gotten their ice cream and Neziah had paid, Ellen took napkins from a dispenser and pointed out the window. "Would you like to go out back to the picnic area? The boys can play on the playground. It's shady and we can eat without worrying about dripping ice cream all over the store."

"*Goot* idea," Neziah agreed. "I just need to remember to come back in and pick up a loaf of bread, and some ginger cookies for my *dat*. He likes a sweet after supper."

"We want whoopie pies," Joel said. He had ice cream on his chin. "The chocolate ones."

Asa was busy licking his ice cream, and for once didn't repeat what his brother had just said.

Neziah glanced at Ellen and then at his son as he led the way to a side door. "No whoopie pies today."

McCann's sold a large assortment of wooden sheds, lawn furniture, children's play equipment, picnic tables and small, portable chicken houses for backyard flocks, all of which were enclosed by a tidy split-rail fence. Store customers were welcome to lunch or snack in the picnic area, and children were free to play on the sturdy swings, climbing walls and slides.

Ellen and Neziah sat down at a picnic table while the two boys ran to explore the play area. For a few minutes they just sat and ate their ice cream and watched the boys. This was something she'd always found admirable in Neziah. He didn't always feel as though he had to keep a conversation going. It was one of the things she remembered fondly from the days when they had courted. The two of them would often go for long stretches of time without speaking. But he had asked her there to talk. She wondered if she should start the conversation.

Neziah pointed out a brown thrasher in the grass on the far side of the enclosed yard. "Bold, isn't he?" He pointed to the little bird. "To be more concerned with what he can scratch out of the dirt than frightened of those two." He indicated Asa and Joel, who'd devoured their ice cream cones and were now attempting to cross a narrow swinging bridge that led to a barn-red tree house at the top of the structure.

"We have a pair of brown thrashers nesting in our orchard," she answered. "I think they raised little ones this summer." She'd always favored the rusty-brown birds with their long tails and bright eyes. Thrashers were in the mockingbird family and usually got along well with other species of backyard birds, unlike the grackles and cowbirds.

Asa had successfully crossed the swaying bridge and was scampering ahead of Joel up the ladder to the small structure on stilts. Joel plopped down on the bridge and dangled his legs over the side of the wooden walkway. "Come on!" Asa yelled in *Deitsch.* Joel shouted back, but Ellen couldn't make out what he'd said.

Neziah finished his last bite of cone and wiped his hands on a napkin. "I'm glad you came for ice cream, Ellen. I wanted to talk to you. Alone."

"*Dat! Dat!* Look at me!" Asa cried from the top of a sliding board.

"I see you!" Neziah waved and looked back at Ellen. "Well, not *exactly* alone," he said wryly. "I'm never alone."

Ellen popped the last bit of cone into her mouth.

He slid a napkin to her. "I wanted to talk to you about this whole courting business. First, I want to apologize for my *vadder*'s—" He shook his head. "I don't even know what to call it."

"You don't have to apologize, Neziah." She wiped her mouth and then her fingers, beginning to relax a little. He was being so kind. She didn't know why she'd been nervous about talking with him about this. They weren't kids anymore. They both knew what they wanted, and neither of them was going to be controlled by their parents. "My *vadder* was a part of it, too," she told him. "I know our parents mean well, but sometimes it might be better if they didn't get so...*involved*."

He smiled and looked down at his hands. "My father, and my brother for that matter, can sometimes border on being meddlesome, but this time I think our fathers might have a point."

Ellen had been watching Asa as he exited the tree house, sliding down a pole. She turned to look at Neziah, thinking she must have misheard him. "You think..." She just stared at him for a moment in confusion. Was he saying she *should* consider both him and Micah for a husband? That couldn't have been what he meant. She could feel herself frowning. "You mean you think our fathers have a point in saying it's time we each thought about getting married?"

He met her gaze. He was the same Neziah she had once thought she was in love with, the same warm, dark eyes, but there was something different now. A confidence she hadn't recalled seeing on his plain face.

"Yes. And I think our fathers are right in saying that you and I, Ellen—" he covered her hand with his "—should consider courting again."

Ellen was so shocked, it was a wonder she

didn't fall off the picnic table bench. Again, all she could do was stare at him. This was the last thing on earth she expected to hear from him. The warmth of his hand on hers made her shiver…and not unpleasantly. She pulled her hand away. "I…" She was rarely speechless. And had never been so with him, but she was so taken aback that she didn't know what to say. "Neziah, I…"

"The past is the past," he said when she couldn't finish her thought. "I think it would be fair to say that we were both young then, emotionally if not in years. But we're older. Wiser. Neither of us is the same headstrong, stubborn young person we once were. I know I'm not." He kept looking at her, his gaze searching hers. "Ellen, I was in love with you once and I think—" he glanced at his boys "—I think I'm still in love with you." He looked back at her. "I *know* I am."

She glanced away. The boys were seesawing. The birds were chattering in the trees. She could hear a young woman speaking *Deitsch* through an open window in the store. The world around her seemed normal, but hearing a man—an Amish man—speak of his feelings was not something she normally encountered. Even her father, who had always been a sensitive man, avoided talk of his emotions when he could help it. "I…I don't know what to say, Neziah," she said finally.

"Then don't say anything. Just think about it. Pray about it. It's important to your parents that they see you married. I don't mean this unkindly, but they're aging. As a parent, I understand the desire to see your children happy and cared for." He leaned back, crossing his arms over his chest. "As for me, enough time has passed since Betty died. My boys need a mother and I need a wife. Everything my father said is true." He shrugged. "We live next door to each other. It would be a good match. We would be able to take care of your parents and my father when the time comes that they can't care for themselves. And I would be a good provider. The lumber mill is doing well, and you've sold two pieces of my furniture in your store in the last two weeks."

Ellen studied his face for a moment, so confused, so overwhelmed that she couldn't think straight. Neziah was still in love with her? That made no sense. They had ended their courtship mutually, agreeing they were unsuited as husband and wife. Neziah had never spoken of love before or after the courtship had ended. He had married another woman, had children. He couldn't possibly have been carrying a flame for her for the last ten years. And yet…he sounded sincere.

Could she really consider courting Neziah? Would she actually consider marrying him?

Neziah would be a good catch for any woman. He was hardworking, intelligent and a faithful member of the church community in the prime of his life. While he might not be as strikingly handsome as his younger brother, Neziah's appearance was pleasant. As a widower, Neziah had kept his beard, but it was close-cropped, and Ellen thought that the few flecks of gray scattered amid his dark whiskers gave him a distinguished appearance.

It was a good face, serious but honest, with strong features and striking eyes. She'd always liked Neziah's dark eyes with their varying shades of brown. When Neziah's gaze locked with hers, she had always known he was giving her his entire attention, that he would listen and give serious thought to what she was telling him. Listen, but not be moved from his own position, she reminded herself.

"Neziah, I…I wasn't expecting you to… This isn't what I was expecting at all." She gave a little laugh. "I thought you wanted to tell me you weren't interested in our fathers' proposal."

"I'm not."

She blinked. She was beginning to feel like she was going too fast on a merry-go-round at the state fair. "I'm confused."

"I'm *not* interested in our fathers' proposal. I've thought this over. I think you and I should begin courting and you should tell my brother to look elsewhere for a wife. The two of you wouldn't be suited for marriage. I've been praying a long time over this and I think *Gott* has answered my prayers. You're the wife for me, Ellen."

She drew back a bit. She didn't like being told what she should do and certainly not by Neziah. "I can't tell Micah I won't see him, Neziah. He was at my house first thing this morning to give me a ride to work. He's very interested in courting me. I told my father... I told Micah I'd consider you both."

He stared at her for a moment, then the smallest hint of a smile appeared. "So you're saying you *would* consider marrying me? You still care for me, don't you?"

This was more like the old Neziah she had always known, trying to force his opinions, his way on her. And yet, not the same. The man she had known, the man she had almost married, had not been one to talk about feelings. Anyone's. "I'll admit no such thing." She felt heat rising in her cheeks, and she got up from the bench.

"Of course you won't. Not yet at least." Another smile. Then he stood. "Joel! Asa! Time to go." He turned to Ellen. "I'm going to go inside and grab the things we need. Meet you out front with the boys?"

She nodded. Once he had gone into the store, she gathered the two little boys and then walked out to the sidewalk. Neziah joined them, carrying a paper grocery sack. The four of them walked the short distance back to the craft shop in silence.

"I'll get your scooter," Neziah said when they reached his wagon. He dropped the groceries into the back. "Is it on the porch?" He didn't sound upset with her. In fact, he sounded pleased with himself.

Walking back to the craft store, Ellen had considered turning down Neziah's offer of a ride home. Right now all she wanted was to be alone and think about what he had said. Neziah was in love with her? Still in love with her, according to him. Was that possible? And how did she feel about him? The truth was, she didn't know. She definitely needed some time by herself, but refusing his ride home seemed childish. "I can get my scooter," she said. "I want to make certain the inner door is locked, anyway." She hurried up onto the back porch landing and then inside.

The freezers were to the right, and she always parked her push scooter against the wall across from them. As she reached down to grab the handlebars of her scooter, her foot struck something and set it spinning away, making a loud clattering sound. It was a soda can. Apparently, someone who'd come to access the freezer space had forgotten it. Ellen tossed the can into the recycle container, went back for her scooter and pushed it out the back door.

Neziah was just coming up the back steps. "I'll take that."

He stowed the scooter in the back of the wagon and then helped her up onto the wagon seat.

The boys were unusually well behaved on the way home. Neziah didn't have much to say, which was fine with Ellen because she'd had quite enough honest talk with him for one day. Her mind was flying in so many directions that she had to take a breath and try to relax and enjoy the summer evening ride, listening to the familiar sounds of the mule's hooves striking the blacktop.

When they arrived safely at her door, she thanked him for the ice cream and the ride home. She said her goodbyes to Asa and Joel and was about to walk away when Neziah called after her, "Will I see you at the widows' supper tomorrow night?" he asked.

She turned back to him. "*Jah*, I'll be helping out."

Normally, she would work late on Thursday evening, but the English high-schooler she'd just hired would work until closing.

"Goot. Goot," Neziah repeated. "See you there, then."

She watched him climb into the wagon; as he headed down the driveway, he touched the brim of his hat and offered the warmest smile. It wasn't big and full of joy like Micah's; it was… Ellen couldn't think how to describe it.

"Ellen?"

Her mother's voice startled her, and she turned to see her standing on the front porch.

"Did Neziah bring you home from the store?"

"*Jah*, he did. I went for ice cream with him and the boys."

Her mother flapped her apron at a stray

chicken. "Shoo! Shoo! Get away from my flowers!" She descended the wooden steps and chased the black-and-white hen away from the porch. "Pesky birds. Why your father wants to keep chickens I don't know. All the time they scratch, scratch, scratch at my flowers."

Ellen pushed the scooter toward the shed. "Maybe it would be better to keep them in the pen, *Mam*." The poultry was her mother's and had always been her mother's. In the fall, her mother had always raised extra ducks to sell to other Amish families for the holiday meals. Ellen knew it would be a waste of time to remind her mother that her *dat* didn't let the hens out of the chicken coop, she did. And it was her father who had often said that the chickens were too much work for her *mam*. But her *mam* loved her chickens and could not be persuaded to part with any of them, other than the old hens that went into the stewing pot or the young roosters that ended their lives as Sunday dinner.

By the time she'd put the scooter away, her mother had returned to the porch and was sitting on the steps with her feet in a pan of soapy water. It was another of her mother's odd habits; in spite of having two perfectly good bathrooms in the house, she liked to wash her feet outside at the end of the day. It was fine in summer, but one day in March, Ellen had come home to find her mam soaking her feet on the porch. The afternoon had been a bitter one, but her mother hadn't seemed to notice that it was too cold for bare feet, let alone washing them outside.

Ellen sat down on the steps next to her. "Tomorrow night is the widows' haystack supper. We'll be eating there, so you won't have to cook anything for supper tomorrow."

Her mother smiled and nodded. "I won't forget. They're raising money for that baby, the one in the hospital in Philadelphia. Poor little *bubbel*. We should all remember him in our prayers. You were always a healthy child, *Gott* be thanked. We were not so fortunate with the others, but you came plump as a partridge, screaming to bring the roof down." Her *mam* patted her hand. "A *goot* girl always. Never a trouble to your parents." She chuckled. "Other than to be so choosy about picking a husband. Happy we are to see you courting Neziah."

Ellen glanced at her mother. "I'm not courting Neziah," she corrected gently. "Or his brother, Micah."

Her mother's eyes widened in distress. "But..." she stammered. "They came to supper. Simeon said... Your father said..." Her eyes narrowed and her jaw firmed. "I'm sure you agreed to marry—" she thought for a minute "—one of them," she finished. She looked at her daughter, obviously confused. "Here's Neziah bringing you home. Taking you for ice cream. What are we supposed to think?"

Ellen slipped an arm around her mother. "You're supposed to think I had ice cream with a neighbor and his boys. And before anyone else tells you, Micah drove me to Honeysuckle this morning in his buggy."

Her mother's mouth gaped open and she clasped her hands. "You're courting *both* of them? *Nay. Nay.*" She shook her head. "That will not do. You must remember what is decent for a respectable young woman. Decide between them. One or the other, but not both Shetler boys. What will the bishop say?"

"What will the bishop say about what?" Her father stepped out on the porch.

"*Mam* thinks I'm walking out with both Micah and Neziah." Ellen rose off the step. "I told her that Micah drove me to the shop, and Neziah brought me home."

Her father raised an eyebrow. “Neziah did, did he?”

Ellen threw her father a look of warning. “But I’ve not agreed to court either of them yet,” she said firmly. “I just said I’d…” She searched for the right phrase. “I said I’d get to know them and *consider* courting one of them.”

“One of them, now, is it?” her father asked. “I thought you said you wouldn’t consider Neziah.”

“You must speak to her, John,” her mother fussed as she removed her feet from the basin. “You must tell her that people will talk if she runs up and down the roads with two beaus at the same time.”

He took her mother’s arm. Ellen picked up a towel from a chair and handed it to him.

“Not to worry, Mary. Our Ellen will do the right thing. She always does.”

Her mother sat down on the chair, took the towel and began to dry her feet. Ellen dumped the water from the basin into the flower bed. “I’m not worrying,” her mother fussed. “It’s an easy choice. Such a *goot*-looking young man, that Micah. Such nice hair. If I were her age and still single, I tell you, John, I would not be thinking too long. Some other girl will snatch him up, and she'll have to take the older one."

Her *dat* winked. "So you think our Ellen should marry Micah because of his nice hair?" he teased.

"*Jah*, yellow hair like Joel's. It's like spring butter. So sweet you just want to pinch his cheeks."

"Joel's or Micah's?" her father asked innocently.

Her mother gasped and her hands flew to her cheeks. "*Vadder!* To say such a thing. The little boy. You know what I meant. Little Joel." She sputtered. "All the time, you make jokes, but this is serious. Our daughter must marry, and she has a nice young man who wants to court her and she has to be difficult."

"When she could have a suitor with butter-yellow hair?" Ellen's father asked. Then he chuckled. "Let her be, *Mutter*. She's a sensible girl. She will do nothing to shame us or herself."

Ellen made eye contact with her father, deciding to simply not address his question about Neziah. "I'm promising nothing," she reminded him. "Just thinking on the matter."

"It's all we ask," he replied. "Nothing would make us happier than to see you make a good marriage and nothing would make us sadder than to see you enter a bad one." He held open the door for her mother. "Now, can we go in and have supper before my lima beans and dumplings are cold as last winter's turnips?"

Chapter Six

Ordinarily, suppers and other fund-raisers in the community were held in an Amish home, the same as worship services. Naomi Beiler, leader of the widows' group, often hosted the widows' benefit affairs, but due to the large number of people expected, she and the other members had decided to serve the meal at one of Honeysuckle's Amish schools. That evening was a haystack supper, a community favorite that provided sustenance and fun for everyone.

"Naomi thinks that we may have a lot of outsiders at the supper," Saloma Hochstetler said to Ellen as the two set plates, glasses and utensils on the first of the long tables set up under the trees. "And an Amish family from Delaware is here visiting relatives. They've been in Ohio with their family, and are on their way home to Kent County. Have you met them? Charley and Miriam Byler? She's about my age. They have the sweetest little boy. And Miriam is so friendly. You'll like her."

"I heard they were coming, but I haven't met them yet," Ellen answered, setting down another fork. "I'll be certain to look for them. We want to make them welcome."

Visiting between Amish communities and friends and families was one of the joys of Plain life. Often people would travel hundreds, even thousands of miles to spend time together. It was always wonderful to exchange news with those who shared the Amish faith from other communities in other states.

"It's not too hot tonight. There's a breeze, so there'll be no mosquitoes. Perfect, don't you think?" Saloma moved along her side of the table, keeping pace with Ellen and continued prattling on.

Ellen smiled. It was difficult to keep her mind on what her friend was saying when all she could think of was the possibility of her looming courtship and marriage, or, she corrected herself, her *possible* courtship and marriage. A flash of heat under her skin made her swallow hard.

Micah or Neziah? She was so certain she and Neziah weren't well suited, but after having ice cream with him the previous day, she wasn't as sure. There was something about him that had stayed with her long after they parted.

She was dying to say something to Saloma about the Shetler boys and the agreement she had made with her father concerning them. It would have been a relief to share her confusion—to tell Saloma about the frank conversation she and Micah had had when fishing. About how Neziah had declared that he loved her over ice cream in broad daylight, but she couldn't bring herself to talk about anything so intimate, not even to a dear friend.

Saloma could be trusted not to gossip, but how could Ellen confide in her when she didn't know her own feelings? She'd already told Micah she would consider courting him. She'd made up her mind that she would not consider Neziah. But then, being with Neziah had stirred up emotions and memories that she'd thought she'd put behind her. She'd barely been able to sleep a wink.

Love. Neziah had said he loved her. He'd sounded sincere, and she'd have given anything to hear that from his lips years ago when they were courting...when they'd almost agreed to have the banns called. How was it possible that he felt this way about her after so long and after all that had happened since: Neziah's marriage, having children, losing his wife in that terrible accident? It didn't seem possible.

"Lizzie told me—" Saloma rolled her eyes, pulling Ellen back into the moment. "Are you listening to a word I'm saying?"

"*Jah*, I am," Ellen said hastily. "Sorry."

"I was saying that the widows put up signs advertising the supper at the restaurant and the general store and the post office. One of the newspapers ran a story on the Blauch baby and how he's in the hospital, so that should bring in more of our neighbors from Lancaster County, English and Mennonite. You know, the regulars who always support our suppers and breakfasts."

"*Jah.* And maybe some tourists will come, as well." Ellen folded a snowy-white cloth napkin beside each place setting. One of Dinah's granddaughters was coming behind them, putting ice in the glasses. Children raced around the tables in spite of their mothers' warnings to not get in the way, and a girl of eleven or twelve years of age sat on the grass urging a chubby toddler to take his first steps. Inside the schoolhouse kitchen, Anne Stoltzfus was frying ground meat with sloppy joe seasoning, and wonderful smells drifted through the open window. "The widows should have a *goot* turnout."

Saloma grimaced. "I suppose, but you know sometimes those strangers don't respect Amish privacy. My *Endie* Rhody had two *Englisher* tourist women walk into her house last week and start taking photographs with one of those telephones that's a camera. Can you believe it?"

Ellen shifted the basket of silverware from one arm to the other. "Your aunt? Really? Which Aunt Rhody?" Saloma had two aunts named Rhody, one who lived in the next church district over and another near Bird-In-Hand.

"Menno's Rhody, the one with bushy eyebrows and the seven boys. Anyway, my *endie* was gathering eggs in her henhouse. She heard a car pull up. You know Uncle Menno sells those funny yard spinners that look like horses and buggies. The wheels and the horses' feet move when the wind blows. Anyway, the English buy them all the time. Nineteen dollars for a little one. Well, before my *Endie* Rhody could get to the house, she heard the kitchen screen door slam."

Ellen hadn't heard about the incident, but she knew of others that were similar. Still, it never ceased to amaze her how insensitive some people could be when they were away from home. "Your aunt found them actually *inside* her house? What did she say to them?"

"I don't know exactly, but she shooed them out and sent them on their way. They— Oh, look who's coming! It's Micah Shetler. *Nay*, don't let him know you're looking!" Saloma grabbed Ellen's arm and cut her eyes in the direction of the road. "I knew he'd be here," she whispered excitedly, still holding on to Ellen. "Isn't he just the cutest thing?"

Ellen glanced at the horse and buggy turning into the schoolyard. That was definitely the Shetlers' family buggy and Samson was pulling it. *"Jah,"* she agreed. "That's Micah."

"Isn't that horse of his beautiful?" Saloma demanded. "If he asked to drive me home, I wouldn't know what to say." She let go of Ellen. "I wish he would. Agnes went out with him a few times, with other couples, not a *date* date. And she said Micah's sweet, not wild, like some people say. But my *mam* would have a hen if I started walking out with Micah. She thinks he's not Plain enough. You know, because he's almost thirty and not baptized yet. My mother thinks that's a disgrace."

Ellen wished she had said something to her friend about her predicament with the Shetler brothers earlier. Saloma finding out later that Micah had driven her to Honeysuckle and that Neziah had driven her home the previous day would be even more awkward to explain now. And Saloma would learn about it. Nothing got by her for long. She would find out, and she would ask why Ellen had kept it a secret. But Saloma babbled on without seeming to notice that Ellen hadn't said anything.

"But you know Micah really well," Saloma continued. She'd paused in setting the table, resting one hand on her hip. As much as Ellen loved Saloma, sometimes her constant chattering and abundant gestures were a bit much. "You're neighbors, and you and Neziah used to walk out together. You know the Shetlers. What do you think? Should I set my *kapp* for Micah?" She chuckled. "Would he make a good husband for me, do you think?" She fluttered her lashes dramatically, making Ellen giggle, too.

Micah drove his horse to the open shed and got out of the buggy. As he was tying Samson to the rail, Bishop Andy approached him with a smiling stranger that Ellen thought might be the visitor, Charley Byler. The three began a conversation.

Ellen moved on to the next table. She hoped Micah would keep his distance at the supper. At least, she *thought* she did. As much as she hated to admit it, a tiny part of her was pleased with Micah's attention. But she didn't want it to cause hard feelings with Saloma.

Only in her midtwenties, Saloma was far from being an old maid, but she worried constantly that no one would ever ask to court her. Apparently, her old community in upper New York State had a shortage of available young men, and Saloma was one of five girls, all but one of marriageable age. Since their arrival in Honeysuckle two years ago, an older sister had married and another, two years younger, had just had her banns cried for a November wedding.

Saloma was a nice-enough-looking girl with blue eyes, rosy cheeks and a dimple in her chin. Her curly hair was tucked into an untidy bun that seemed ready to come down at any moment, and her silver, wire-rim glasses usually perched precariously on her nose. Other than Saloma's habit of talking nonstop, Ellen could see no reason why she didn't have more beaus. She was hardworking, good-natured and vivacious, though she did, sometimes, appear too eager to like others of the opposite sex and be liked in return. Ellen's *mam* thought that Saloma bordered on being fast, but Ellen knew better. Saloma's flirting was harmless, and she would have been shocked and hurt if she suspected anyone thought otherwise.

More buggies were arriving, as well as families on foot. The night's fare was a haystack supper, which meant that food tables would be set buffet-style with huge bowls of seasoned ground meat, shredded cheese, cooked rice, shredded lettuce, onions, tomatoes, peas, raw shredded carrots, chopped celery, green peppers, sliced pineapple, crumbled potato chips, Ritz crackers and corn chips and sunflower seeds. Guests could choose any combination they wanted and top it with melted cheese, salad dressing or sour cream.

Serving at a haystack meal was easy because each person took his or her own plate, helped themselves and returned to the table, where pitchers of iced tea, lemonade and ice water were readily available, as well as yeast rolls, butter and homemade jams and jellies.

Part of the fun of the evening's meal was that, unlike Sunday communal dinners, there was no hierarchy in seating arrangements. Tonight the only rule was that everyone ate together, and people sat male, female, male, female. It didn't matter if you were married or single; the point was to interact with friends, guests and relatives in a relaxed atmosphere and make everyone feel welcome. Ellen hoped to keep busy in the kitchen or refilling the bowls of haystack filling. Thus, she reasoned, she could tactfully avoid being seated next to either of the Shetler brothers. Unfortunately, her wish wasn't to be.

No sooner had Ellen and Saloma helped to carry out the last bowl of cheese sauce than Dinah appeared behind them, thanked them for their help and waved them toward a half-empty table of younger people. "You girls go on and enjoy yourselves," she urged. "It was kind of you to help out, but it's time you had some fun."

"But you may need someone to go for refills," Ellen offered.

Dinah chuckled. "I believe Lizzie, Naomi and I can handle that, dear. You two go along now. Find some nice young man and sit by him."

"You heard her," Saloma whispered when

Dinah bustled away to seat an English family who'd just arrived. "Maybe I can find an empty seat next to Micah or that sweet Abram Peachy. He was dating someone from one of the other church districts, but I heard she's going with a stone mason from Bird-In-Hand now."

"You'd better hurry," Ellen said. "If Abram's available again, he won't be for long. Look, there he is." She smiled at Saloma and moved away.

There was quite a crowd gathering for the fund-raiser. Ellen spotted Neziah's Joel seated between two girls; she didn't see Neziah, Micah or little Asa. She drifted toward the place where the elders were seated, noting that her mother and father, Bishop Andy and a local Mennonite couple had settled at a table. Simeon was there, as well, Asa on his knee. Dr. Gruwell, a popular pediatrician who made house calls to the Amish, was laughing at something Ellen's *mam* had just said, and his wife was deep in conversation with Neziah and Micah's *Grossmutter* Lydia.

Where to sit? Ellen's gaze drifted beyond the schoolhouse to an orchard. When she was small and troubled, she would retreat to a big black cherry tree at the edge of the woods line. She would climb high into the branches, find her favorite fork in the trunk and sit there looking out at the valley until she figured out a solution. She'd loved the solitude, the peaceful sound of the birds and the stirring of green leaves around her. What she needed was an hour or two in a treetop to think.

So many decisions to make…

First, did she want to be married to one of the Shetler boys? Second, which one would she prefer, Micah or Neziah? Marriage to Micah would never be dull. They had so much in common, and their household would always be merry. Or, should she try to reclaim what she'd once felt for Neziah? She sighed. Round and round like a snapping turtle in a barrel. Her thoughts kept coming back to memories that she'd tried so hard to erase.

"Ellen! Come here a moment." Dinah motioned from the end of the food table. "I want you to meet this couple from Delaware." When Ellen joined them, Dinah introduced her to Charley and Miriam Byler.

"It's good to have you here with us," Ellen said. As Saloma had told her, both Charley and Miriam were friendly. Ellen liked them at once. "Don't you have a little boy?"

"We do." Miriam laughed, taking a chair beside her husband. "But he's making the rounds with his cousins, Ava and Zoey King, and I can't seem to get him back. I wish I could scoop the twins up and take them back to Seven Poplars with me. He's a handful, and they're wonderful with him."

"Wayne King and Charley are cousins," Dinah explained. "The Bylers are staying with the Kings."

"Would you like to sit with us?" Miriam asked. Ellen nodded, and she, Miriam and Charley proceeded to take their plates to the buffet tables. Miriam chatted on, telling about their extended vacation, first to Ohio to see an aging aunt, and then to Honeysuckle. "Believe me, Charley will be busy when we get home. My brothers-in-law and my stepfather have filled in for him on the farm. But my sister Anna will be having a baby next month, and I'd like to give her a hand with canning. Still—" she sighed "—it's been fun seeing all the family and all the sights."

They returned to the table, and Ellen took an empty seat between Charley and Wesley King, the eighteen-year-old brother of the King twins. Charley pulled out his chair then backed away. Ellen's eyes widened in surprise as Micah slid into the seat, taking Charley's place. Laughing, Charley circled the table and sat across from his wife. As he sat down, he and Micah exchanged looks and both grinned. Ellen was sure that it had been a setup.

"Nice supper." Micah's eyes twinkled with mischief.

"Jah," Ellen said. "And excellent company." She couldn't help smiling back at him. She'd been had, but now that he was here, seated close enough for his trouser legs to brush her skirt, it wasn't so bad. In fact, she decided, not unpleasant at all. When had being with Micah not been entertaining? Between him and Charley, they soon had the whole end of the table laughing at their jokes and stories.

Charley was relating an amusing incident about a neighbor's goats when Micah leaned close to her. "Would you ride home with me, Ellen? After the supper?"

"I have to be up early in the morning," she hedged. She wasn't ready to agree to a long buggy ride that might end with Micah wanting to come in and stay until midnight.

"Straight home," he promised. She noticed that Micah was dressed in his good church pants, a crisp white shirt and a vest, not in the clean working clothes that most of the men were wearing. He was wearing his courting clothes.

She felt a flush of excitement. "I rode with my parents."

Micah poured water into her half-empty glass. "Your *dat* won't mind. I'll tell him that you're with me, so he won't worry."

"All right," she agreed. It had been years since she'd ridden home from a frolic or a supper with a young man, and she couldn't resist.

Micah raised his glass of iced tea and clinked it against a grinning Charley's lifted one. "I told you she would."

"Would what?"

There was no mistaking that deep voice. Ellen turned to where Wayne King had been seated a moment ago, and there was Neziah, slipping into his place. The King boy was nowhere in sight. Ellen shook her head in disbelief.

"Evening, Ellen," Neziah said.

"Hello, Neziah." She smiled at him, surprised by his boldness. "Have you met Miriam and Charley Byler?"

Charley stood and offered his hand across the table to Neziah, and by the time introductions were complete, the three men were talking, and Ellen was able to eat her supper.

The food was good, but the dessert would be even better, and she hadn't taken a large portion of the main course because she wanted to leave room for peach cobbler and hand-cranked ice cream.

Neziah didn't speak directly to her until she and Miriam rose to start clearing away the empty plates. He laid a big hand on her wrist. "The boys and I were wondering if you'd like to ride home with us?"

Ellen felt her face grow warm. "I can't. I promised Micah—"

"Too late, big brother," Micah interrupted, leaning forward. "You're going to have to be faster than that. I'm taking Ellen home."

Ellen stepped away from the table and glanced at Neziah. "I'm sorry," she said. "He asked me first."

"Sure," Neziah said.

Micah leaned over again and this time slapped his brother on the back. "Cheer up. Tomorrow's another day."

Gathering a stack of plates, Ellen started toward the schoolhouse. Miriam kept pace with her. "I hope Charley didn't do anything wrong, giving up his chair to Micah. I think he just assumed that you and Micah were walking out together."

Ellen looked at Miriam. She liked her, but she didn't really know her, and it would be difficult to explain the situation to a stranger. "It's complicated," she admitted. "Micah *has* asked me to walk out with him, but…" She took a deep breath. "But so has his brother, Neziah."

"Ah, his *brother*," Miriam said. It was growing dark, but Ellen could make out the young woman's thoughtful expression. "And how do you feel about that?"

"I don't know." Ellen grimaced. "I've known them both all my life, and they're both good men. Either one would make a good husband."

Miriam made a sympathetic sound. "I understand completely. Before Charley and I started seriously courting, there was someone else, a man I had great respect, even affection for. I spent a lot of time worrying over my choosing between them. Both had good qualities to be a husband, but they were different in many ways."

"How did you decide?" Ellen asked, moving closer to her new friend.

"It wasn't easy. I spent a lot of time praying. I knew that God had a plan for me."

Ellen nodded. "I know He does for all of

us. But sometimes it's difficult to know what God is saying to us, and what's our own will."

"Jah," Miriam agreed. "What's important is that you take your time, and not be influenced by what others—even your own family—want for you. You have to think carefully, consider what each of you has in common." She smiled warmly. "And you have to follow your heart."

Other women approached, arms filled with dishes and silverware. "We best get these dirty things into the dishpans," Ellen said. "They'll be putting out dessert."

"Can I help with the washing up?" Miriam offered.

"*Nay.* The boys' youth group has volunteered for cleanup tonight."

Miriam followed her inside. The school kitchen had no electricity and no dishwashing machines, but it did have two double sinks, two large gas ranges, a propane-powered refrigerator and lots of counter space for preparing food. A long table with a butcher-block top ran down the center of the spacious room. Tubs of vanilla ice cream, pies, cakes, cookies and cobblers stood there ready to be dished up and carried outside.

Saloma came in with a huge smile on her

face. "Abram sat with me," she whispered to Ellen. "And he asked to take me home." She elbowed her teasingly. "I saw you sitting between Neziah and Micah. Which one do you like?"

Ellen shrugged. "Maybe neither of them."

"But it's a *goot* start, isn't it, Miriam?" Saloma said. "First you talk, and then you see if you are attracted to each other. Ellen lives next door to the Shetlers. Pretty convenient, if you ask me." She giggled, reached for a tray and began to arrange paper plates on it.

Ellen cut slices from a coconut cake and slid them onto plates. "How are you serving the ice cream?" she asked Dinah.

"Some of the men have brought tubs of ice. We'll put the ice cream in those and dip it out as people come through the line," Dinah answered. "If you would just carry those trays of pie and cake, it would be a big help."

Ellen and Miriam were caught up in the serving and didn't get another chance to continue their conversation. Instead, with Saloma's help, they carried trays of desserts to some of the elders. Ellen found her father and told him that she had a ride home with Micah.

He beamed and patted her arm. "Take your

time," he said. "No need to hurry home. A nice night for a buggy ride."

"We're coming *straight* home," she said.

Simeon joined them, Asa trailing him. "Micah tells me that he's taking you home," he said cheerfully. "Glad to hear it."

"I want ice cream," Asa said.

Simeon laughed. "All right, if your brother hasn't eaten it all. Joel already had two slices of cake with ice cream."

"Boys are always hungry," Ellen's mother said. "I love to see a boy with a *goot* appetite."

Ellen was just going when Charley came up with his sleeping son. "I think we'd better get this one home to bed," he said.

Miriam said her goodbyes and hugged Ellen. "We're going home in the morning," she said. "I wish we'd had more time to spend together. You must come and visit us in Delaware. My *mam* has a big house, and there's always room for visitors. Bring your parents, too."

"I'd like that," Ellen said, "but the shop keeps me pretty busy."

"You should take time off once in a while," Miriam insisted. "Come whenever you like. The invitation is always open." She took her little boy from Charley. "As much as I want to get home to my family, it's hard leaving so many new friends." She and Charley walked away.

Soon everyone was leaving. The teenagers were folding chairs and benches, and the last of the guests were finishing their desserts. The evening had been a success, and Ellen expected that the widows' group had raised a record amount of money for the Blauch child. Pulling together was one of the greatest strengths of an Amish community, and Ellen couldn't imagine living anywhere else. Not everyone in Honeysuckle was well-off financially, but they were all rich in friends, a shared faith that never failed them, the warmth of family and a true sense of belonging.

"Ellen?" Micah stood behind her in the gathering darkness. "Are you ready to leave?"

She glanced around. There seemed to be nothing more that she was needed to do. *"Jah,"* she said softly. There was something solid in Micah that she admired. For all his teasing and lightheartedness, she felt that he really cared for her.

"You're not angry with me for trading seats with Charley?"

"Nay." She shook her head. "I don't mind."

"Good. We'd better be off. Samson's getting restless." He led the way to his buggy.

Ellen's heart beat a little faster. She felt a small shiver of excitement as Micah helped her up into the buggy. She sat up straight on the bench seat and smoothed out her skirt as Micah unhitched the horse and came around to get in on his side. He gathered up the reins and clicked to Samson. "Walk on."

Micah guided the horse into a line of other buggies that were exiting the schoolhouse lane. "You look awfully pretty tonight, Ellen," he said.

"Jah," came Neziah's agreement from the back of the carriage. "Very pretty."

"Neziah?" Ellen and Micah both exclaimed together.

"What are you doing here?" Micah demanded over his shoulder.

"Just riding home, same as you." Neziah leaned forward so he was almost between Micah and Ellen. "You don't mind, do you, Ellen? *Dat* took the boys with him, and I thought I'd just keep you and my little brother company."

Ellen couldn't help but laugh, and soon both brothers were laughing with her. And the ride home that she'd been both anticipating and dreading at the same time turned out to be more fun than she'd expected.

Chapter Seven

"What did you say?" Ellen raised her voice, hoping Saloma could hear her amid the hubbub around them. It was midmorning on Saturday, and they were standing in a line of eager visitors waiting for seats on *Storm Runner*, a popular roller coaster at Hershey Park. To be heard above the crowd, they had to compete with the metallic reverberations of the rides and the excited conversations of the multitude of visitors who'd come, as they had, to enjoy a day at the amusement park.

"I said, we should go eat after the ride." Saloma moved closer to Ellen. "I'm starving." She took a sip of her oversize soda pop and passed it to her sister Irene.

Two of Saloma's single sisters had come with them, making five girls, including herself and newlywed Susan Brenneman. Susan's husband, Ivan, Saloma's date, Abram, and Micah made up the rest of their party. As a married couple, Susan and Ivan were considered proper chaperones for a Saturday's outing to the amusement park, even though they were younger than Ellen and Micah.

Micah touched Ellen's elbow. "Move up," he urged her. "We'll be next." Being Micah, he'd been the one to arrange the trip. Usually everyone in the party would chip in to hire a van and driver, but today it was Micah and Abram's treat. They'd left home early, and because Hershey Park was less than an hour away from Honeysuckle, the group had arrived just as the gates opened.

The amusement park was the last place Ellen had expected to spend her Saturday, and she'd been uncertain if it was responsible to take off work and accept Micah's last-minute invitation. Saloma had mentioned at the haystack supper that she, Verna and Irene were going today with some friends to celebrate Verna's upcoming birthday. She hadn't said anything about Abram or Micah being part of the group.

Micah had surprised Ellen with an invitation Friday when he stopped by her shop.

Since Micah was as persuasive as his father, it was difficult to refuse him, once he'd seized on a plan. The truth was, she had a secret passion for Hershey Park, and she loved the rides, the faster and more thrilling, the better.

"You'd never get Neziah on this," Micah said when the smiling attendant waved them forward. "He gets nauseated on roller coasters."

Ellen shrugged as she allowed Micah to help her into the car. What Micah said was true, but she didn't want to be critical of his brother. Neziah had brought her to Hershey Park when they were walking out together because she'd wanted to come. Because Neziah didn't like the wild rides, though, Ellen had spent most of the day with his little brother, Micah. "Not everyone likes extreme rides," she said. "Nothing wrong with that."

He grinned at her. "It's something we have in common, loving the thrill. And when it comes to roller coasters, you're crazier than I am. You must have nerves of steel."

Ellen chuckled. "Maybe it's just a lack of good sense."

The attendant ushered Verna and Irene and the Brennemans into the seats behind them, but Saloma and Abram had to wait for the next ride. Ellen gripped the over-the-shoulder restraint as the coaster slid away from the boarding station and came to a stop on the track. She'd taken the precaution of knotting her bonnet strings tightly to keep her head covering from blowing off.

She heard the recorded sound of a heartbeat, then a voice from the loudspeaker said, "Get ready, here we go!"

The coaster rocketed forward, and Ellen felt a rush of excitement. Verna and Irene screamed. Their screams mingled with those of other riders, but Ellen only laughed with delight and prepared herself for the first inversion. The ride looped and dipped, flying faster than she'd ever gone on wheels, and was so exhilarating that she wished it would go on forever.

All too soon the coaster finished the last twist and plunge, and the ride was over. The group from Honeysuckle climbed out of the cars, ignoring several tourists who stared at them. "Must be from the city," Micah commented. He tugged his straw hat on and followed Ellen down the walk to wait for Saloma and Abram, whose car had just launched.

"I think Ellen and I will go on by ourselves for a while. Unless you girls want to dare the Skyrush?" Micah offered.

Ellen glanced at him. Leaving the group wasn't exactly following the unwritten rules of a date, but they were in a public place so she didn't see the harm.

Irene giggled. "That was enough for me. When Saloma gets off, we want some cotton candy."

"How about if we meet up for lunch at that place that has the good pizza?" Ivan pulled a small black cell phone from his pants pocket. "Call if you need us. Have fun."

"Call?" Ellen looked at Micah. "You have a cell phone?"

"Just a little one," Micah admitted sheepishly as he tapped his pocket.

"Oh, look!" Irene pointed. The roller coaster had just made its first inverted loop and a man's straw hat went spinning off to sail through the air and finally land in the grass at the base of one of the *Storm Runner*'s massive supports.

Micah laughed. "That looks like Abram's hat."

"How can you tell?" Irene joked and shaded her eyes with a hand to peer at the Amish hat, a small tan object against the green of the close-cropped lawn.

Micah laughed and turned to the group.

"Sure none of you want to come with us?" There were no takers, so he and Ellen walked away in the direction of the Skyrush.

"There's a dolphin show," Ellen said, keeping pace beside him. "Would you like to see what time the performances are? After we ride Skyrush?"

"If you want," he said without much enthusiasm. "Thirsty?" He stopped and pointed to a refreshment stand. "They have good lemonade."

"Jah, danki." Micah bought the drinks, and the two found a shady spot to sit and watch the passersby. "It was nice of you to ask me here today," she said.

The last-minute invitation had caused her to suspect that Micah might have had another girl in mind when he made the plans for the excursion, but she wouldn't mention that. She supposed that Simeon's plan had surprised Micah as much as it had her. Sunday past, her life had been set in a pattern, and now… Ellen sighed with pleasure. She didn't like to be pushed or pulled into anything, but now that she'd had a chance to get used to the idea, she could see all sorts of exciting possibilities. Maybe Simeon was right. Maybe God had spoken to him, and maybe this was exactly what He had planned for her all along.

Micah favored her with a broad smile, and she felt her stomach knot.

"So you're having a good time?" he asked.

She nodded. "I am. I love Hershey Park. It's such a nice family place."

He removed his hat, brushed his hair back out of his eyes and rested the hat on his knee. "Did you mind coming away from the others?"

"Nay," she answered. "I wouldn't have come if I did."

"I suppose you wouldn't." He spun the hat slowly in a circle, and Ellen suspected that he was trying to summon the nerve to tell her something.

As she waited, she thought to herself how handsome Micah looked, with his blond hair and brilliant blue eyes. His short-sleeve shirt was lavender, his trousers blue denim and suspenders black leather. She noticed other women looking at him, and it pleased her that she wasn't the only one to find him attractive. *I could be his wife*, she thought. *I have only to say* jah, *and in a few months the deacon will cry banns for us*. But was it what she wanted? Maybe it was exactly what she'd been waiting for. Maybe Micah Shetler was the man she'd been waiting for all her life.

"Ellen…" He hesitated, and his Adam's apple moved beneath the skin of his tanned throat. "I started the classes…with Bishop Andy. For baptism." He glanced up and smiled sheepishly. "He said it was high time."

"And you feel right with your decision?"

Baptism in the Amish faith was a huge step, not to be taken lightly or irreverently. Giving your word before God and the church community meant that you were accepting the Amish lifestyle for the rest of your life. Like marriage, such a decision was final. It was a great responsibility. She had wanted to be baptized since she was fifteen, but her parents had urged her to wait until she was twenty and certain. In the years since she'd pledged her faith, she'd never wavered. Accepting God's word and trying to live as He instructed had been and was her greatest joy. She couldn't imagine any other path but this narrow and steep one.

"It feels right," Micah said soberly. "Like coming home after a hard day's work, or watching the sun come up after a stormy night."

"I'm happy for you," she said and meant it.

"I want you to know that I'm serious about settling down," he went on with continued sincerity. "I want you for my wife. We'll be happy together, I promise you." He glanced around, his sweeping gesture taking in the whole amusement park. "If you accept my proposal, I'll buy us season tickets and bring you to Hershey whenever you like."

She laughed. "But it wouldn't be so special, if we came all the time. Part of the fun is *thinking* about coming. And when we're married, *if* we're married," she corrected, "we'll be too busy to take many days off. We'll have to be responsible members of the church community and set a good example for the younger folk."

"I thought we were doing that already, or, at least, you were." His twinkling eyes grew serious. "So let's be done with this. Will you marry me, Ellen?"

"We're not even courting yet," she admonished teasingly. When he didn't laugh, she went on. "I'm considering it, Micah. I am," she told him, "but this has all been so sudden. It's a lot to consider. The whole idea only came up a few days ago."

"It's not been just days. You've known me for a lifetime. It might be too soon if we'd just been introduced, but you already know all my faults and my good qualities."

She smiled at him. "And you know mine, as well—the faults, anyway."

He nodded, as if considering. "Bossy, outspoken, stubborn."

She knew he was teasing, trying to get a rise out of her. "You must be pretty desperate to think of marrying such a terrible woman."

He stroked his clean-shaven chin. "How do you think I'll look with a beard?"

"We were discussing my faults."

"Were we? How could that be when you don't have any? You're smart, pretty, hardworking and my father approves of you. What more could I ask for?" He made a wry face. "And you didn't answer my question. I'll be even better-looking when I let my beard grow in, won't I?"

She chuckled. "I don't know. I suppose it will be all right if it doesn't come in sparse like Marvin's." Marvin Smucker, a young man who worked in Simeon's sawmill, was so fair that his hair looked white, and when he'd married, his beard had grown in sparse and stringy.

Micah groaned. "Don't wish that on me. My

brother has a fine growth on his face. Why wouldn't my beard be equally fine?"

"Because Neziah has had to shave every day since he was sixteen, and you..." She tried not to laugh. "Not so much."

He put his hat on and pushed it back at a rakish angle. "How would you know when I started shaving?"

"Well, didn't you just say we've known each other all our lives?" She raised her cup to finish her lemonade. "Shall we tackle that Skyrush line?"

"Absolutely." Micah took the empty cups and deposited them in a trash container. "And then I suppose I'll have to go with you and watch those fish do tricks."

"They aren't fish," she said, "they're dolphins, and watching them perform would be very educational."

"If you say so. But to me, they're just big fish."

They rode Skyrush twice before meeting the others for lunch. Ellen had checked the time for the next dolphin show, and they all went together. The performance was a big hit, so much so that even Micah had to admit that for fish, the dolphins were pretty clever. They rode the Ferris wheel, and then another roller coaster called Fahrenheit. It was thrilling, but Ellen had to agree with Micah that the newer Skyrush was the best one. At his insistence, they rode Skyrush one last time before leaving the park around five, and then stopped at a family-style restaurant for supper before heading home.

The van stopped at the end of her lane, Ellen said her goodbyes to her friends and thanked the driver.

Micah got out with her. "Mind if I come up a while and sit on the porch with you?" He asked.

She smiled at him. "I'd like that." She waited while he spoke to the driver and paid him from his wallet. Then he joined her again.

He reached for her hand, and she let him enfold it in his. His fingers tightened around hers. Together they walked up the lane. It was the soft time between dusk and dark, and the air was filled with the chirp of crickets and the croaking of frogs. The chickens had gone to roost, and the horse was settled in his stall for the night.

"I had a really good time today," she murmured. "Thank you for asking me." She felt a little breathless, and wondered if the sensation was from the walk up the steep driveway, or from the warmth of Micah's hand.

"Ellen!" Her mother called to her from her rocker on the porch. "*Vadder. Vadder!* Our girl is back from...back from the singing. Did you youngsters have a good time?"

Ellen's father came out the door. He went to her mother's chair and placed an affectionate hand on her shoulder. "The amusement park, *Mutter*. Ellen went to Hershey today with—"

"Neziah!" her mother supplied. "I knew that. Just the wrong words popped in my head. Come sit with us. Did you bring the boys? I do love little boys."

"Mam," Ellen said gently. "Micah took me. Simeon's other son. Not Neziah. Micah. This is Micah."

"Little Micah. Are you the blond one or the dark-haired, chubby one?" Ellen's mother clapped her hands together. "Come and sit down and I'll see if I can find you some raisin cookies and milk."

Ellen swallowed hard. She looked at Micah, a lump rising in her throat. "*Nay, Mam*, he can't stay. He has to go home now." She gave Micah's hand a squeeze and pulled away, hoping that he would understand.

"Jah," he agreed quickly. "But thank you.

And thank you for going with me, Ellen. I'll see you at church tomorrow."

"Not far to go this week," she answered. Church was being held at their neighbor's, two farms down. "I'll see you there."

"Thank you for seeing our girl home," her father called from the porch. "Good night."

Ellen walked up the steps, bent and kissed her mother's cheek.

"Did you enjoy yourself, dear?"

"*Jah*, I did," Ellen said. And she had, but the excitement of her day faded fast. Her mother's remarks worried her. She wanted her father to make a joke of it, to say that they'd put their heads together and decided to play a joke, but he didn't say anything. He just sat in his rocker and sighed. She could feel his distress without him speaking a word.

Ellen rested her hand on the back of her mother's chair. "Are you tired, *Mam*?" she asked.

"She did a lot of baking today," her father explained. "I think it's just that she's tired. Cooking for tomorrow's church dinner. I told her she didn't need to make so many muffins and cookies. We always have plenty."

Ellen felt a wave of guilt for not being there

to help her mother. She'd planned to bake tomato and cheese pies tonight. No cooking could be done on a church Sabbath, and not much on a visiting Sunday, every other week. The Sabbath was supposed to be a day of prayer and rest so Saturdays were usually busy ones for the women, preparing food that could be served cold at the break in worship service.

And, she thought, even more guiltily, *if I marry Micah—if I marry anyone and leave home, who would be here to help* Dat? Her mother was not getting any better. The occasional memory losses and confusion were becoming more common. Trying to brush off the incidences as normal with age was no longer possible. Her mother had some failing of the mind…and it would only get worse with time. How could she think of leaving the household when her parents needed her more than ever?

A misty rain was falling the following morning when Ellen rose to prepare a light Sunday breakfast of muffins, cold cereal, juice and hard-boiled eggs. Her father would have to hitch up the horse and buggy, and the Petershwims would have to host the dinner inside, buffet-style, rather than outside on tables under the trees. It would make for more work for the women and probably more confusion, but the rain would be good for the late crops. Most of their neighbors were farmers, and farmers always welcomed rain in late summer. Ellen didn't mind. She loved the feeling of gathering for worship with her friends and neighbors with rain or snow pattering on the roof and against the windows. It always made her feel safe and content, even if the ride home was somewhat less than comfortable.

She threw a light raincoat on and went out to feed the horse and chickens. She'd heard her parents moving around in their bedroom, and she wanted to have everything ready when they came out to breakfast. Back inside, she washed her hands, put the coffeepot on and poured the tomato juice. She'd dressed for church earlier. All she had to do was trade her work apron for her Sunday apron, cape and bonnet. She'd been up late the night before finishing food preparation, so she had missed a few hours of sleep, but she felt good this morning. The promise of a day of peace and worship always lifted her spirits. The problems that had seemed so overwhelming last night had receded. She would find her answers in prayer, and whatever the outcome was, God would be her rock, as He always had been.

She had just gotten the butter and jam from the refrigerator when she heard a knock at the door. *Who would be coming so early on a church Sunday? Pray God it wasn't an emergency.* Wiping her already dry hands on her work apron, she hurried to open the door. To her surprise, Neziah was standing there, wet black wool hat in hand. "Neziah."

"Ellen." He shifted from one foot to another. "I thought I'd come over and drive you and your parents to church this morning. That way, you won't need to take your horse out in the rain."

"It's early yet," she said, and then felt foolish. Would he think she was ungrateful? "Please, come in. We're just sitting down to breakfast."

He smiled and ducked his head as he came into the kitchen. It was a low sill, and if a man as tall as Neziah didn't duck, he'd get a rude awakening. "I thought you might be eating, but I wanted to get here before your father hitched up the buggy. Save him the trouble."

"It's thoughtful of you."

He glanced at the stove. "And hoping maybe I could have a cup of that coffee I smell brewing." He grimaced. "*Dat* heated up last night's coffee. Says making it fresh is work, and work is against the rules on the Sabbath."

She couldn't resist an amused expression. "If I remember, you once told me that yourself. Didn't you?"

Neziah hung his hat on a hook by the door and went to the cupboard for a large white mug. "I probably did," he admitted sheepishly. "I admit I was pretty strict the year or two after I was baptized." He offered her another hopeful look. "But I've mellowed since then. I can't see where making a decent pot of coffee to get a man's blood moving in the morning goes against the Lord's law."

She rested her hands on her hips. "Neziah Shetler. You do astonish me sometimes."

"Do I? Good. Because no matter how many amusement parks and frolics my brother takes you to, in the end, you'll come to see that you and I are the best match."

"You think so, do you?"

"I do." His dark eyes grew serious. "I changed in more ways than my choice of Sunday coffee, Ellen. I'm not a foolish boy any longer." He hesitated. "But I am still the man I think you loved."

She tried to think of what to say to that, but found herself speechless. The Neziah she'd known had been unmoving on such things as whether his wife could work outside the house in a public place. It had been one of the chinks in their relationship that had led to their breakup. And what was this with his talk of love? Did he mean love in the same way she did? "I don't..." she began. "I mean—" She spied her father coming through the door. *"Dat."*

Neziah turned to greet her father as he entered the kitchen. "John, a blessed Sabbath to you. I've come to drive you and your family to services."

Her father smiled and offered Neziah his hand. "Have you now? Isn't that thoughtful of him, Ellen? Well, don't just stand there with your coffee cup. Sit and have breakfast with us. I insist."

"I guess the boys didn't want to come with you?" Ellen asked.

"Oh, Joel wanted to come but I told them to stay put." Neziah pulled out a chair and folded his long body into it. "My boys will ride to services with Micah and my *vadder*. Asa was still abed when I left the house. You don't want to wake him too early or you've got a cranky child on your hands all day. Let him wake easy and he gives no trouble."

"Sounds wise to me," her father said. He took his normal place at the table. "Your mother will be right out. She's good this morning. Real good."

"I'm glad to hear it," Ellen said.

Neziah eyed the muffins hungrily, but she knew he wouldn't touch one until after the silent grace. "Did you make these muffins?" he asked Ellen.

She shook her head. "*Nay*, *Mam* did."

"Well, I won't complain. She always was a fine cook."

Was, Ellen thought. She hadn't tasted these and hoped that her mother hadn't confused the salt with the sugar again, as she was wont to do. "Don't say you won't complain until you've tasted them," she warned.

Neziah's gaze met hers. "I'll not complain," he repeated. "I'd give your mother no reason to be embarrassed no matter what she fed me.

Or you, either." His smile widened. "I told you, I'm a changed man."

"We'll see about that," Ellen teased, and the two men joined her in laughter.

Chapter Eight

It was a short distance from John Beachey's place to Uriah and Nellie Petershwims's big stone farmhouse down the road, but Neziah drove cautiously, as always. His mule Jasper ignored the rain and the loud motor vehicles that occasionally passed the slow-moving gray buggy. Neziah was uncommonly fond of Jasper. He was a steady beast of burden, sure-footed and streetwise. Neziah could brush off his brother's and his friends' jests about *mule speed* and *long-eared transportation* for the knowledge that those he cared most about were safer with the big Missouri mule between the shafts. Micah's fancy horse might be showy for the girls, but the animal was too high-spirited for Neziah to want him for a driving horse, especially where the safety of his sons was concerned.

His mother and his late wife had died in a traffic accident when the van they'd been riding in had been struck by a tractor trailer, and Neziah had seen several fatal buggy accidents. He didn't like the idea of taking his chances with flighty horses who might not be steady enough to remain calm when a motorcycle or a wailing fire truck approached. Micah accused him of worrying like a *grossmutter*, and maybe he did, but he was never one to take unnecessary chances. He placed his faith in the Lord but felt that a man had to do his share by showing common sense.

"Looks like we're one of the first to arrive this morning," Ellen's father commented as he climbed down out of the buggy and brushed lint off his black wool coat. Her father was wearing identical clothing to Neziah's—his best go-to-meeting garments, which included the formal *mutze*—a long coat with split tails normally worn only to worship.

Neziah gave the order to Jasper to stand and got out to help Ellen and her mother with the baskets of food they'd brought for the midday meal. Ellen favored him with a warm smile, which went a long way toward easing the discomfort of what had become a downpour. "I'd be glad to carry these to the house," he offered, indicating the containers of muffins and the tomato pies. Even in the rain, she shone like the first star of evening. Most women would be fussing about getting wet, but Ellen took the day in stride with good humor.

"No need," Ellen said. "We can manage." Her father took a tray with the pies, and two of the Pettershwim girls came out with umbrellas to cover them in their run to the house.

"*Will komm*, Neziah," the one in the brown dress said. "Your brother's coming today, isn't he?" She gave him a toothy smile.

"We made schnitz pies yesterday," squeaked the one in lavender. "I know how he loves them."

He returned the greeting politely, trying to recall which of Uriah's daughters they were. There were four girls still at home with their parents, though they were all of marrying age. They always looked alike to him: average height, plain, freckled faces, reddish-blond hair, faded blue eyes that peered out at the world through thick, wire-rim glasses. The Pettershwim daughters all had small hands and feet, squeaky voices and not a single one had eyes that danced like Ellen's.

The girls' father was a man of substance

in the community, owning five hundred and twenty acres of prime Lancaster County farmland, a dairy and a harness shop. He had approached Neziah on the subject of his available daughters on more than one occasion. Uriah had pointed out that he was well able to provide good dowries for his daughters. Neziah knew the size of the jointure down to the dollar because not two months ago, Uriah had offered him his choice of any of his girls and the harness shop.

He hadn't been interested. Uriah's daughters were pleasant enough and they were devout members of the church. Any of the four would probably be kind stepmothers to his sons, but he wasn't willing to go into another marriage for practical reasons. He'd set his hopes on Ellen now, and if he couldn't have her, he might not marry at all.

As he guided the mule away from the house, Neziah scanned the long, open shed for his brother's horse and their other family buggy. He'd warned Micah to hitch up the driving mare, a steadier horse than Samson. He hoped Asa and Joel hadn't been too much trouble this morning. Sometimes, getting them fed, dressed and tidy for church seemed harder than a nine-hour day at the sawmill. They needed a mother to see to their needs, that was certain, but not just any woman. They deserved someone who would accept them as her own, love them and take them in hand. It was a great responsibility, and he wasn't certain he could convince Ellen to take on the task.

Keeping an eye out for his boys, Neziah led Jasper into the stone shed, removed his bridle and snapped his halter rope to a round iron ring in the old wall. He unharnessed the mule and pushed the buggy back far enough so as not to make Jasper feel confined. Some men wouldn't bother to unhitch their animals, but there would be a three-to-four-hour service this morning, the break for the midday meal and then at least another hour of final services. Neziah wouldn't see any animal of his standing so long in discomfort, especially with the inclement weather. Jasper was a social creature, and he was content with whatever horse or pony was tied beside him in the shed. Lastly, Neziah took a section of burlap, wiped the wet from Jasper's back and fed him an apple from his pocket. The boys would see that he and the other horses and mules were watered and given hay.

Other families were arriving, and friends

and neighbors soon joined Neziah. He waited in the shelter of the shed until his brother and father came in and was pleased to see that Micah had heeded his advice and had hitched up the mare instead of his Samson. He chatted with them all for a few moments before dashing with his sons through a lull in the rain to the huge stone barn where the men were gathering. Asa and Joel ran to play with other boys, and Neziah joined the men. It was always pleasant, the visiting with other men before church: discussing crops and weather, congratulating new fathers, inquiring after the health of older folk in the community and listening to the latest jokes.

They all waited in the barn until the bishop and the two preachers entered the house. When the last elder had taken a seat inside, the married men and widowers filed into the rambling farmhouse followed by younger men and finally the male children. Earlier, teenage boys had removed furniture and carried the rows of benches into the keeping room and two parlors. The big stone house was spacious, giving ample space for an aisle down the middle of the largest room, separating the women's section from the men's.

Neziah settled Asa on his knee; Micah took

charge of Joel. The boys couldn't be still for the entire service, but they would wander with other children their age in and out of the kitchen, have a snack and return, hopefully without causing a commotion. Normally, Asa, because of his young age, would have remained with his mother on the women's side. Since Betty's death, Neziah had tried to keep his sons with him during church, even though the women always offered to take them. It just seemed like the right thing to do.

Once the men were seated, the married women entered in much the same order, with the older or infirm given comfortable chairs near the front. Next came the unwed women, followed by the teenaged and younger girls. The widows sat with their own age group, or near friends or family. Many of the women carried babies or small children.

Neziah had eyes only for Ellen. She was tall and graceful, her posture erect, her hair neatly twisted into a bun, her modest *kapp*, apron and dress without a wrinkle. Neziah's throat tightened as he watched her. He admonished himself. It was the Sabbath; his thoughts should have been on the opening hymn, but all he could think of was Ellen and how it would be to drive her to service every worship Sunday and to have her seated beside him.

An elderly man, the song leader, known as the *vorsinger*, rose shakily to his feet, opened the *Ausbund* and began the first hymn of the morning a cappella. There was no accompanying organ or piano, as musical instruments were considered worldly. As every voice joined in the sixteenth-century Anabaptist hymn, the bishop and the two preachers retired to another room to plan the morning's service. Once, an English acquaintance had remarked to Neziah that Old Order Amish worship hymns sung in the high *Deitsch* dialect sounded like medieval chanting. To Neziah, it was natural and right, and the combined voices of his community filled him with peace. Both he and his brother had been blessed with their father's singing voice, and Neziah took more pleasure than he should have from adding his resounding bass to the cherished hymn.

The song had many verses, and it was nearly a quarter of an hour later that it ended and the *vorsinger* led them into "Das Loblied," the traditional second hymn of the service. It was then that Asa wiggled free from his grasp, crawled under the bench ahead of them and darted down the center aisle to where his grandfather was sitting. He climbed up on the bench beside Simeon and began to dig in his grandfather's pocket for the peppermints he usually carried there. Neziah was mortified. His first instinct was to go after the boy, but doing so would only disturb the service more as he'd have to climb over four other men to reach the aisle.

His father bent and whispered to Asa, but instead of heeding Simeon, Asa persisted in digging in first one pocket and then the other. More people were noticing. Then Asa found a wrapped peppermint, laughed and carried his prize back to the aisle. Neziah knew that he had to act, but as he was rising, Ellen suddenly appeared in the aisle, scooped up a protesting Asa and carried him out of the room. With a sigh of relief, Neziah returned to his place and took up the hymn again.

Hours later, when the community stopped for the midday meal, Neziah approached Ellen as she carried a platter of sandwiches from the pantry to the kitchen counters. Due to the weather, the dinner would be inside, but with so many people and not enough tables, there was a lot of commotion. "Thanks for seeing to

Asa," he said. "Where is the scamp? When I get my hands on him—"

"He's with Micah." She deposited the sandwiches, wiped her hands on a towel and motioned for him to follow her back into the pantry.

"He's only four," she said. The long, narrow room lined with shelves was in semidarkness, lit only by a single window high on the wall. Jars of canned peaches, green beans and tomatoes rose head high, and cured hams and slabs of bacon hung from the ceiling along with strings of onions and bunches of dried herbs and flowers. Ellen walked to a table loaded with trays of sandwiches. "It was a naughty thing to do during worship, but he's little more than a baby."

"He knows better," he answered. "It's my fault. I let go of his hand to turn the pages of the *Ausbund*."

"But there was no harm done."

She was so close that he could smell the clean scent of her starched apron and *kapp*, and something more. Honeysuckle? He took a step closer. "Ellen…" he began.

She turned to pick up one of the trays. "It was nothing, Neziah. I was on the end of a row. It was easy for me to get to him without bothering anyone. Little boys will be boys."

He raised an eyebrow. "Of course, if the boys had a mother, like you, they wouldn't be into mischief all the time."

She looked at him and pursed her lips. "Don't think you can guilt me into this, Neziah. I'm not the kind of woman who needs or wants to be controlled."

Now she had her dander up, which hadn't been his intention at all. "I was joking." He felt foolish. He didn't want to argue with her. Not ever again. "I didn't mean—"

"Ellen!" a woman called from beyond the sliding door. "Have you got more sandwiches?"

"I have to go," she murmured, holding the tray between them.

"I can carry that," he offered.

She gave him a quick smile that seemed more polite than anything else. "You best not. Excuse me."

He stood there for a minute chastising himself. It had been silly to make that remark. He hadn't meant to guilt her into anything; he really *had* been just teasing. *Attempting* to tease her. Why had he spoken before thinking, before realizing how it might sound to her? When they'd been courting, there had been arguments over what she had seen as controlling behavior in him. And in all fairness, she'd probably been right. But he wasn't that man anymore. Why didn't she see that? It was his own fault for trying to make a joke. Micah was the jokester in the family, not him.

He debated if he should go find Ellen and apologize or just let it go. Maybe he could bring it up when he took her home. But would it matter what he said? Was he kidding himself to think Ellen would ever choose him over Micah? If he were her, who would he choose?

He emerged from the pantry into the kitchen to find it empty. Or so he thought. As he crossed the kitchen, just out of the corner of his eye, he registered movement on the dessert table. As he turned, he saw a pie sliding across the white tablecloth...with the assistance of a small hand. Then a second hand appeared. The child's fingers closed around the rim of the pie pan and the lemon meringue pie vanished.

It would have been funny, had Neziah not known to whom the hands belonged. He strode across the room and lifted the hem of the spotless white tablecloth.

Two pairs of guilty eyes widened in shock.

The pie rested on the floor between them, ruined by little fingers. Joel burst into tears and covered his round face with quivering hands covered in meringue. Asa's mouth gaped, revealing partially chewed pie.

"What do you think you're doing?" Neziah demanded, reaching for the nearest boy, who happened to be Asa.

Asa was too quick for him. He scooted out from under the table and fled past a sturdy woman carrying a tray of bread, cheese and jam.

"Vas is?" Nellie Pettershwim exclaimed. The bishop's wife, coming just behind her, gasped. A third woman, behind her, laughed behind her hand.

"Joel. Come out here," Neziah said in an attempt to regain his composure.

Joel wailed louder, started to crawl out and managed to put a knee in the pie.

Neziah pulled him out gently, stood him on his feet and took a firm hold of his hand. "I'm sorry. Leave the mess, Nellie. I'll clean it up, after I scrub this one off." Joel had so much meringue on his face that he looked as though he was wearing a beard. Lemon custard trailed down his shirt and soiled his pants and shoes. A large gob of lemon clung to one knee.

Neziah looked from the boy to the circle of amused faces that had gathered around him and wished he were anywhere but there. And then, he couldn't help himself. He began to laugh, not simply an embarrassed chuckle that anyone could understand, but a deep, rolling belly laugh.

Which was how Ellen found him when she came back in the room, exposing himself for what he was: an indulgent father who allowed his sons to misbehave at church and then didn't even have the decency to discipline them as they so soundly deserved.

"I don't see that what they did was so terrible," Ellen's father said the next morning at breakfast. They had been talking about Neziah's boys and their exploit with the pie. He held out his cup and she refilled it with steaming hot coffee. "Better to laugh than to have the opposite reaction," he added. "If it had been your grandfather, it would have been off to the woodshed for me. I'd not have been able to sit for a week."

"*Grossvadder* Beachey was strict?" Ellen asked. She had never known him, other than by reputation, because he'd died before she was born. She walked to the stove to bring over the scrambled eggs and scrapple. Toast, stewed prunes and tomato juice were already on the table.

"Very strict," her father said. "He used to quote from the Bible all the time, 'Spare the rod and spoil the child.'"

"So it says. Thankfully, you were of a different opinion. For if anyone was a gentle father, you were, *Vadder*." Her mother smiled at her husband. "Let us give thanks."

This was one of her *mam*'s good days, and Ellen was grateful for that. Her mother had even insisted on cooking most of the meal, and the eggs were fluffy and the scrapple crispy on the outside and perfectly done. Ellen looked around the table and felt a surge of love for her parents. They had raised her with gentleness and patience, and she'd never doubted how much they both treasured her. She slid into her chair and clasped her mother's soft hand. All three closed their eyes and lowered their heads for the blessing.

"And what little boys *wouldn't* want a whole lemon meringue pie to themselves, if they could get away with it?" her mother asked when grace was finished. She laughed. "I might have done the same thing if no one had been looking!"

Ellen's father laughed and added milk to his wife's coffee.

The theft of the pie hadn't surprised Ellen as much as Neziah's reaction. She would have thought that he would have insisted on punishing the children. The old Neziah certainly had been more rigid. It was to his credit that he'd carted the boys off, cleaned them up and seen that they had at least the appearance of a good dinner before the final service. And he'd made not the slightest reference to the incident when he'd driven them home after church. *Maybe he has changed*, she thought.

But the reasons they'd broken up were still lodged firmly in her memory. Many times in the past ten years she'd reminded herself that she'd been wise to call off their courtship when she did...or they did. She had believed that Neziah would be happier with someone whose inclination was more biddable than her own, someone like Betty, the wife he had later chosen. He and Betty had been happy, as far as she could see, and probably would be happy still if she hadn't lost her life at such a young age.

"You remember that I wanted to go into the

shop this morning?" Ellen said when there was a lull in the conversation. She had bills to pay and bookkeeping to do. The craft shop was always closed on Sundays and Mondays, but she liked to go in for a few hours on Monday because she could get so much done with no customers to tend to.

"*Jah*, you go on, dear," her mother said. "I'll clean up the dishes. If you go now, you can be home in time for dinner. I'm making succotash with tomatoes and onions. It's a Delaware recipe my sister Sara sent me in her last letter. She lives in Kent County now, you know. Moved there from Wisconsin."

"Your sister?" her father asked. "You talking about Sara Yoder? Isn't she a second or third cousin?"

"*Jah*, *Vadder*, didn't I just say so?" She waved toward the door. "Go on, go on, Ellen. I'll *rett* up this kitchen faster than a horse can trot."

Ellen glanced at her father, and he nodded. "You heard your mother," he said. "We'll be fine. If she needs help, I'm here."

Ellen arrived in Honeysuckle early enough that it was still pleasantly cool. Early September could be overly warm, but it was still cloudy after the previous day's heavy rain, and she suspected there might be another shower before dark. She waved to one of the neighbors walking his dog and pushed the scooter around behind her store. All was quiet. No horses tied at the hitching rail and no hummingbirds at the feeder. The glass feeder with its faux red flowers was almost empty. She'd have to boil up a fresh batch of sugar and water for the hummingbirds this morning. She and Dinah loved to watch the tiny birds hovering in the air and zooming past the windows of the shop.

Ellen pushed the scooter up to the enclosed back porch and opened the wooden door. It was dim inside, and she paused to allow her eyes to adjust to the semidarkness. When she could see again, she wheeled the scooter past the first of the big freezers.

She sensed, rather than saw, the dark lump along the far wall. Alarmed, she stopped short, peering at the object, a blanket or— Suddenly, Ellen's heart began to beat faster. There was a low murmur, and then a figure leapt up out of what appeared to be a sleeping bag.

Uttering a startled cry of alarm, the intruder scrambled past her. "I'm sorry! So sorry!" She rushed through the open doorway and into the backyard. Ellen dropped the scooter, which fell to the floor with a crash. She hurried to the door in time to see the girl with a ponytail, wearing English clothing, fleeing across the backyard toward the line of trees that separated the store property from the house behind them.

"Wait!" Ellen called after her. "Come back!" She picked up a worn pink sneaker the girl had dropped. "You won't get far without your shoe!"

Chapter Nine

The trespasser stopped and turned around. “I’m sorry,” she repeated. “I didn’t steal anything. I promise.”

Ellen came down the back steps still holding the young woman’s shoe. “I didn’t accuse you of taking anything.” Now that she had a better look at her, Ellen was certain she’d seen her before, but not in jeans and a Philadelphia Eagles T-shirt. “You’ll need your sneaker.” Ellen held it. The footwear had clearly seen better days. The canvas material was worn thin; the lace had broken and was held together with knots.

Ellen heard the scrape of a window raising on the second floor of the house. *“Vas is?”* Dinah called down. “What’s all the shouting? Is everything all right down there?”

"Everything's fine." Ellen smiled and waved up at her. "Everything's fine."

Dinah looked down at the girl suspiciously, then at Ellen and slowly closed the window.

Ellen returned her attention to the girl, who was definitely older than she seemed at first glance, probably late teens or early twenties. It was difficult for Ellen to guess the age of *Englishers* because of their dress, hairstyles and makeup. But this girl wasn't wearing makeup, not even lipstick.

She was small and rail-thin with a heart-shaped face and large brown eyes that were shiny with tears she was obviously trying to hold back. Ellen suddenly remembered where she'd seen her before; the jeans and T-shirt had thrown her off. Last time she saw the girl, she'd been wearing a below-the-knee, blue gingham dress with a white apron and scarf—the uniform that all the waitresses wore at the Mennonite restaurant down the street. "Please, take your shoe." Ellen's heart rate had returned to somewhere near normal, and she tried to keep her voice soft as she moved nearer. "I'm not angry. You just startled me."

"Please don't call the police." The young woman was trembling from head to foot. "I'm not a thief." She moistened her lips nervously with the tip of a small pink tongue. "Please don't have me arrested."

There was something so vulnerable in her eyes that Ellen felt her stomach knot. She didn't look like a dishonest person or a dangerous one, but she *did* look desperate...and possibly hungry. "I'm not going to call the police," Ellen said. "Please, come inside. I'll put on a pot of tea, and we can talk about it."

The girl shook her head as she reached for her shoe. "If I could just have my sleeping bag, I promise I won't ever bother you again."

"You work for Margaret, don't you?" Ellen rested her hand on her hip. "At the restaurant? I've seen you waiting on tables, but we haven't met. What's your name?"

The girl stood on one foot while she hastily tugged her shoe over her bare foot. "I shouldn't have sneaked into your house, but..." She wiped her hand on her jeans and extended her hand. "I'm Gail... Bond."

Ellen studied her. There was a definite *Deitsch* accent, enough that she suspected the girl's last name might be something less English. "Well, Gail Bond, you'd best come inside with me before Dinah gets even more curious.

There's no need for us to alarm the neighbors, is there?"

Gail shook her head.

"Come on." Ellen waved her toward the door. "Troubles always seem lighter over tea." She led the way back to the house, half expecting the girl to cut and run. Inside the enclosed porch, Ellen removed a ring of keys from her pocket and unlocked the door that led to the back rooms of the shop. Picking up the basket of food her mother had sent for Dinah, she stepped into the back hall.

Gail followed hesitantly as Ellen led her through a storeroom and into the large, old-fashioned kitchen with its rose-patterned linoleum floor, vintage Hoosier's cupboard and round oak table. "The whole building used to be a single-family home once," Ellen explained as she switched on an electric light.

The kitchen of the original house remained, altered over so many years and changes of owners, and rebuilt after the fire destroyed the floor and built-in cabinets. Nothing was fancy, but the twenty-year-old stove and aging refrigerator worked well enough, and there was hot and cold running water.

"You're Amish." Gail glanced up at the

overhead light fixture. "You're not supposed to use electricity."

"*Nay*, I'm not supposed to use electricity," Ellen agreed. She filled the teakettle with water and put it on the stove to heat. "But because this is a business, we have to have a telephone, electricity, even a computer. Our Bishop Andy is understanding. He allows modern conveniences for commercial establishments, within reason. Please, sit down." She waved toward the table.

"I really shouldn't," Gail protested, hovering in the doorway. "It was wrong of me to sleep here. The only reason I did," she added hesitantly, "was because it rained yesterday, and I didn't have anywhere else to go."

Ellen thought about the sounds Dinah thought she had heard, and the empty soda can she herself had found. "But this isn't the first time you slept on my porch, is it?"

Gail shook her head slowly.

"Thank you for being honest." Ellen pointed to a closed door. "That hallway leads to the bathroom. It's private. There's no one here but the two of us. Why don't you take a few minutes to freshen up while I make our tea?" Ellen lifted the lid of her basket and removed a container of deviled eggs, several biscuits, a quart jar of canned peaches and a generous helping of sausage.

Gail eyed the food. "I couldn't. You've been kind enough. I should go. I can't be late for work."

"What time do you have to be at the restaurant?"

"Eleven. For the noon shift. I'm not full-time, not yet, but—"

"It's early yet. You have plenty of time. I won't take no for an answer," Ellen said. "You know Margaret wants her staff to be spotless. Why don't you take a shower and wash your hair. There are towels under the sink. We'll have tea and a bite to eat when you're done."

Gail eyed her warily. "Why would you be so nice to me after what I did?"

Ellen thought for a minute. "Because you'd do the same for me."

"I hope so." A shy smile brightened her thin face. "No, I would. I know I would," she answered. "But promise you won't call the police?"

Ellen responded in *Deitsch*. "Nonsense. Of course I won't. And if I'd spent the night on a dusty floor, I'd want to wash up. There's shampoo, soap in there, too. Please, make yourself at home." She smiled at her. "My guess is that you've had a rough time."

Gail didn't have to answer. The look on her face was proof enough.

"How old are you?" Ellen switched back to English.

The girl stared down at small hands, nails bitten to the quick. "Nineteen."

"Really?" She could be younger, and Ellen didn't want to encourage an underage runaway.

"Nineteen years and two months." The certainty in Gail's answer made Ellen believe that she was being truthful. Gail hovered by the table, hands trembling, clearly wanting to stay, clearly needing a friend.

"And you're Amish, like me."

"*Was* Amish. I was raised in the faith." Gail swallowed and looked down at the floor. "I ran away…" She raised her head and met Ellen's gaze. "You must think that I'm a terrible person."

Ellen chuckled. "I'll think you're a foolish person if you don't go in there and have a shower."

Gail was in and out of the shower in less than ten minutes, face scrubbed shiny clean, hair pulled back tight into a finger-combed ponytail, looking all of fourteen. She came back into the room shyly, glancing around as if she expected to see Pennsylvania State Troopers ready to snap handcuffs on her. "How did you know I was *Deitsch*?" she asked when she decided the coast was clear. "Is it the way I talk?"

Ellen chuckled and waved her to the table. Actually, Gail looked enough like some of her younger cousins to be part of the family. It was hard to miss the fair German complexion and the ruddy cheeks. But more than that, it was the *look* that most young Amish women had, an appearance of unworldliness that you didn't see in the English. "Tea first and then talk," she suggested.

It took some coaxing, but eventually Ellen got Gail to eat two deviled eggs, a biscuit with sausage and a dish of peaches. Ellen was certain that the girl hadn't had breakfast, and she suspected that there had been no supper the previous night.

"When did you last eat?"

"After work Saturday. Margaret lets us have anything from the buffet on Saturday night. They don't serve any of the leftovers on Monday. Someone picks it up for animal feed."

Ellen sipped her tea. "If you've been working, why are you homeless?"

Gail grimaced. "I was renting a trailer with two other girls out on Fox Hole Road. I paid my share every week, but I came home from work one night to find everything gone, even my clothes. All I had left was what I had on me and twelve dollars. The next day the landlord padlocked the doors. I guess Jackie kept my money and never paid the rent." She shrugged. "I thought I could trust her."

"And this Jackie used to work at the restaurant?"

"For almost a year. She was a cashier."

Ellen had heard from Margaret that she'd had to let a girl go because her register never balanced out correctly at the end of the day. "How long ago was this? That you lost the trailer?"

"About a month ago."

"Where have you stayed since then?"

"Here and there. Once, I slept in a barn. It wasn't bad, but it was smelly, and I didn't want to go to work smelling like sheep. But then I saw people going in and out of your back porch, so I knew it wasn't locked." Gail looked down at her hands, clearly embarrassed. "Usually, I'm out by six-thirty, but your store isn't open on Mondays, so I slept later." She wrinkled her nose and rose to take her plate and teacup to the sink. "Too late, I guess."

"Aren't you scared?" Ellen asked. "Living on the street?"

"Sometimes, maybe a little, but people in Honeysuckle are nice," Gail admitted. She turned from the sink. "Please don't tell Margaret. If she fires me, I don't know what I'll do. It's hard getting a job without papers, and my father wouldn't give them to me."

Ellen understood. Some Amish parents refused to hand over birth certificates and social security cards in an attempt to force their kids to come back home. Amish teens often had only an eighth-or ninth-grade education. Boys who wanted to leave the Plain life had carpenter skills. They could get construction jobs, but most girls knew nothing but homemaking and childcare. The English world could be a dangerous place for a young woman without skills and life experience, especially one who trusted strangers too easily.

Gail washed her cup and plate and set it in the drying rack on the counter. "I should go. This was really nice of you to let me shower. And to share your breakfast with me."

"I'm glad I had something to share."

"I'm going to go." Gail walked to the doorway and picked up her crumpled sleeping bag and big backpack. "Thanks again. I mean it."

"Where will you go tonight?" Ellen asked, carrying her teacup to the sink.

"Don't worry about me. I'll be all right."

Ellen walked toward Gail. "Have you thought about going home?"

"Every day." She hung her head, then slowly lifted it to look at Ellen. "But I'm not going to." She exhaled. "My father is not a 'spare the rod' sort." She looked down at her feet and then back up at Ellen again. "I'll save up, rent a room somewhere and maybe buy a car. Then I might want to go to school, get a high-school diploma." She straightened to her full height. "I can't thank you enough for being so nice to me."

Ellen walked her out through the back and watched her cut across the grass toward the street. Ellen was just walking down the hall toward the front of the shop when Dinah came down the stairs. "Who was that?"

"Um… Gail. You might know her from the diner? She's a waitress."

Dinah made a sound of disapproval but didn't respond. She hustled into the main shop, carrying a broom. "After I've dusted and swept I have some visiting to do. I'll be back late in the afternoon to unpack the boxes that came Friday."

"It's your day off, Dinah. You know I don't expect you to work on your day off," Ellen said, walking around the counter to grab her accounts notebook. She tried to do her accounting on the computer the way her accountant had showed her, but she liked to keep tallies on paper, as well.

There was a knock at the door and both women glanced in that direction. The Closed sign hung in the window.

Ellen bent to see who was at the door. "It's Simeon," she said with surprise. "Let him in."

Dinah went to the door, turned the dead bolt and opened it.

"You're closed today," Simeon said, smiling at them both. "And here the two of you are, hard at work as usual."

"Not so hard," Dinah said, latching the door behind him. "Just sweeping up a bit of dust."

He gave Dinah an appraising look. "I don't know why you want to live in Honeysuckle, away from the community. An attractive woman like you." He winked at her. "Don't you think it's time you remarried?"

"I like my independence," Dinah proclaimed

as she resumed sweeping. "You giving advice on getting married is the pot calling the kettle black, Simeon Shetler." She rapped one of his crutches with the bristle end of the broom to make him move. "Even as troublesome, long-winded and free with sweet talk as you are, I imagine someone would have you."

Ellen grinned and went back to looking for her notebook in the bin under the counter. If she didn't know better, she'd think the two of them were sweet on each other.

"You may not believe me, Dinah, but I'm only speaking the truth." Simeon leaned against a set of shelves his boys had made for the store the previous year. They were pine and meant to be utilitarian, but they were beautiful just the same. "You look ten years younger than you are," he went on. "And you can outcook and outsew any young woman in Lancaster County."

"Go on with you," Dinah fussed. "I wasn't born in a celery patch. Everyone knows you can charm the crows off the fence posts with your blather." But Ellen knew by the flush of Dinah's cheeks that she was pleased.

Simeon grinned and glanced at Ellen. "Neziah and I brought that painted hope chest he's been working on. He walked over to your house this morning to tell you it was done, and your mother said you were here. I was going to the mill for feed, so we just brought the chest along."

"Does Neziah need help carrying it in?" she asked.

"*Nay*, we brought Abram with us."

Neziah was a fine craftsman. He built his chests, stools and small tables out of white pine and then painted old Pennsylvania Dutch patterns on them in primitive reds, blues and yellows. His stylistic doves and flowers were particularly popular with the English tourists.

"I can hold the door open, at least." Ellen went out the front door and from the front porch saw the two men unloading the pretty piece of furniture from the back of the wagon.

"Morning, Ellen," Neziah said. "The finish on this is dry, so I thought you wouldn't mind if we delivered it today." He smiled up at her. She returned his greeting and exchanged a few words with Abram.

"Where are your boys?" she asked as the two men carried the chest up onto the front porch and into the store. "Here, let me get the door for you."

"Micah took them fishing," Neziah answered. "The last time we took them to the feed mill, we almost lost one in the millpond and the other in the machinery. Didn't want the same thing to happen today. I try to watch them, but they're unruly."

Abram laughed. "You can say that again. Joel put two worms in my lunchbox last week."

She smiled, remembering Sunday's pie episode. "I hope you didn't get in trouble with the bishop about yesterday."

"Nay," Neziah said. "Bishop Andy came by the sawmill early this morning. Wanted to order oak posts for his new stable. I asked him if he'd heard about my pie snatchers, and he said he'd spent a lot of church services as a boy trying to figure out how to do exactly the same trick and not get caught."

"We're fortunate to have such a wise spiritual leader," Ellen commented as she showed them where to put the chest.

"*Jah*, but don't forget," Simeon reminded them. "Bishop Andy was God's choice. He doesn't make mistakes in those he leads to head up the faith." He walked slowly with the aid of his crutches to admire the chest. "I think the blue and yellow ones are the best. This should sell quick, don't you think?"

"I believe it will," Dinah said. "I had a customer earlier this month who asked about a hope chest. I didn't even know that English girls collected linens and such for their weddings anymore."

"If you have anyone show interest, you can tell them that Neziah can carve the names of the bride and groom on the front," Simeon said.

Neziah nodded. "Or make something special to order."

"Come back to the office with me, and I'll give you a receipt," Ellen said.

"No need for that, is there?" But he followed her, leaving his father, Abram and Dinah to continue talking about the items that sold best to the tourists.

"It's a beautiful piece," Ellen said, turning on the light in her office. "I don't know where you find the time. You keep pretty long hours at the sawmill."

"Not as much as I'd like," he said. "The mill is our livelihood. I took up the job of sawyer because it was my father's craft, but the woodworking, that I do for pleasure. It calms me—sanding, fitting together the joints. I like taking a length of wood and turning it into something useful."

"And beautiful," she reminded him as she entered his bridal chest in her ledger.

"*Jah*, if you say so. That, too."

He moved closer to her desk, and she looked up at him. He'd put on a clean blue shirt and dark trousers to come to town, but the scents of fresh sawdust, leather and evergreen boughs hovered around him. She knew that scent, and with it came a wave of memories, memories she thought she'd forgotten.

"Ellen, I wanted...*we* wanted to invite you and your parents to supper tonight. It won't be fancy. None of us are great cooks, but it would make me happy if you would join us."

She nodded, wishing he wasn't standing so near. "Will Micah be there, too?"

"*Jah*, he will. Just our family, though. My father, Asa and Joel, my brother and me."

She took a deep breath and let it out slowly. She'd thought to have this evening to herself. But the days were fast coming one after another. One month, she'd promised her father. She'd said she'd give this seeing both Shetler boys a month. But she knew very well that her father, that all the men in her life, including the Shetlers, would expect to hear her opinion after that time. And while no one had suggested she need to choose one of the brothers by October, she knew that's what everyone expected of her. Which left her with what? Three more weeks? Of course, she could choose to stop seeing both Micah and Neziah, but that was seeming more unlikely as time passed. She was becoming accustomed to thinking of herself as someone who would marry in the immediate future…a woman who could look forward to being a mother and managing her own home.

"Thank you for asking me," she said softly. "I would like to come, but…" She hesitated.

"But what?" He leaned over her, making the room seem suddenly small.

"But…" She smiled up at him. "I think it would be best if I came alone this evening, if you don't mind. It might be easier for all of us if we didn't feel that my mother and father were watching every move, listening to every word."

He smiled in response to her smile and nodded. "A good idea. A very good idea." He rested a hand on her desk. "They *do* seem in favor of you marrying a Shetler. I just hope it isn't Micah they're rooting for, because I would make you happiest."

She got to her feet. "I think I'm the one to decide that. It is my future, after all."

"Not just yours, but mine and my sons'. And Micah's, too."

He reached out and brushed her cheek tenderly with a callused thumb, a touch as gentle as the one she'd used when she'd caught a Luna moth trapped inside the screen porch and set it free. Ellen's mouth went suddenly dry at his familiarity.

"You need to think this through carefully," he said quietly. "Because whatever you decide, nothing will ever be the same for any of us again."

Chapter Ten

At six o'clock that evening, after she'd finished the milking and seen that her parents were sitting down to a light supper, Ellen started down a lane that led from her father's property to the Shetlers'. It was an old logging road: narrow, dirt and wooded on both sides. She'd taken care to use mosquito repellent liberally before she began the walk. She carried a wicker basket with cinnamon-raisin sticky buns and her birding binoculars.

Evening was the best time to sight unusual species. She'd heard warblers in the orchard, but the little birds had been fluttering from one heavily leafed branch to another, making it difficult to identify them. She'd seen a magnolia warbler on Saturday and wanted to log it before they took on autumn coloring and became what birders referred to as *confusing fall warblers*, because they looked so much alike. Like many other birds, warblers migrated from north to south, and birds that had spent the summer in Pennsylvania would soon be leaving for warmer climates. Lancaster County was a good place for birding, but not as good as the coastal areas farther east. Someday, Ellen hoped to be able to travel to Chincoteague, Virginia or the Delaware Bay during fall or springtime migrations.

As she walked, Ellen thought about the girl who had been sleeping on her porch. It pained Ellen to think that the girl might spend another night in a barn. Should she have done more for her than just given her a meal and let her take a shower? Had she failed in charity by merely giving her food and a place to bathe and then sending her off with nothing more than a prayer? Where was the line between helping a stranger in need and putting one's self and family in danger?

Ellen had never hesitated when it had come time for her to join the church, but for Amish young adults, it was a personal decision. Naturally, families wanted their children to accept baptism in the faith, but no one could make that decision for them. In the Honeysuckle community many families had a child who'd chosen the English world, and so long as they hadn't joined the church when they left, they were usually welcomed home with open arms. If she knew Gail better, there wouldn't be a question about helping her—unless Gail had accepted the faith and *then* run away. Then Gail would have been under a ban. No one in the community would be able to eat with her. They weren't even supposed to speak to her. It wasn't meant as punishment but as a way to bring the lost sheep back to the fold; anyone who returned to the faith was welcomed with open arms. Gail hadn't said if she had been baptized or not, and Ellen hadn't asked. Should she have?

Perhaps, after a year or two away, Gail would decide to return to the faith. Staying away was difficult because church was the heart of Old Order Amish lives. Or maybe family was the heart of the church. Ellen couldn't imagine living without the quiet beauty of community worship or living apart from those she loved.

That was one reason Simeon's suggestion was gaining so much favor with her. Amish wives accepted that they would go wherever their husbands chose to live. Some families who'd lived in Lancaster County for generations were pulling up roots and moving out west, where there was cheap land to be had. She'd read that their county had some of the richest farmland in the world, and very little was ever sold. And the majority of that farmland was already in Amish hands, land never to be sold, but passed down to sons and grandsons.

The sound of hooves and the creak of wheels pulled Ellen from her reverie. As she glanced up, Butterscotch came trotting around the bend ahead. Simeon waved from the two-wheeled cart. Joel smiled at her but kept both hands tightly on the reins.

"Guder owed," she called. *Good evening.* She'd half expected either Micah or Neziah to walk out to meet her, but she was surprised to see Simeon and Joel. Simeon waved and returned her greeting. "I'm driving!" Joel shouted. His grandfather slipped an arm around the boy's shoulders and aided him in gently reining the little palomino to a walk and finally a halt. "I drove all the way here," the little boy boasted. "Did you see me? *Grossdaddi* hardly helped at all!"

"Wonderbor," Ellen said, brushing the golden mane out of the pony's eyes and strok-

ing his face and velvety nose. "Your *dat* will be pleased with you."

"We thought you might like a ride up to the house," Simeon explained. "Mosquitoes are pretty fierce out here in the evenings."

"Haven't been bitten," she replied, coming around to climb up into the cart beside Joel. "Mosquito spray."

"Micah always tells me to put it on," Simeon said. "But I hate the smell of the stuff. And it always feels greasy on my skin." He took the leather reins from Joel, gave the pony the command to walk on and turned the cart at the first wide place in the lane. "The boys are putting supper together," he explained. "I have to warn you, I'm not sure what they'll come up with. Neziah wanted to make a chicken stew, and Micah argued for spaghetti."

"*Onkel* Micah burned the biscuits," Joel volunteered. "Asa had to throw them to the chickens."

"Whatever we have, I'm sure it will be fine," Ellen said.

"Neziah and Micah are both trying their best to impress you," Simeon confided. He made a clicking sound, and Butterscotch broke into a trot. "Either one would be a good match for you. Neziah inherits the house, but

Micah won't come to a wife empty-handed." He stole a glance in her direction. "You know I've made provision for his future. There's land for him here, and he'll always have a job with Neziah. He's a hard worker, and you'd never do without."

She turned her head to face him. "I'm making no promises, Simeon. I haven't said I'd be willing to marry either of your sons."

"*Nay*, you haven't said, but you and I know you will. Come on, you can tell me." He ran his fingers through his beard thoughtfully as he studied her. "Which one is your favorite?"

"My *mam* likes Micah for me, but I think *Dat* favors Neziah," she replied. "Although he hasn't come right out and said so."

"But you," Simeon persisted. "Which one do *you* like best?"

"It's not a matter of which I like best, is it? If I choose, I have to choose who would make the best husband for me. Who God has chosen for me."

"*Onkel* says you like him best," Joel put in. "Because if you marry our *dat*, you get stuck with Asa and me." He made a face. "*Grossdaddi* says we are not *goot* boys."

Ellen wasn't sure how to reply to that. Joel was young, but he took delight in being mischievous in order to get attention. So if she agreed with him, she would only add to the problem. "I think that when you go to school and see how the bigger boys behave, you will do better," she pronounced. "Especially since you are the older brother, and Asa watches you to see how he should act."

Joel seemed to consider that for a moment then nodded.

"Would you like to have a new mother?" Ellen asked him thoughtfully. "Or do you like having your *dat* all to yourself?"

"Just me and Asa and *Dat*," he said loudly. "*Onkel* says that a *mutter* will make us wash behind our ears and eat cauliflower and Brussels sprouts every day." He screwed up his face. "I don't like them. Yuck."

She met Simeon's gaze and they both laughed. "It doesn't sound like Micah's playing fairly," she pointed out.

"It sounds like he wants you for his wife," Simeon countered.

Ellen returned her attention to Joel. "I don't have Brussels sprouts with me, but do you like raisin-cinnamon buns and *kuchen*?" she asked. When he nodded, she lifted the cloth on top of the basket, letting Joel get a whiff of the sticky buns her mother had sent. "So, if a *mutter* cooks healthy vegetables," she told him, "she can also bake delicious goodies that small boys enjoy."

Simeon chuckled. "She has you there, Joel. This boy can eat his weight in raisin buns."

"With sugar icing!" Joel exclaimed, and his round little face creased in a grin. "Can I have one now?"

Ellen shook her head. "After supper, and only when your *vadder* or *Grossdaddi* says you may."

Joel frowned and his lower lip came out, but when neither of the adults paid attention, he reached for the pony's reins again. "I want to drive," he insisted. "Let me drive, *Grossdaddi*!"

"*Nay,* enough for tonight." Simeon held on to the reins. "Maybe tomorrow if you get into no trouble tonight." He glanced at Ellen. "You have a *goot* way with *die kinner.* You will make a fine mother, and I know my Irma would be pleased whichever of my sons you choose to marry."

The pony cart jounced into a rut in the dirt road, and Ellen took hold of the seat to keep her balance. "*If* I choose either," Ellen reminded him. But from the satisfied expression on Simeon's face, she knew that he took her agreement to wed either Neziah or Micah as something she had already accepted.

Ellen remembered the Shetler household back when Neziah and Micah were small and their mother, Irma, was in full control of the house. It had been a tidy, pleasant place, smelling of newly baked bread and polished floors. Lines of laundry had stretched outside on Mondays, which was always wash day, and she'd often seen the brothers on hands and knees scrubbing the porch or washing the windows. But this evening, she was clearly in a home managed by three men and occupied by active children.

Wash hung on the line still, although it was past the time to bring it in. And had her mother seen the manner in which the clean clothes had been hung, she would have thrown her apron over her head and wailed in disapproval. Most things had merely been thrown over the line, rather than pinned neatly. There was no order. Towels dragged on the ground, and men's trousers were interspersed with boys' nightshirts, washcloths, undergarments and scrub cloths. Sheets had been tossed over shrubs, and one had slid off and lay in a damp pile on the ground. Worse, blackbirds sat on the clothesline, soiling clean, or what should have been clean, garments and linens.

Inside the house, an effort had clearly been made to sweep the floor and put the kitchen in order. Someone had scrubbed the floor; the bucket full of dirty water and the mop remained in a doorway. The windows needed cleaning, and cobwebs hung from the ceiling. Thanks be, there were no food scraps or unpleasant smells in the kitchen, but in order to reach the table, Ellen had to step over or dodge a whirl-a-gig, a child's toy wagon missing one wheel and turned upside down, and a collection of wooden toy animals. The wagon was attached to Asa, or Asa to the wagon, by a rope looped around his waist, and he was demanding that someone replace the missing wheel.

Neziah stood at the stove stirring a huge kettle of what, Ellen wasn't certain, but he welcomed her in and waved her to a seat at the table. Micah came in right behind them, scooped up Asa and the wagon and carried them both down the hall. "Evening, Ellen," he called over his shoulder. "Glad you could come have supper with me."

There was a loud squawk and Asa squealed with laughter. Joel rushed through the kitchen into the front room and immediately joined the fun. Something heavy fell or was pushed over, and Micah came out with a brown hen tucked firmly under his arm. "Asa let Rosy in again," he explained, stray feathers trailing behind him. Asa, protesting loudly, was right behind him. Micah carried the chicken to the back door and deposited her on the porch. "Rosy cannot come into the house, Asa. Chickens belong outside."

"I want Rosy!" Asa cried.

"You heard your uncle," Neziah threw over his shoulder from the stove. "No chickens in the house. Now, wash your hands for supper. You, too, Joel."

"Something smells good. What are we having? Stew or spaghetti?"

"Neither," Neziah said. "Vegetable soup." He smiled at Ellen as he carried a loaf of store-bought white bread and a cracked saucer containing a stick of butter to the table. "I hope you like vegetable soup. Have a seat."

She glanced at the bread as she sat and wished she'd brought a loaf of her homemade honey-wheat bread with her. She'd almost tucked it into her basket, then thought better of it, not wanting the Shetlers to think she thought they couldn't set a meal to a table.

Micah commanded the seat next to hers. "It's sort of a spaghetti, stew, steak and vegetable soup," he explained. "What would you like to drink? We have milk, coffee or water. Or…" He winked at her. "Water, coffee or milk."

"Water, please." She noticed gratefully that the faded tablecloth was clean and the mismatched dishes and bowls spotless. The place settings were haphazard. Her spoon had a bent handle, the fork was missing a prong and her knife was tarnished silverplate.

Simeon took a seat at the head of the table. "Crackers? Are there crackers for my soup?" he asked.

"I'll get them." Micah jumped up and went to the cupboard. He rummaged through several tin cans and then another cupboard before producing an unopened box of saltines. He returned with a triumphant grin, and the boys cheering him. But before he reached the table, Neziah pulled out the chair his brother had just vacated and sat beside Ellen.

"Tricked by my own father," Micah declared dramatically. "You're on his side, aren't you, *Dat*? You like him best."

"He does," Joel said. "Jah, *Grossdaddi*

likes our *dat* bestest." He giggled. "But I love you, *Onkel*."

Asa pounded his spoon on the table. "Me, too! *Onkel! Onkel!*"

Ellen looked from Micah to Neziah, saw that they were all in on a family joke and laughed with them. Then Simeon motioned for grace, and everyone, even Asa, grew quiet and closed their eyes. When the silent prayer time was over, both Neziah and Micah rose to serve the heavy pottery bowls of thick vegetable soup.

"We like to talk about our day when we finally all get together for supper," Micah said as he placed Ellen's nearly overflowing bowl in front of her. "Did you see anything interesting today?"

"Or bad?" Joel giggled. "We have to tell if we did something bad, too."

"Bad, too," Joel's echo, Asa, added.

Ellen's first thought was to tell them about the stranger sleeping on her porch, but she wasn't certain that was a proper supper topic. Instead, she told them about the magnolia warbler.

"There was a flock of yellow throats here earlier in the week," Neziah said. "And I think I saw one myrtle warbler with them."

"Today," Simeon reminded him. "You're supposed to tell about today."

"What did you see today, *Grossdaddi*?" Joel asked.

"Hmm." Simeon stroked his beard again. "What did I see? I know. I saw a small boy driving a pony cart. A *goot* job he did of it, too."

"*Grossdaddi!* I wanted to tell that," Joel exclaimed. "I did, *Dat*. I drove Butterscotch by myself."

"Did you?" Neziah asked, wide-eyed. "Bet you did a fine job."

"So what else did you do today?" Simeon asked the boy. "See any blue cows?" Both children giggled. "*Nay?* No blue ones? What about flying cows?"

The game went on around the table with much laughter and teasing. Ellen found herself more relaxed than she'd thought possible. She'd been afraid that coming for the evening meal would be uncomfortable, but it was the opposite. She was pleasantly surprised to discover that she felt at home in this house, at ease with these three men, as she had been when she was a child. Even Asa and Joel seemed endearing. They were scamps, certainly, but if their upbringing the past few years had been lenient, it was plain for anyone to see that they were loved and loved back in return.

I could be really happy here, Ellen thought. *I could be an aunt or a mother to these boys and a daughter-in-law to Simeon.* He was a good man and he'd raised decent sons who were devout and faithful to the community.

But which son? she fretted. Which man was the one the Lord wanted her to marry? Because she *would* take one of them. It wasn't an abstract question anymore. Simeon had been right in the pony cart when he'd driven her through the woods. The question was no longer *if* she would choose one of his sons. It was: *which one* would she choose?

"Let me help with the dishes," she offered when they had finished off the last of the cinnamon sticky buns.

"Not tonight," Simeon said, rising from the table. "Come with me, boys. We'll see if I have any peppermints left in my candy can." He glanced at Micah. "You two can do the cleaning up. Ellen is our guest. Plenty of time for her to tend the kitchen when she marries one of you," he called as he left the kitchen, boys trailing behind him.

"I don't mind," she said.

"You heard *Vadder*." Neziah rose and began gathering up the plates. "Tonight you're our guest."

"You wash, I'll dry," Micah told his brother. "After I walk Ellen home."

Neziah gave him a stern look. "I invited her. I'm walking her home. But not yet. First we visit, talk, like people do."

"And then I walk her home," Micah said.

Neziah's voice grew louder. "You do *not* walk her home. I do."

Ellen stood there in the middle of the kitchen not sure what to say or do. Micah and Neziah sounded a little like Joel and Asa fussing.

"Are you two arguing again?" Simeon called from the parlor. "Micah, stop giving your brother a hard time. Neziah will walk Ellen home. When *you* invite her, you can walk her home."

"Fine," Micah said.

Neziah picked up a damp towel off the sink and tossed it at Micah. "*Jah*, Micah. Stop interfering between me and Ellen."

"I could say the same about you," Micah replied with a grin.

"Boys!" Simeon bellowed.

Eventually, amid much horseplay and teasing between the brothers, the dishes did get washed, dried and put away. Neziah made fresh coffee and they joined Simeon on the porch, where they watched twilight settle around them. The children, tired after a long day, curled up in the nearest male lap until Neziah announced that it was time for baths and bed.

"I can handle that chore," Micah offered. "If you're to have Ellen home before dark, you'd best start out now." Asa and Joel protested, begging to go with their father, but Micah picked up one under each arm and carried them off amid much giggling and pleading for a bedtime story.

Neziah and Ellen ended up talking with Simeon a while longer and they didn't set off down the woods' lane until an hour later. She offered the use of her flashlight, as it was completely dark, with only a partial moon and a few stars illuminating the sky.

"*Nay*," Neziah said, waving away the flashlight. "I know every bend in the path. Unless you prefer we use it."

"I trust you."

Micah groaned from the dark, somewhere behind them. "Your first mistake, Ellen. Never trust him," he called. "He's sneaky." And when neither answered him, he said, "I could come along and protect you, if you need me."

Neziah shook his head and chuckled at his brother's antics, but then his thoughts became more serious. It had seemed in the beginning as if Micah had seen this as just another contest, but he was beginning to think his little brother really did care for Ellen. That worried him. What if she fell in love with him? And in all fairness, what wasn't there to love about Micah?

"Ignore him," Neziah told Ellen.

"I'd make a *goot* chaperone!" Micah persisted, following them a few yards into the woods.

"We don't need one," Neziah called back.

"You'll be sorry!" Micah shouted. "Remember, I warned you, Ellen."

Ellen laughed and looked up at Neziah. "Maybe he's right." She turned on her flashlight, shining the yellow beam on the rutted track ahead of her. "Maybe we should invite him to come along."

"He's not right," Neziah argued good-naturedly. "This is my time with you, and I'm not going to share."

They walked for a while in easy silence.

The sounds around them were familiar and comforting to Neziah…the chirp of crickets, frogs croaking and the rustling of small animals in the leaves and undergrowth. He and Ellen had often walked together in silence during their earlier courtship. Because they both enjoyed bird-watching, it came naturally to them. Talking frightened away some of the species they were attempting to identify. Of course, they'd not see many birds at night, but the dark was nice.

When Neziah was certain they were alone, he said, "It wasn't so bad, was it?" he asked. "Tonight?"

"I had a really nice time," she answered.

He took her hand. It felt small and warm, familiar but strangely exciting at the same time. "There's a fallen log, here, just ahead on the left. Will you sit with me for a few moments?"

He felt her hesitation, but something more…

"Maybe we *should* have taken Micah up on his offer as chaperone," she said teasingly. But he knew she was serious.

"*Nay*, I'd never do anything to threaten your honor. I love you, Ellen. I think I've always loved you."

"I loved you, too, Neziah, but…"

"But?" He led her to the log and they sat, only a few inches of space between them. He was afraid that she was going to say that she loved him like a brother. And that wasn't what he wanted.

"I don't know, Neziah," she admitted. "We're talking about love. Love we had for each other a long time ago. You've been married since then. You were a married man."

"And that bothers you?" he asked quietly. He had known they would have to talk about Betty at some point; he just hadn't be eager to do so. It was a strange place for a man to be. A widower with the possibility of a second marriage with the first woman he ever loved.

"I… It doesn't bother me," Ellen said. "It's just…I…" She exhaled.

"You want to know about Betty. About Betty and me."

"No. No, of course not." She sounded flustered. "That wasn't what I meant. I only …" Again she didn't finish her thought.

Neziah brought her hand to his lips and gently kissed her knuckles. "I don't mind talking about Betty. I think you're right. We do need to talk about her."

He smiled in the darkness, liking the feel of her hand in his. He'd held her hand quite a bit in their courting days, but he didn't remember it feeling this way. So simple. So good. So right. "If you accept my proposal, I'd not have any secrets between us, Ellen." Reluctantly, he let go of her hand.

"All right." Her voice sounded small.

He tightened his hands into fists, then relaxed them and leaned forward and rested them on his knees. "The accident was such a shock. Losing her that way. I've grieved for her over the past three years."

"I understand. It must have been terrible, losing Betty and your mother in that accident, being left with no mother for the children." She let out a long breath. "I didn't know her that well, but she seemed patient and cheerful, hardworking."

"She was," he continued, torn between sharing what was in his heart and being disloyal to Betty. "Ours was a solid marriage. I had great respect for her, and I felt deep affection, as well. It's important that you know that."

Ellen didn't reply, so he went on.

"I will always keep a special place in my heart for her. Every night I pray with my boys, and I try to keep the memory of their mother alive for them."

"As you should."

His throat constricted with emotion. "But it really is time we moved on. Joel has forgotten her, and Asa never really knew her. There's only me, and sometimes…sometimes I have trouble remembering her face."

"Neziah, you don't have to tell me these things. You're embarrassing me."

He rose to his feet, unable to remain seated. "That's not my intention. But I think I need to explain my relationship with my wife if I have any hope that you'll agree to marry me."

She was quiet, sitting in the darkness. He went on. "Betty was nothing like you. She was a gentle girl who accepted without question the traditional role of wife. It was what I believed I wanted when I asked her to marry me. She was brought up in a strict community in Missouri. She had been taught to turn to me as head of the house to make all decisions, even domestic ones that my mother would make without going to my father. Betty and I never argued. Whatever I wanted, she was content."

Insect song chirped and peeped all around them.

"But over time, I learned that it wasn't what I wanted at all," he said. "I would have honored her and our marriage so long as I lived.

But…" He stopped and started again. "The love between us was different from the way I feel about you. I've felt guilty sometimes, thinking I should have been a better husband to Betty. Thinking that I don't deserve a second chance to be with you."

Neziah stood in front of her, listening to the sounds of the woods. "I wanted to come to you after my year of mourning had passed, but I didn't know how. I didn't know what to say to you. And the more time that passed, the more impossible it seemed. For me to come to you. Then, a few weeks ago, I went to my father and confided my shortcomings to him."

"Oh, Neziah." She sighed.

The way she said his name made his heart thump in his chest. He had to make himself go on. With every word he spoke, he was afraid he would turn her away from him, but he knew he had to say these things. "You know what he told me?"

"What?" she murmured.

"He said it was time I put aside my mourning for Betty. 'Life is a gift from God,' he said. 'You were faithful to your vows while your wife was with us. You take nothing away from that by seeking happiness in marriage again. My son, if you had been the one lost in that wreck, I would give the same advice to Betty. None of us knows what the Lord has planned for us, but we must strive to accept and make the most of whatever that may be. To do less is to squander the precious gift of life.'"

They were both quiet for a moment. "And he was right," she said.

Neziah sat back down on the log and stared into the dark. "You think so?"

"I do. And I think that, no matter what happens between you and me, Neziah, I think you should take his words to heart and find the wife who's meant for you."

"Does that mean you prefer Micah over me?"

"I didn't say that."

He felt his heart swell with…hope. "So I'm still in the running?"

She turned to him and in the darkness he could feel her more than he could see her. "Now you sound like Micah. This is not a contest." She rose. "I should get home."

He jumped up. "I guess we need to talk about what happened with us. When we ended our courtship. Do you want to talk about that, Ellen?"

To his surprise, she gave a laugh. "I think

we've had enough serious discussion for one night, don't you?"

He smiled and fell in step beside her. "Can I hold your hand?" he whispered.

She laughed again and gave him a little push. And then he felt her small, warm hand slip into his, and he grinned all the way to her farmhouse steps.

Chapter Eleven

By seven-thirty Tuesday morning, Ellen was halfway to Honeysuckle on her push scooter. So far, no motor vehicles had passed her, and she'd seen none of her Plain neighbors walking or driving. It was one of the things she liked about leaving early for the shop. She spent so much time in the company of others that she treasured time alone with her own thoughts.

It hadn't been a particularly restful night, and she'd had a lot on her mind this morning when she left her barnyard. She'd enjoyed her visit at the Shetlers, and the walk home had been exciting, but also unsettling. She believed Neziah now when he said he still loved her. The question was, did she still love him or had that period in her life passed? What if her future was with his brother?

The problem was that both Shetler brothers were good men, and she cared for each of them. Being with Micah felt so exciting and new. But she found a certain comfort in being with Neziah, a comfort that came from having a past with a person. She was so confused. How could she tell if her affection for Micah was budding love? Or what if what she felt for Neziah wasn't real, but simply a longing for what they once shared?

And the Shetlers hadn't been the only thing that had troubled her night's rest. She hadn't been able to stop worrying about the homeless girl she'd found on her porch the previous morning. She kept wondering if she had shown Gail due charity or if she'd taken the easy way out, simply giving her a meal and saying a prayer to ease her own conscience. Should she have done more for Gail than offer a few platitudes?

In the middle of the night, Ellen had risen from her bed and gone to the window to stare out at the moonlit barnyard. Standing there, she had wondered where Gail was. Had she taken shelter in someone's stable again, or had a friend offered a spare bed? Did she even have any friends in Honeysuckle? Had Gail eaten or had she gone to sleep on an empty stomach? What if something awful had happened to her in the night and Ellen could have prevented it?

Ellen balanced both feet on her scooter and rolled down a hill, enjoying the feel of the wind in her face. She felt so strange, as if her life had lost its balance, though not in a bad way. Still, it was unnerving. So much was happening so fast. It was only the previous Tuesday that Simeon had made his proposition and changed the entire direction of her life. She felt as though she were caught up in the swirl of wind and tumbling leaves that came before a thunderstorm. One minute, she had been resolved to remain unwed and care for her aging parents, and now she was being courted by not one, but two suitors. Two *serious* suitors.

It was hard to believe that when November came, the traditional time of weddings, she might be one of those happy brides celebrating her marriage with her family and community. It was a dream come true and one that filled her with excitement. The truth was, all the time she'd been assuring herself that it wasn't God's plan for her to wed, she'd been secretly studying each eligible male visitor to Honeysuckle. She'd watched the faces and listened to the voices of strangers for years, but never thought to look next door.

The sound of a horse and buggy coming up fast behind her caught her attention. She laughed aloud, guessing that it was either Micah or Neziah, but she refused to look back over her shoulder to see which one. Whoever it was must have gone up to her house only to find her gone.

Of course, she could be wrong and then she would feel silly. It might be some other member of the Honeysuckle community, but she didn't think so. She supposed that she should feel guilty that she was keeping either Neziah or Micah from starting his workday on time, but instead she felt deliciously giddy.

In her teens, Ellen had read a few forbidden English romance novels where couples walked together through clouds of apple blossoms. Sometimes, sweethearts parted over some misunderstanding and then when all seemed lost, he came galloping back on horseback to fall on his knees and propose marriage. In other stories, the handsome young man and the girl met when he rescued her from danger. They had been chaste stories, nothing like the revealing covers she saw on book racks in Lancaster, but daring enough to make her heart race.

For herself, Ellen had long since given up on romance. She had thought that if she did ever marry, because of her age, it would be to an older widower, someone with grown children or a man who needed a younger wife to nurse him in his later years. Suddenly, everything was different, and she was being swept up in a whirlwind romantic courtship with not one but two men, both of whom professed to love her. She had to admit that she was enjoying every moment of it.

The rhythm of hooves on the pavement grew louder, and seconds later, Micah's showy driving horse drew up beside her. "Morning!" Micah called from the buggy.

"Morning." Ellen pushed harder, and the scooter kept pace with the buggy.

Micah removed his straw hat and waved it at her. "I've come to drive you to town!" How handsome and dashing he looked, with his yellow-blond hair and square, clean-shaven chin.

Breathlessly, she slowed and the horse and buggy pulled slightly ahead. Micah reined in the horse to remain alongside her. "Move over! You're blocking the road," she shouted above the sound of Samson's hooves striking the blacktop.

"I know." He grinned. "It will be all over Honeysuckle if anyone sees us. You better get in."

She wanted to say something clever in reply but she was quickly becoming winded. Surrendering gracefully, she stopped pushing, let the push scooter roll to a stop and got off to walk. Micah reined Samson to a walk and then a halt.

"Does this mean you need a ride?" he asked innocently.

She laughed. Minutes later, her scooter was in the back, and she was sitting on the front seat of the buggy beside him. He shook the reins and gave Samson the signal to walk on. "I thought you'd wait for me this morning because you were feeling so guilty about letting Neziah walk you home last night," Micah teased.

Ellen straightened her *kapp*. It had slipped down, and she'd nearly lost it when she was racing along the road to keep up with the buggy. Why was it that Micah always brought out her reckless nature? She smiled to herself. Life with him for a husband would never be humdrum or boring. He was exciting, and

Ellen liked excitement. Didn't that mean they would be a good match? "Why aren't you at the sawmill?" she asked, choosing to ignore his question.

"I had to see you this morning. Wanted to ask you if you'd go bowling with me tomorrow night."

She looked straight ahead. A van full of tourists stared at them through the open windows of a minivan as they passed. Micah grinned and waved. Ellen saw several phones pressed against the windows. Pictures, she supposed. Someone was always trying to take pictures of them, as if they were exotic animals at the zoo. She'd often thought of buying a camera and snapping photos of the tourists, but she supposed that it wouldn't be good for business. You never knew when a tourist might become a customer at the shop, and she was attempting to be a successful businesswoman.

"So, will you?" Micah asked. "Bowling? Pizza after?"

"Just the two of us?"

He shook his head. "Abram's going. And Nat. They're bringing dates. I don't know who, but there will be other girls, so you don't have to worry about me trying to steal a kiss or anything."

She should have chastised him for his inappropriate joke, but when she looked at him he was grinning. She couldn't help smiling back. "All right. You know I love to bowl."

His grin grew broader, if that were possible.

"I warn you, though," she said. "I might be better than you."

He chuckled and urged Samson into a trot. "That was pretty easy. Neziah thought you wouldn't agree to go with me so easily."

"And if I didn't?" she teased.

"I'd just keep pestering until you agreed." His blue eyes twinkled with mischief. "My brother should know by now that I'm impossible to resist."

Micah left her at the back of the shop with the promise to pick her up the next evening at six-thirty. That would give her time to close up, go home and make certain her parents had their supper before she left to go bowling. In spite of her boasting to Micah, Ellen hoped that she wouldn't be too rusty at the game. She loved bowling, but she hadn't been in more than a year.

As Ellen pushed her scooter up onto the

back porch, she couldn't help wondering if Gail would be there again. But everything was as Ellen had left it the previous day. There were no empty soda cans, no sleeping bag and no evidence that anyone had been there since she'd left. She unlocked the inner door and went into the shop. All was quiet; Dinah hadn't come down yet. She put coffee on to brew for Dinah, then went into the office to turn on the computer. There, her gaze fell on a box of baby clothes that she hadn't had time to price and put on display yet. Drawn to the contents, Ellen opened the box. Inside were infant sleepers, dresses, sacques and caps, hand sewn of the softest cotton in green, yellow, lavender and cream. The sewing was exquisite, the style of the clothes simple and traditional.

She lifted a newborn-size sacque and pressed it to her cheek. Longing to have a baby of her own blossomed in her chest, and she found her eyes welling up with tears. If she married, God willing, she could have a child of her own, one that she could dress in such tiny garments.

The sound of a door opening and footsteps made Ellen dash away the moisture from her eyes and quickly return the baby clothes to the box. “Morning, Dinah,” she called, feeling silly by the intense emotion that had bubbled up inside her. “I’m in the office.”

“Wee gayts,” Dinah answered. “A good day to you, too.” Her cheerful face appeared in the open doorway. Dinah was wearing her work apron and carrying a bucket and cleaning cloths. “I thought I’d wash those windows in the front room before we open. They looked smudgy yesterday. I can’t abide dirty windows.” She set her bucket on the floor. “Coffee smells *goot*. Will you have a cup with me before I start?”

Ellen murmured assent. There was little chance of any dirt collecting when Dinah was around. Although she’d been thinking of having a cup of tea, she joined Dinah, accepting a mug of the strong coffee. Dinah liked hers black. “My husband liked it that way,” she explained, “and in time I came to think that was the only way to drink it. He’d say, ‘If a spoon won’t stand straight up in the cup, the coffee’s not strong enough.’”

“I guess we didn’t have any visitors last night,” Ellen commented.

“Quiet as a graveyard. Just the way I like it.”

They talked about what Dinah had cooked

herself for supper the previous evening and then discussed the best way to can peaches. Three-quarters of the way through her coffee, Dinah leaned forward, elbows on the table. "How was last night's supper at the Shetlers'?"

"Fine." Ellen studied the mug between her hands. "It was nice. They're a nice family."

Dinah pushed her glasses back up her nose. "So which one are you planning on? The serious, older one or the young, sassy one?"

"I don't know, Dinah." She glanced up at her friend. "And that's the truth."

"My advice is to use your head as well as your heart. Marriage is nothing to go into lightly. You get out what you put in. It's past time you had a husband and a family of your own, and either of those boys will do, so long as you can pick one and never question your choice. Trouble comes when a woman weds one and yearns after another." She rose from her chair, went to the sink and rinsed out her cup. "Best I get to those windows." She patted Ellen's shoulder as she went by. "Pay no heed to my nosing into your business. Just an old woman who lives by herself and talks too much when she has someone to listen."

"I value your advice, Dinah. You're one of my best friends, and you're a wise woman."

Dinah gathered her cleaning supplies and removed a bottle of ammonia from the cabinet. "I walked down to the restaurant last night," she said. "Asked Margaret right out about that girl."

"What did she say?"

"Wasn't disposed to say much. If the girl doesn't have her papers, she shouldn't be working there. The government has rules. If you ask me, Margaret suspects Gail's Amish and is giving her some rope."

Ellen stood. "She must like her or she wouldn't be bending the rules for her."

"Oh, she likes her, I could tell that. Says Gail has never been late for work and never missed a day. Honest as a bishop. Apparently, a customer left her purse on the counter in the restroom. She had a lot of cash in it. Gail found it and turned it in. She offered the girl a reward, but Gail turned it down."

Ellen brushed her forehead with her fingertips. "I couldn't sleep last night for worrying about her," she admitted.

Dinah frowned. "Best you let it go, Ellen. You've enough on your shoulders without taking on more. And..." She glanced around as if she thought they might be overheard. "What if her people shunned her?" She shook her head. "No *goot* can come of poking into some stranger's troubles." She picked up her bucket and carried it into the front showroom.

Ellen returned to her office work, but she couldn't concentrate. Restless, she shut the computer down, priced the beautiful baby clothes and put them on display. She was headed for the office again when someone knocked at the front door. She hoped it wasn't a customer because they weren't open until nine. "Dinah?" she called.

"It's just Simeon," Dinah said. "He told me he'd be bringing some more of his boxes in today. We sold the last of what we had."

Simeon made small boxes out of cedar and pine and inlaid them with designs in cherry. Suitable to hold jewelry or trinkets, they were attractive and reasonably priced and sold as quickly as he crafted them.

"I can let him in," Ellen said, turning in the doorway.

"I can handle this." Dinah set down her mop. "No need for you to bother."

Ellen hesitated, thinking about what Dinah had said about Gail. "Okay. I think I'll take an order to the post office. I'll be back in a few minutes." The post office wasn't her primary destination, but she did need to mail off some aprons that had been ordered. As she left the office, she glanced into the front room and saw Simeon and Dinah deep in conversation. On the back porch, she put the carefully wrapped package into the scooter's basket and made her way to the small post office a block away.

After collecting the mail and mailing her package, Ellen continued on to the Mennonite family restaurant. She just wanted to say hi to Gail if she was there. Check on her. She propped the scooter against the porch and started up the steps. As she reached the door, it swung open, and Gail nearly collided with her.

"*Ach!* I'm so sorry," Gail said. Her cheeks reddened. She wasn't in her waitress uniform and was wearing the same clothing she'd had on when Ellen had surprised her on her back porch.

"Good morning," Ellen said. "Are you off today?"

"*Nay.* No," Gail corrected. "They don't need me until later."

"Have you found a place to stay yet?"

Gail shook her head. "Not yet, but I know I will soon." She glanced back at the restaurant.

"You aren't going to say anything to Margaret about me sleeping on your porch, are you?"

Ellen shook her head. "I hope you don't mind me asking, but...where *did* you stay last night?"

"With a friend," Gail said quickly. But she averted her eyes, and Ellen wasn't sure she believed her.

"You know, you might talk to Margaret. Her church helps people sometimes."

Gail shook her head and backed away. "I don't want charity. Don't worry about me. I'll be fine." She forced a half smile. "I know you mean well, but really, I'm *goot*. I can take care of myself." She turned away and waved. "Have a good day."

"You, too," Ellen called. And then, under her breath, she murmured a prayer for Gail and all the vulnerable young women like her.

Chapter Twelve

Friday evening, Micah arrived to pick Ellen up, said all the right things to her father and had her mother laughing and blushing like a fourteen-year-old before they drove out of the yard. Ellen had looked forward to the bowling expedition from the moment Micah had invited her. Bowling dates for twentysomething young people were not exactly encouraged but were allowed by the church elders so long as they were group activities. Mennonite parents in the neighborhood regularly took their children to bowling alleys for birthdays and other special occasions, but it was rare that Amish families participated. Ellen's father had been an exception, and she'd gained some proficiency and a love for the sport by going with him when she was a teenager.

"You look pretty tonight," Micah said as he guided Samson out onto the blacktop at the end of Ellen's lane.

She murmured a thank-you and sat up tall on the leather seat, pleased that she'd worn one of her newest dresses, a modest, pine-green dress and a matching green headscarf. She wasn't trying to look English, but knew that she'd attract less attention from strangers than she would if she wore her prayer *kapp*. She'd brought twenty dollars in a plain black purse, a precaution she'd taken after Neziah had once forgotten his wallet and they'd had to convince the English manager of a pizza restaurant that he would return the following day with enough money to pay the bill for their refreshments. That had been more than ten years ago, but the memory of Neziah's and her own embarrassment remained vivid in her mind.

A mile from the house, Micah reached under the front seat, pulled out a battery-operated radio and tuned in to a Christian rock station. Ellen knew she should have scolded him. She was a baptized member of the church, and listening to the radio, no matter what station was playing, was definitely forbidden by the community. Music, other than hymns and *praise songs* sung without accompaniment, was forbidden as being too worldly. But Micah wasn't baptized yet, so officially, he was still in his *running around* stage.

Rumspringa was the time in a young person's life when they were permitted to experience some of the English lifestyle. A few kids—mainly boys—took it too far, getting driver's licenses and buying motor vehicles, even moving away to sample a reckless lifestyle among the English. Micah hadn't done that, and he was studying for baptism, so chastising him for the radio might make her appear too strict.

Those were the excuses that rose in Ellen's mind, and she almost convinced herself that they were good ones. But she'd never been one to be less than honest with herself, and the truth was, the beat was really catchy, and she enjoyed the guitar, drums and whatever other instruments were accompanying the male singers.

"Great song, isn't it?" Micah asked as the final notes rang out from under the seat. Before she could answer, a young woman's voice began another song, every bit as enthusiastic and exciting as the first one. "That's Myra Grace. She's terrific, isn't she?"

This music was a long way from the spirituals sung at youth singing frolics, and further still from the *Deitsch* hymns that played such an important part of the Sabbath worship services. But she couldn't deny that this Christian rock thrilled her and filled her with emotion. *"Wonderbor,"* she said, and meant it.

"So you like it? For real?" Micah asked. He patted the seat next to him. "You could sit a little closer, you know. I don't bite."

She shook her head and laughed. "I'm fine where I am."

Micah guided his horse to the shoulder of the road as an oversize truck carrying farm machinery approached. "We're picking up Abram and Linny," he said. "Do you mind?"

"Nay." She didn't know Linny well. She was much younger and belonged to another church district, but she'd seemed pleasant enough when Ellen had met her at a farm auction recently. "So, Abram is walking out with Linny now?" she asked him. "I thought he and Saloma—"

"Oh, Saloma's coming, but with Marvin Yordy and another couple from Marvin's church district. Abram likes Saloma well enough, but he's still dating different girls.

Abram's a long way from settling down yet. He's a few years younger than me."

"Are you certain you're ready?" she asked. He glanced at her with a slow, heartfelt smile and nodded. "Even if it means giving up your radio and cell phone?" she reminded him.

One blond eyebrow shot up. He pushed his hat back and asked, "How did you know I had a cell phone?"

Ellen laughed, folding her arms and replying, "Hershey Park. You told me."

Micah grimaced. "Right." Then he shrugged and grinned.

He was trying to charm her and Ellen knew it, but he was hard to resist. Life with Micah would always be full of laughter and fun. She could almost picture a small boy or girl with Micah's dimple and bright, inquisitive eyes. He was a good uncle to Neziah's sons, and he would make an excellent father, if a bit indulgent. Micah was slow to anger and quick to forgive. She'd have to be a fool not to let herself love him.

The clatter of hooves alerted Ellen to the approach of another horse-drawn vehicle coming up behind them. When she glanced in a side mirror, she saw an open courting buggy pulled by a gray horse. After a moment or two, the topless buggy's sole occupant reined his horse to the left lane, drew alongside and passed them, his showy gray stepping high. Ellen recognized the driver as one of Solomon Schwartz's sons, maybe Jonah. It was difficult to tell which one it was at a brief glance. There were several brothers of running-around age, all about the same height and all with longish bowl haircuts. The Schwartz boys took turns using the open buggy and driving the fine gray mare. Everyone knew that she was fast, and the Schwartzes were fond of saying that she had been a winning pacer before being sold at an auction when she grew past racing age.

Micah frowned as the open buggy passed them. "Show-off," he muttered.

As horse and driver pulled back in line ahead, the Schwartz boy turned, grinned and waved at Micah before turning on a string of blue-and-red lights that flashed on the back frame.

It was definitely Jonah, Ellen decided. She rolled her eyes. "Juvenile." She looked over at Micah. "Seriously," she continued. "Joining the church will make a lot of changes in your life. Are you sure you're prepared for it?"

"I'll be sure the day you agree to marry

me." Micah's eyes narrowed, and he urged Samson to move a little faster. They quickly closed the distance to the rear of the buggy ahead of them.

"Micah," she warned. "Don't get too close."

He caught her hand and squeezed it, but he didn't take his gaze off the flashing lights and rolling buggy just ahead. "You mean everything to me, Ellen. It's what I want. You as my wife, baptism, a life that has meaning."

She gauged the distance between Samson's nose and the string of blinking lights. Micah's horse wasn't happy, because his ears were back and he was leaning forward in the harness. "Don't do anything foolish," she murmured. "This is a busy road."

"Don't worry," he assured her. "I'd never take chances with you in the buggy." He was saying all the right things, but his expression was exactly the same as it had been the day one of the sixth-grade boys had dared him to walk the ridgepole of the bishop's barn, two stories up.

"And you think we can be happy together, live according to our faith, make our families content?"

"I do," Micah answered. "If I didn't, I'd never have agreed to my father's proposition. I've been waiting for a woman like you, a wife, children, responsibilities. We're a lot alike, you and me. And you're steady. We'll make a *goot* match." He hesitated. "I know that you and Neziah…you know." He shrugged and glanced at her. "Anyway, he's probably a better man than I am, but he's too serious for you. Being Amish, living Plain, doesn't mean we can't still enjoy ourselves, does it?"

"Nay," she agreed. "It doesn't."

"Goot!" With a triumphant grin, he slapped the reins over Samson's back and reined the horse left, surprising Jonah and quickly gaining on the open buggy ahead of them.

"Micah!" Ellen braced herself against the front dashboard as one of their wheels hit a pothole, and the buggy jolted hard enough to make her fly an inch off the seat.

"Get up!" Micah shouted, and Samson's head went up and his stride lengthened. "Hold on tight!" In barely a minute, Micah's horse inched up and then drew nose to nose with the gray mare.

Jonah's eyes widened in surprise as he saw them passing him. Grabbing his long buggy whip, he snapped it through the air over the mare's withers. The gray leaped ahead, and the race was on.

Ellen knew she should be protesting, insisting that Micah stop this nonsense, but she found the race thrilling. Seemingly evenly matched, the two horses stretched out, hooves pounding the pavement. First one buggy edged ahead, and then the gap narrowed between them before the other took the lead. "Faster! Faster!" Ellen cried, her heart pounding with excitement. "Go, Samson!"

Wheels spinning, buggies rocking from side to side, they pounded through an intersection. Two Amish teenage boys, waiting at the stop sign on the left side of the crossroad, waved and whooped excitedly at the horse race. Jonah, on Ellen's right, stood in the two-wheel open carriage, reins in both hands, yelling encouragement to his gray mare.

Fifty yards, a hundred, and finally Jonah's horse seemed to be tiring. Inches, and then by a head, and finally a length, Samson pulled ahead. Far down the road, Ellen caught sight of a blue garbage truck. "Micah, rein in. There's a truck coming!"

Jonah saw the truck at almost the same time. He pulled back on the leathers, slowing the gray so that Micah could safely pull into line ahead of him. Micah eased Samson's pace to a slower one, and by the time the English vehicle passed them, the two buggies were proceeding at a steady pace.

Ellen sank back on the seat, exhilarated. "You won! Your Samson is faster than his gray."

Micah looked at her and grinned as he turned to wave triumphantly at Jonah, who whooped and waved back good-humoredly. "Ellen Beachey! Listen to you," Micah admonished. "And you're supposed to be an example for other young women?" He glanced down at the toggle switch on the buggy dashboard. Mischief danced behind his intense blue eyes. "I dare you," he challenged.

Ellen didn't hesitate. Before she lost her nerve, she threw the switch that powered Micah's string of battery-operated, flashing red-and-blue lights. She leaned far out and waved at Jonah. "Slowpoke! Dusteater!"

Micah roared with laughter and she couldn't help joining in, laughing until tears ran down her cheeks. *Maybe he's right,* she thought. *Maybe Micah is the one I belong with.*

Hours later, Micah guided Samson up Ellen's steep driveway. The house was quiet, lights out, with no sign of either of her parents. He reined in the horse in the deeper shadows of the oak trees at the edge of the yard and slid closer to her on the buggy bench. "Did you have a *goot* time tonight?" he asked her.

"I did."

It was strangely intimate, just the two of them sitting so close in the buggy. The moon was up, and a blanket of stars glittered in the navy blue sky. "I did, too," he said.

"You don't mind that my score was higher than yours?"

"*Nay.* I'm proud of you."

"The preachers tell us that pride is a bad thing."

"Pride in one's self, not for someone else's accomplishments. Besides, we beat everyone, didn't we? We left them in the dust."

She laughed. "Like Jonah and his gray mare."

"Exactly." He chuckled and slid an arm around her waist. Ellen leaned close, so close that he thought he smelled the scent of her shampoo. Peaches. Happiness surged up in his chest, seeping through him from the crown of his head down to his toes. Samson shook his head, and the harness jingled. Micah could imagine that this was *their* home and they were coming home together after a frolic or visiting friends. Being with Ellen made him content, made him eager to join the church community and join in marriage.

He caught her chin between his thumb and forefinger, turning her face toward his, and bending to kiss her.

"Nay." She pressed two fingers to his lips. "It's not seemly that we behave this way."

He let out a slow breath. "You want to kiss me, don't you?"

"*Jah*, I do, and that's all the more reason we should show restraint." She gently took his hand and lowered it.

"You're not a girl, Ellen," he said. "We're old enough to know our own minds. I'd never do anything that would shame you."

She sighed. "But *I* might. I care for you a great deal, Micah, but some things are best kept for marriage."

Her voice was soft and sweet, no longer the teasing Ellen or the one so quick with a crisp comeback. The sound of it made him go all shivery inside. And maybe she was right. If he allowed himself to pull her into his arms, if he kissed her with all the pent-up emotion he felt, would he be able to remember what was proper for a courting couple and what went beyond what was decent?

"It's all right," he said, and his words came

out deep and scratchy. "I like the idea of marrying a chaste woman, one who can teach our children by example the right way to live." He chuckled. "But then again, maybe it would be better to share at least *one* kiss before we take our wedding vows. What if I'm a terrible kisser?"

She laughed. "I doubt that, and I doubt that you think so."

"Would it be so dangerous? One good-night kiss between friends?"

She got down out of the buggy. He scrambled after her and found her hand again.

"Between friends might be harmless," she told him, "but with a man I'm considering marrying, maybe more than I want to dare."

"Other girls don't consider a few harmless kisses so dangerous."

"I'm not other girls."

He nodded, knowing when she had the best of him. "I know you aren't, Ellen. You're special. And if you'll marry me, I promise I'll try to be the man you deserve."

She squeezed his hand and pulled free. "Thank you for tonight," she said.

"Will you come with me again? Soon?"

"Maybe." Her face was in the shadows, but he sensed that she was smiling at him.

"Can I walk you up to the house?"

"If you like."

A funny hollow feeling settled in his stomach. A minute ago, he'd felt sure of her...sure of his chances, but now he wasn't so certain. Was she teasing him? "*Nay*, Ellen, only if you want me to."

It wasn't that far to her back porch. He wished it were a mile. Neither spoke until she stopped at the bottom step.

She turned to him in the darkness. "Have you kissed a lot of girls?"

Her question surprised him. "*Nay*, only two. But nothing serious. Not something I should be ashamed of." He straightened. "And don't ask me who, because I'll give no names. All I can say is it was nothing I, or they, took seriously."

"You're sweet, Micah." She raised up on her toes and kissed his cheek. "Good night."

He touched his fingertips to where her mouth had just been on his cheek. "Night."

In seconds, the door closed behind her, and he stood there wondering if things had changed between them. Inside, he felt like they had. Something important had happened this evening, but whether it was for good or bad, he couldn't tell. As he made his way back to Samson and the buggy, he tried to think what was different in their relationship.

He was still puzzling over Ellen's responses when he reached his father's stable. As he approached the barn, he saw a tall figure leaning against the double doors. "Neziah?"

"*Jah.* You're late getting home. Everything all right?"

"Right as rain," Micah said.

"You went bowling with Ellen?"

"*Jah.*" He got down and led Samson through the double doors into the barn. Neziah followed him, and Micah began to worry that maybe something was wrong. It wasn't like his brother to be waiting for him this way. "*Dat* all right? Kids?"

Neziah took down a lantern from inside the barn door. Micah heard the scratch of a match, and then a circle of yellow light glowed from the kerosene lamp. Neziah hung it back on the wooden peg. "Everything is *goot* here." Neziah began to unharness Samson. "Okay to give him water now?" He stroked the horse's neck. "He feels a little warm. You weren't driving him hard on the way home, were you?"

"Walked him from Ellen's. Water's fine." He backed the buggy into an empty space near the stalls and waited while Neziah hung up the harness.

"Much traffic on the road tonight?"

"Not much." He found a curry brush and began brushing Samson's neck and chest in long, sweeping strokes. Neziah went out of the barn and returned with a bucket of fresh water from the well. He carried it to Samson's head and offered it to the horse. Samson drank until he was satisfied, then blew a spray of wet slobber over Micah's trousers. *"Danki,"* he said. "Fool horse." But he grinned as he said it and took care as he brushed along Samson's back. "You know that gray that Jonah Schwartz drives, the one that used to race on the tracks in Delaware and New Jersey?"

"Strong legs, that mare."

Micah drew the brush along Samson's rump. "She's not as fast as they say."

"Who isn't?" Neziah asked.

"Jonah's horse." He threw the brush into the open aisle outside the stall and turned to Neziah. "Are you jealous? Because I took Ellen bowling?"

"Took a long time at her house. After you got her home, I mean."

"How do you know when I got her home?" Micah asked. Feeling out of sorts, he found the brush and put it back on the wall where it belonged. Their *vadder* liked things in place. If he found it on the barn floor tomorrow, he'd ask questions.

"Saw your lights coming down the road," Neziah said. "Quite some time ago."

"Not that long. We were talking." He made a sound of exasperation. "You *are* jealous. We went bowling. Two other couples went with us. Then we had pizza and sodas. Then we came home. End of story."

"That's all?"

"I didn't kiss her, if that's what you want to know."

"But you tried, didn't you?"

Trying to tamp down his irritation, Micah led Samson to the back door that led to the fenced-in compound and turned him out. It was a warm night, and he would be more comfortable outside than in his stall. "What Ellen and I do on our date is none of your business, big brother."

"It is my business," Neziah insisted. "Because Ellen's going to be my wife."

"And that would bother you? If she ever kissed me?"

"It would."

Micah closed the half door and locked it so

neither Samson nor any of the other animals could get back into the main area of the barn and raid the feed barrels or the haystack in the night. "I didn't kiss her, Neziah, but it's not something you should be asking. You might *not* be marrying her. She could well choose me, instead of you."

"No need for me to worry about that, little brother. It's me she'll marry, and you'd best get used to the idea."

"We'll see about that." Micah walked off into the dark, making the decision it was time to pin Ellen down and set their wedding date.

Chapter Thirteen

On Saturdays, merchants in Honeysuckle hosted a farmer's market and auction at the northern end of town. It was one of Ellen's favorite aspects of the village, and she rarely missed a market day. Vendors came from all over to rent outside space for tables, selling everything from household items to vintage furniture to seasonal food. That day, the tables were a feast of colors with red-and-gold mums, and baskets of early apples. There was also an area where farm equipment, both horse-drawn and motorized, was auctioned off. And there were always tables of odds and ends. Ellen liked to look for old handmade items: wooden butter churns, oil lamps and small antiques, things that customers who visited her shop were eager to buy.

The real draw for tourists and the Amish community alike were the food stalls inside, offering choice cuts of beef and pork, cold cuts, locally made cheese, baked goods, ice cream and homemade moon pies and funnel cakes. A pizza truck and other mobile snack stands sold scrapple and sausage sandwiches, hand-cut fries and non-alcoholic drinks. Picnic tables stood inside and outside under the trees, so that shoppers had a place to sit and talk or enjoy a simple meal. Like most Saturdays, Dinah had come early to the market to meet friends from her widows' club for breakfast, and she was happy to keep an eye on the store and their new *Englisher* employee while Ellen took a break.

As Ellen was walking between tables, she came upon Saloma and her sister Joanie sitting at one of the tables in the shade. Ellen saw from the outline of Joanie's dress that she was expecting a child, and Ellen couldn't help the smallest wince of envy. Joanie was younger than she was by at least five years, but she'd found a husband she adored and was already starting a family. One by one, most of Ellen and Saloma's friends had married. With God's help, Ellen prayed, she would make the right choice and become one of those wives before the first snowfall.

"Sit down, sit down," Saloma urged. "Joanie was telling me about a new job that her husband has just gotten. He won the contract to build a big barn for an English family that bought the old Peterson farm. He'll have to hire more people to help him, but the work will keep them busy for three or four months."

"I'm so happy for you, Joanie." Ellen set her cup of lemonade on the table and slid onto the bench across from the two sisters. She didn't say anything about the coming baby. Pregnancy was a subject not spoken about outside the family until the last few weeks.

"Ellen's walking out with the Shetler brothers," Saloma said as she finished off her scrapple sandwich and wiped her mouth with a napkin. "Both of them." Joanie looked dubious, but Saloma laughed. "It's true. Tell her, Ellen."

Ellen smiled and shrugged. "I don't know that we're walking out, but I have been seeing a lot of both Micah and Neziah," she admitted. "My parents would like to see me marry one of them."

Joanie narrowed her gaze. "And you? Is it what you want? I can understand you considering Neziah's suit, but Micah…" She spread her hands, palms up, in a gesture that said a lot about her opinion of Micah without putting her criticism into words.

"Well, I hope she *doesn't* pick Micah," Saloma said eagerly. "Then maybe I'd have a chance. He's so cute."

"*Jah*, he is." Joanie glanced at her sister. "But cute doesn't put groceries on the table. Micah has a reputation for being flighty. And he hasn't joined the church yet." She turned her attention to Ellen. "Are you sure he's ready for the responsibility of baptism and marriage?"

"We've been talking about that and I think he is," she answered.

"I know you and Neziah courted once before," Joanie said. She opened a Ziploc bag of homemade potato chips and offered some to Ellen. "Maybe that's where your heart will lead you. He seems to be the steadier of the two."

Ellen selected a potato chip and ate it slowly. They were salt and vinegar, her favorite. "I do know Neziah better, but…" She shook her head. "I'm not sure. They are both solid men, and Micah…he's so easy to be with. So much fun, you know?"

"Pray on it," Joanie suggested. "When I accepted my husband's proposal, there was someone else who'd written to me to ask me to be his wife. He seemed like a better choice. He was well set up, with a big farm."

"And an interfering mother," Saloma put in. "A widowed mother who would have tried to run their marriage."

"*Nay*, sister," Joanie admonished. "Caring for elders is a privilege, not a duty. That he had responsibilities that I would have shared wasn't something that would have kept me from accepting his offer." She smiled and touched the place over her heart. "It was a feeling in here, and the sense that the man I chose is who God wanted for me. Sometimes important decisions can seem overwhelming, but remember, if you hold with our faith, you are never alone. Listen with your head and your heart, and you'll know who is right for you."

"*Goot* advice." Ellen nodded as she munched on another potato chip.

Talk then turned to less personal subjects as they finished their snacks, and she was just about to go inside to purchase goat cheese for her father when she saw a familiar figure strolling between two vendor stalls. Certain that the young woman in the blue dress was Gail, Ellen said her goodbyes to Joanie and Saloma and strolled nonchalantly across the market to intercept her.

"Oh, hey," Gail said when she nearly bumped into Ellen. She stopped short, a mixed expression of eagerness and embarrassment on her face.

The girl looked tired. Dark circles beneath her eyes smudged her fair complexion, and she was scratching several large mosquito bites on her arm.

"Gail. It's good to see you." Ellen noticed that Gail had a stuffed backpack over her left shoulder and was carrying the rolled-up sleeping bag under her other arm. It was everything she owned, probably. "How are you doing?" Ellen asked. "Are you on your way to work?"

"Not until four." Gail shifted her feet nervously and lowered the backpack to the ground. "I…I like to see what people have for sale."

"Me, too." Ellen smiled at her, hesitated, then spoke her mind. "Would you think me rude if I ask where you slept last night?"

Gail flushed and averted her eyes. "Not on your porch. Honest."

"But where?" Ellen pressed. She couldn't

shake the feeling that this meeting hadn't been by chance. Sometime in the night, she'd awakened in a cold sweat. She'd suspected that she'd had a bad dream but couldn't remember any of the details. Gail had certainly been at the heart of her concern. All the way to the shop this morning, she'd wrestled with her conscience. Dinah's advice about not being too trusting of strangers was wise, but… Could it be that they'd both been too cautious?

"I can take care of myself," Gail said, edging away. "You don't have to…"

"Wait." Ellen laid a gentle hand on Gail's forearm and gazed directly into the girl's eyes. It was obvious that Gail was struggling to keep from crying.

Gail swallowed hard. "A sheep barn," she admitted, looking down at her feet. "Without permission."

"Well, that won't do," Ellen said. "It's going to get cold soon and I want to help. Will you come back to the shop with me?"

Gail looked uncertain.

"Please. I have a proposition to make," Ellen said in a rush. "If you don't mind a little work."

Gail shook her head vigorously. "I'm not afraid of work. If I could earn a little extra, it would help me save up for the security deposit to rent a room. They come up sometimes, you know, in the paper."

"I think I can do better than that," Ellen told her with a smile. "Come on."

Gail stood there for a moment and then, with what could only have been a leap of faith, she fell into step beside Ellen.

"There used to be an apartment up on the third floor of my shop," Ellen explained as they walked. "It's not much, but it's yours if you think it will suit you."

"Really?" Gail's eyes widened. "You'd let me stay in your shop?"

"I couldn't ask any rent for it. It's a bit of a mess. We've been using it for storage." She glanced at Gail, whose face now seemed bright. "Maybe in exchange for the room you could help by sweeping the sidewalk of leaves, scrubbing the porch, little chores that I hate to ask Dinah to do."

Gail beamed. "I'd be glad to help in any way I can."

It was only a short walk back to the shop and once they'd reached it, Ellen led the way around to the side of the building to the foot of an exterior staircase. "The rooms will need a *goot* cleaning and airing out, but there's a cot in the storeroom. You're welcome to stay here as long as you need to, until you find something permanent. I'll warn you, though, the place hasn't been dusted in over a year. It's probably full of cobwebs."

"Spiders I can deal with," Gail declared, gazing up the metal staircase that somewhat resembled a fire escape. "They don't bleat at night like sheep."

She laughed, and Ellen laughed with her. Then Gail grew serious. "How can I thank you enough?" Tears suddenly glistened in her eyes. "This is the nicest thing anyone has ever done for me. *Ever.*"

"I'm glad that I can help. I just feel bad that I didn't think of this sooner," Ellen told her. "I'll have to tell my father and Dinah that you're staying here, of course, but I'd appreciate it if you didn't say anything to anyone else about it. Let's just keep it a secret between us."

"Because you'd get into trouble with your church…for helping someone who left their community." Gail nodded. "I understand." She offered a trembling smile, and her cheek grew pink. "I guess you already figured it out, but my name isn't Bond. It's Bontrager. Abigail Bontrager."

Ellen returned the smile. "I'm pleased to meet you, Abigail Bontrager."

She shrugged. "Everyone will know soon enough that I fibbed, anyway. My brother found my birth certificate and my social security card and sent them to me, so Margaret won't get in trouble for letting me work there."

"So your family knows where you are?" Ellen asked.

Gail shook her head. "Just my brother, and he won't tell. He's leaving home, too, as soon as he turns eighteen. One of my mother's uncles is going to hire him to work on his dairy farm. He's going, but he's not turning English."

"And you are?"

"Maybe, I'm not sure. It's something I have to think about." Again, she stared at her canvas sneakers. "I'm just, you know…trying it out."

"Your community would take you back," Ellen said thoughtfully. She crossed her arms over her chest. "You can always go home, if it's what you want."

Gail sighed. "*Nay.* I can't. I won't."

"But surely your mother and father—"

"You don't know my father." Gail shook her head. "He would never forgive me, no matter what the bishop or the elders said." She glanced up at Ellen, making eye contact. "Not all fathers are kind ones."

There was something in Gail's tone that made Ellen think there was more to her story. She was suddenly grateful for the man who was her father. She had always known how blessed she was, but sometimes it took a reminder, such as this girl in the faded dress, to remind her that she should give thanks every day for the family God placed her with.

Gail glanced up the stairs, clearly eager to investigate her new quarters.

Ellen reached into her apron pocket, plucked out a ring of keys, sorted through them and removed the key that would unlock the door at the top of the steps. "You go on up and look around," Ellen said, handing the key over. "I'll see about that cot and some bedding and cleaning supplies. I need to let Dinah know you'll be staying here."

After looking in on the high-school girl behind the counter, Ellen climbed the stairs to Dinah's apartment on the second floor. Dinah was busy making oatmeal-raisin cookies to take to a friend and invited Ellen to have a cookie just out of the oven that was as big as the palm of Ellen's hand. They were one of Dinah's specialties that always went over well at potlucks and schoolhouse auctions.

Ellen accepted the sweet, warm cookie, spiced with cinnamon and told Dinah about inviting Gail to stay in the third-floor apartment. Her decision didn't go over as easily as she had hoped. Ellen tried to convey Gail's plight sympathetically, but Dinah's brow furrowed and her eyes narrowed behind her glasses. If she'd been a hen, Ellen could picture her feathers ruffling.

"You can't be serious," Dinah exclaimed. "I don't believe you handed a total stranger the keys to your shop and told her to make herself at home. You're too trusting, Ellen."

"She's Amish, the age of your own granddaughter. She's just a young girl who needs a friend. And having her up there on the third floor is no danger to us or the business." Ellen shrugged. "I didn't give her the keys to the shop, just to those unused rooms in the attic. The inside door from the third story to the hall is locked. What harm could she do?"

Dinah pursed her lips and again Ellen imagined an angry chicken, beak poised to peck.

"It isn't as if we haven't had prowlers before. Have you forgotten the fire that nearly ruined your father? I warrant that was no accident."

Ellen waved away her older friend's objection. "That was years ago. Gail would have been only a child. Surely you don't think she started the fire."

Dinah shook an accusing finger. "You're a softy for a sad story."

Ellen took a big bite of her cookie. "Doesn't the Bible teach us to offer kindness to strangers?"

"What will your father say?"

"He'll respect my decision." *As should you,* Ellen thought, though she didn't dare say it for fear of hurting Dinah's feelings.

"I don't know that he'll agree with you. It sets a bad example, harboring a girl who's run away from her people."

"It will be all right. I promise." She got up from the table to hug Dinah. "You're not fooling me. You aren't as prickly as you'd like to pretend. You've a generous heart."

Dinah squeezed her back and pushed her gently away. "I hope I do," she murmured, "but when you've lived as long as I have and seen people behave in ways they shouldn't, maybe you won't be so trusting."

* * *

The following day was the Sabbath, but not a day of community worship. It was a visiting Sunday, one where friends and relatives would call on each other and spend time together, resting from the week's labor. Sometimes Ellen and her parents spent a quiet day together on visiting Sunday, but this week it was far from quiet at their home. Dinah's friends from the widows' group had gathered there to plan their next benefit and to give thanks for little Raymond Blauch's continuing recovery at the hospital. Ellen had invited Dinah to welcome the widows to her house rather than the apartment over the store because Dinah's space was small, and negotiating the stairs was difficult for some of the older women.

It was a beautiful September day with a breeze that carried the sweet smell of ripening apples from the orchard and ruffled the hair of the laughing youngsters who chased each other around the yard. Some of the widows had brought children and grandchildren, and several other families who were not members of the widows' club had stopped by. The older women tended to gather in the kitchen and front room, while the teenagers and younger women congregated on the porch or in the yard, where they could see and be seen by the younger men, who stood and talked in the shade of the barn and windmill.

"Anne will stop by later if its another false alarm," Naomi Byler informed Ellen, speaking of the local midwife. Naomi, widow of the former bishop, was the unofficial leader of the women's group. She'd settled into a comfortable rocker in the kitchen where she could observe the comings and goings and make certain that no one was behaving in a manner improper for a Sunday. "This is Dora Stoltzfus's first child. She's not due until the first of October, but her husband's gone to fetch Naomi three times this week. Twice it was the middle of the night."

"Poor Anne," Dinah remarked as she made room on the counter for a bowl of applesauce. "I don't know what's worse, anxious young mothers or worried first-time fathers."

"The fathers for certain," Ellen's mother said. "My John made such a fuss when Ellen was born that the midwife said he was in more danger than I was." Her friends laughed and were quick to share stories of their own childbirths, some funny, others harrowing. Ellen's mother wasn't a widow, but she'd known most of the women, including Dinah, for a lifetime, and they were all dear friends.

To Ellen's amusement, what had begun as a typical Sunday with a few guests dropping by had grown to a large gathering. Ellen's parents had neglected to tell her that they'd invited the five Shetlers, and with the promise of a fine dinner, nothing short of a flood or snowstorm could keep Simeon and his sons and grandsons away.

It was a matter of fact that the widows' group included some of the finest cooks in Lancaster County, and it was a point of honor that every woman brought the results of her best recipe for their potluck dinners. Casseroles, trays of sandwiches, baskets of yeast bread, platters of cold ham and chicken, jars of pickled beets, salads and plates of stuffed eggs covered the counters and spilled over onto the kitchen table. Ellen's *mam*'s prize hand-carved buffet was lined with pies, cakes, puddings and apple tarts.

"More food here than a wedding supper," Ellen's father had teased as the largess continued to arrive. But there were no complaints from him. Ellen knew that he was looking forward to the delicious meal and the leftovers that would remain behind when the widows went home. He'd always enjoyed company, and playing host to his friends and neighbors pleased him greatly. If the female chatter became overpowering, the weather was nice enough that he and his comrades could always retreat to the barn or to the fields for peace and quiet.

Ellen had just found another folding chair on the porch for an elderly latecomer when she caught sight of Micah standing near the grape arbor. She paused to wave and smile at him, and he motioned for her to join him. She carried the chair inside and then went back out.

As she approached Micah, he stooped to pick up a soccer ball that had bounced off a tree and tossed it back to Joel, who gave a whoop and dashed off with three other boys in his wake. Micah moved back into the arbor and gestured for her to sit beside him on the high-backed swing. There, shielded from the house and yard by the still-green grape vines, they could have a measure of privacy without breaking the rules of propriety.

"It's crazy in the house," she said and gratefully took a seat. "Dinah says that it's rare that nearly everyone can make a meeting." The grass was cool under her bare feet, and she was all too aware of Micah's commanding presence. A few bees buzzed and flew overhead, but the Concord grapes had ripened and vanished for the year. Only bare stems and a few dried remnants of the fruit that had hung so heavily on the vines remained. She'd always loved the grape arbor. As a child, it had been her favorite place to read. Now she found another reason for it to give her sweet memories.

"I wanted to talk to you about something," Micah said. He folded his arms and regarded her seriously. "I heard that you're letting some runaway sleep in your shop."

Ellen grimaced. "That didn't take long. I expected the news to make the rounds by church Sunday, but..." She shrugged. "Who told you?"

"*Vadder.* What are you thinking, Ellen? You don't know this girl, and you don't know if she's under a ban from her church."

She was so surprised by the tone he was taking with her that it took a moment for her to respond. "You haven't even met Gail. She's a *goot* person in bad circumstances. She had a place to live but her roommate didn't pay her share of the rent and they were both evicted."

"I have to admit I'm surprised. You're usually so sensible, Ellen." He frowned. "And I don't know what's gotten into your father that he'd allow—"

"Micah!" She stared at him, more than a little annoyed that he'd speak to her as if she were one of his naughty nephews.

Just then, Neziah appeared at the entrance to the grape arbor. "Melvin's here," he told his brother, "and he's looking for you. Something about a horse race?"

Micah glanced at Ellen as he rose from the swing. "We'll talk about this later," he said. "I think you need to give it serious thought."

Speechless and now more than a little irritated, she watched Micah walk away. Neziah took his seat on the swing next to her. "I was looking for you."

She turned toward him and held up a hand. "If you've come to talk to me about Gail, I'm not in the mood to discuss it."

He looked at her oddly. "Are you talking about the Bontrager girl?"

"Is there anything that anyone in the community doesn't know about my personal business? Yes, I did offer to let Gail sleep at the shop, and I'm standing by my decision. I'm not a child, Neziah. I've thought about this for days. I've prayed about it, and God showed me His way. Gail's a sweet young woman, and she's going through a bad time. What's wrong in extending a hand of—"

"Ellen, Ellen." He raised his hand again, this time in a calming motion. "I didn't come to criticize you."

"Micah certainly did. I'm thirty-three years old!" She took a breath and started again. "Old enough to make my own decisions. Was I supposed to let Gail sleep in a barn? What if something terrible happened to her? The world outside our community isn't a safe one for a young woman alone. Aren't we supposed to show charity?"

He smiled down at her. "Can I say something, or do I just get to listen?"

She sighed loudly. "Go ahead. Get it off your chest. Tell me why I've made a foolish decision and why I'll live to regret it."

His smile became laughter.

"I'm glad you think my actions were—"

"Admirable? Brave? I came looking for you, Ellen, because I heard about Gail Bontrager, and I wanted to tell you how proud of you I am. It's easy for people to talk about extending a helping hand, but actually going out on a limb for a stranger? You don't see that often. Not even in our community, where it should be taken for granted. It's where the Mennonites put us to shame, don't you think? They go out into the English world and help those who need it most."

"Wait!" She seized his hand. "You're saying you don't think what I did was wrong?"

He raised her hand to his lips and kissed it. He looked at her with his cinnamon eyes. "*Jah*, Ellen. I agree with what you did. I think it was right and *goot*. I would hope that, put in the same position, I'd make the same choice you did."

She stared at him, suddenly feeling lightheaded. "Neziah, I never expected *you*..." She stopped and started again. "When we walked out together, you admonished me for attending those Bible classes where we were free to talk about interpretation. You didn't want me to speak out against tradition. You told me that you'd never allow your wife to work outside your home...to associate with the English." She looked down and then up at him again. "You've changed," she murmured.

"I hope I've gained a *little* wisdom in ten years." He stroked the back of her hand. "What can I say? I was wrong about you working in the craft shop. I was wrong about the Bible class. I was wrong not to give you the respect you deserved. I'll make no excuses for myself except to say that I was young and foolish."

She pulled back her hand, unable to think clearly while he was holding her hand so intimately, as small tingles of excitement were running up her arm. "You disagree with what our bishop teaches?"

"Nay." Neziah shook his head. "I didn't say that. But I sometimes *do* question our interpretation of it. I think sometimes I've thought too much about the rules and have forgotten the message that the Lord came to deliver to us. What does Jesus say is the greatest of the laws? 'Love one another'?" He steepled his hands, as if searching for the right words. "I was born Amish. My blood and bones are those of the martyrs who came before us and died for our faith. I could never live outside our church. But I would be less than what I believe God wants if I refused to question or to think for myself."

She felt as if a weight pressed on her chest. Was what she had believed all this time about Neziah's rigid mind-set wrong? She scrambled for clarity. "Do you still believe that a husband should be the head of the family?"

"Jah," he said. "I do. I believe that it is God's plan for us. I think the man should be

the head of the household, but I believe just as strongly that the woman should be the heart. Can a head live without a heart?" He smiled at her and extended his hand. "Ellen, I know it hasn't been long since—"

A child's scream brought them both to their feet. Neziah dashed out of the arbor, and Ellen hurried after him.

"Neziah!" Simeon shouted. "Come quick! It's Joel! He's hurt bad!"

Chapter Fourteen

Neziah ran toward his father. *"Vas is?"* he shouted. "Where?"

His brother came around the stable holding Joel in his arms. Blood poured from the boy's mouth and nose, running down his chin and dripping onto the ground.

Asa, shrieking at the top of his lungs, darted after them. "He's dead! Joel's dead!"

Neziah raced across the yard toward his injured child. *So much blood.* What could the boy have done to hurt himself so badly? Other men crowded around, forming a barrier between him and Joel, but he shoved his way through and held out his arms to Micah. "What happened?" he repeated. "Is he breathing?"

At that instant, Joel began to kick and scream at the top of his lungs.

Neziah gathered his son against his chest. *Not dead. Not dead.* Despite Asa's continued wailing that Joel was dead, it was evident that the howling child in his arms was very much alive. *But how badly was he hurt?* Neziah looked at Micah expectantly.

"He fell off the chicken house roof. He may have struck his face on a cultivator before he hit the ground."

A cultivator? His son had fallen on a cultivator? Neziah's blood ran cold. *They would need an ambulance. A doctor. Had his head struck the metal prongs?* The front of Joel's shirt was bloody. Did he have broken ribs? A fractured skull? Everyone was talking at once. His father was bellowing orders. Asa was still wailing. A woman shouted questions from the porch.

Neziah had always considered himself levelheaded. When one of their hired hands had severely cut his arm at the sawmill, he'd been the one to apply a tourniquet, bandage the wound and drive the man in a wagon to the nearest phone where he could call 911. He knew how to react to an emergency. Or so he'd thought. But now, with his child, Neziah felt as though he were wading through waist-deep mud. He couldn't get his mind and hands to coordinate. He knew he needed to examine his son's wounds, but it was difficult to see for the tears welling up in his eyes.

"Let me see him." Ellen appeared in front of Neziah. How she'd gotten through the press of men and the frightened children, he didn't know, but she was suddenly there, calm and soft-spoken. "Stand him up," she said. "He's choking because you're holding his head on an angle."

"But if he has serious injuries, won't that make it worse?" he said.

"Look at him, Neziah. Listen to him. No child on his deathbed has that much lung power." She waved her hand at the onlookers. "Please. Give us room to get a *goot* look at what's wrong."

Given a definite task, his father, Simeon, was all too ready to take charge. "You heard Ellen. Back up, everyone. Give the boy room to breathe."

Joel was sobbing now. His mouth and nose were still seeping blood, but when Neziah stood him on his feet, nothing seemed to be broken. Joel clung to his father's leg and tried to talk, but fell prey to a bout of hiccups and clamped a hand over his mouth.

"You're all right," Ellen soothed, stroking Joel's bare head. "Let me see."

"But...but Asa said..." Joel's garbled attempt at speech was muddled by a combination sob and hiccup. Joel glanced down, saw all the blood on his shirt and started screaming again.

"Can someone bring me water and a clean towel?" Ellen squatted down. She rubbed Joel's back in slow circles. "Shh, shh, it will be all right."

Lizzie Fisher, a veteran of mending scrapes and spills because of her seven young stepchildren, had already guessed what they would need for an injured child. The small but capable woman slipped between the men and shyly offered a basin of water and several towels.

"Shh, shh," Ellen murmured. She dipped the corner of a towel in the water and began to dab it on Joel's face.

"Matthew...said...said I'm *dead*," Joel sobbed. His upper lip was swelling fast, and his words came out barely coherent.

Matthew Fisher was eight and one of Lizzie's brood. In Joel's mind, whatever the older boy said must be true, despite the fact that Matthew was known for his vivid imagination. "You aren't dead," Neziah said. He ruffled his son's hair. He wanted to keep holding him, to kiss his tear-streaked, bloody face, but Amish men didn't publicly show affection. Alone, he would have followed his instinct and embraced Joel as he did every night when he tucked him into bed. With his father and the other men and women watching, it didn't seem right. "You're going to be fine," he said gruffly.

"I don't want...want to go to the hospital!" Joel protested. "*Nay* shots." His sobs were coming slower now. The hiccups continued, but the bleeding from his nose and mouth had clearly slowed.

Ellen dabbed gently at Joel's face with a wet cloth. "You're going to be fine, Joel," she said, glancing up at Neziah. "He's fine. He just knocked out his two front teeth when he fell."

"I don't know. They said he fell on a cultivator," Neziah said. He didn't want to overreact. They didn't run to doctors and the hospital the way *Englishers* did because they didn't believe in insurance, but Joel's well-being was more important than medical bills. "Maybe he should go to the hospital."

"I think he looks worse than he is." Ellen's tone was reassuring. "If he'd fallen on the cultivator, he'd be hurt a lot worse. Look at him," she said. "Legs whole, arms intact." She mopped at Joel's upper lip. "Nose took a bump. Probably had the wind knocked out of him, but he's not acting like he lost consciousness. The total damage seems to be a nosebleed and two baby teeth dislodged before their time."

"His front teeth?" Neziah asked woodenly. "He knocked out his front teeth? That's all?" He took a deep breath, willing his heart to slow. How was it that Ellen could make everything okay in the space of a few moments? And then he felt shame that he hadn't given thanks to God. Surely, it was the Lord who'd prevented far worse from happening. Praise be, he thought. *For Your mercy.*

"Shouldn't we try to find the teeth?" Micah asked. "Take him to the dentist and see if she can...do something."

"Put them back in," Neziah finished. "Thomas told me that his brother's child knocked a tooth out, and a dentist put it back in. It didn't even turn black."

"Try to put Joel's teeth back in after they've been laying in the chicken yard?" Ellen shook her head. "They're baby teeth. He would have lost them by next year, anyway."

Joel's lower lip quivered. His nosebleed had slowed to a thin trickle. "My teeth?" It came out more like *m'teef.* He blinked back tears. "I fell," he said.

"Apparently fell off the roof," Micah repeated. "Matthew said that the soccer ball got stuck there. Joel climbed up to get it, but then he was walking on the edge to show how brave he was. He must have gotten too close to the edge."

Asa, who'd squeezed between his uncle Micah's legs nodded. "Joel climbed on the roof."

"No serious harm done," Simeon announced to his neighbors. "Nothing to worry about. Boy just knocked out a tooth." The group began to disperse—the single women gathered to whisper to each other and the young men to relate similar incidents from their own childhood.

"*Two* teeth," Neziah corrected quietly. He didn't want to show disrespect to his father, but neither did he want the incident dismissed as nothing.

"Luckily not his second teeth," Lizzie added. She held the basin of water for Ellen, waited until she'd dried Joel's face and then carried the basin and towels back to the house.

"Thank you, Lizzie," Neziah called after

her. "I appreciate it." Joel's fall must have brought back terrifying memories. Lizzie's husband had died in a fall out of his hayloft.

Micah knelt beside Joel and gave his nephew a playful nudge on the shoulder. "You gave us quite a scare."

Joel tried to smile, revealing the hole where his top teeth had been.

"We were on our way to throw a few lines in the water when the kids started yelling that Joel had fallen off the roof," Micah said to Ellen as he got to his feet. He pointed to Abram, who'd come up into the yard driving a farm wagon heaped with loose straw. Nat, holding several fishing poles, was sitting on the board seat beside him. On the back of the wagon, Saloma's younger sister and two other unmarried girls were sitting with their bare feet dangling over the edge. "Dinah said we won't be eating until after they finish their meeting, so we're going down to the creek for an hour. Want to come along?"

"Come on!" Saloma's sister called to Ellen, with a wave. "It will be fun."

Ellen glanced down at Joel and shook her head. "*Danki*, but I'll stay here and keep an eye on him."

"Are you sure?" Micah asked. He seemed disappointed.

She brushed at a small bloodstain on her apron. "*Nay*, you go. I think Joel could use something cold on that lip."

Micah's brow furrowed as he glanced from Ellen to Neziah. "You can take it from here, can't you, brother? You don't want her to miss out on the fun, do you?"

It was exactly what Neziah wanted. He wanted Ellen to skip the fishing and stay here with him and Joel, and he was ashamed of himself for thinking it. He averted his eyes. "You should go." He rested a hand on his son's shoulder. "I can handle this from here."

"I want to go fishing, Uncle Micah," Joel declared. "I wanna go!"

"No children this time," Neziah murmured to his son. "Just adults. Maybe next time."

Ellen waved to Micah as he walked away. "Have a good time."

Neziah watched Ellen as his brother joined the young folks in the wagon. "You sure you don't want to join them? Joel can't be too hurt if he's begging to go fishing." He picked up his son. "Let's see if we can talk the women out of some ice for that lip."

Ellen followed him to the house, but Neziah noticed that she was watching the wagon full of young people as it bounced across the field toward the creek. The thought that she was missing out on the fun to care for his boy didn't sit well with him. Marriage to him would mean the heavy responsibility of motherhood from day one. There'd be no honeymoon as most newly married couples had; there would be no trip out of state to visit relatives and spend time getting to know each other as man and wife. Ellen would immediately be a mother of two, with less time for leisure and the lightheartedness that often went with being a newlywed. He knew Ellen would never complain, but he wondered if he was asking too much of her. He loved her and wanted her to be his wife, but was he being selfish? Was he thinking of his own happiness at her expense?

The following week was so busy that Ellen wasn't sure where the days went. Business at the shop had increased measurably, and she and her mother were trying to preserve the abundant harvest from the garden before any went to waste. She found herself rising before dawn to begin regular household chores and breakfast, and returning from the store to can vegetables or to prepare them for drying, late into the evening.

All week, either Neziah or Micah drove her to work, and when she left the shop at the end of the day, one of them was waiting to drive her home. Usually it was Micah, but Neziah came once. The intention was nice and it was fun waiting to see who would be there to greet her, but a part of her missed her quiet times, scooting along on her push scooter. When she rode with Micah, she didn't have to talk. He always had plenty to say, and it was always entertaining. Her rides with Neziah and the children were very different; Asa and Joel chattered on like a pair of bluejays, and she and Neziah shared bits of their day, with Neziah often consulting her on some issue with his boys. Still, she found herself comfortable around both brothers, making her looming decision even more difficult.

With the resilience of childhood, Joel's injuries healed quickly. He'd started school, and—according to Micah—his accident and his missing front teeth made him quite popular among the other first-graders. Neziah had explained that he'd considered keeping his oldest son home another year, but since he had an October birthday, the teacher had convinced the family that school would be good for Joel. Secretly, Ellen agreed. He was a bright child, and keeping him occupied and facing new challenges every weekday would prevent him from coaxing too many sweet treats out of his grandfather.

One of the things that Ellen and Neziah and the children had done together that week was to go to the general store and pick up healthy snacks and fruit to go in Joel's lunch. Not to be left out, Asa had asked for his own lunchbox. Apparently, packing lunch for both boys for the following day had become part of bedtime routine at the Shetler house. And Ellen was pleased to learn from Micah that individual bags of potato chips and packaged whoopie pies had been replaced with apples, cut-up carrots and raisins. Most Amish children walked to school, but since Joel's school was located on a narrow, twisting road more than a mile away, Simeon drove Joel, in the pony cart, to and from the one-room schoolhouse daily.

Neither her mother nor her father had said anything to her about her promise to decide if she would court Neziah or Micah before the month was up, but one of them had drawn a circle in red marker on the calendar that hung in the kitchen. She suspected the culprit was her *mam* because the circle had a small tail at the bottom like a capital *Q*, her mother's trademark. Of course, her father was known for his practical jokes, and when Ellen was a child, he'd sometimes play tricks on her. He'd never own up to his teasing, but always blamed her *mam*. Her *mam* would shake her head and say, "You'll never know, I suppose." Her mother was always loyal, even when it meant taking the blame for mischief she hadn't created.

In any case, the circled date was always the first thing she saw when she came downstairs in the morning, and the last thing she saw before going up to bed. "Nothing like a little pressure," she had muttered under her breath the first time she had spotted it. But she didn't really blame them. They were, as always, thinking of her best interests. She hoped she'd be as good a parent as they had been, and she never failed to thank God for them in her evening prayers.

Saturday found Ellen with both families, her own and the Shetlers, at a community apple-cider gathering. That year, a few varieties of apples had come ripe early, so the work frolic was being held nearly a month earlier than usual. The husband of one of Dinah's daughters owned a large apple orchard, and it was their custom to host a community gathering every fall.

The older men and women, aided by teenagers and younger women with babies, watched over the children, providing pony rides, apple bobbing and taffy pulls. There were sack races, tug-of-war contests and games, all intended to keep the little ones entertained while their mothers made huge kettles of apple butter over open fires. The younger men were equally busy. They were in charge of making enough apple cider to share with the entire Amish community. It was a much-awaited day of work and play, visiting and plenty of food to offset the business of cider-and apple-butter making.

With so many hands to help, even the tasks of stirring the bubbling apple butter and sorting and grinding bushels and bushels of ripe apples were enjoyable. Ellen and Micah had arrived early and contributed their share of labor before noon so that they could take part in the corn-toss games, the wood-chopping contest, the egg and spoon races and the corn-husking and shelling competitions. Ellen had come in first in the blindfolded egg-and-spoon race, and Micah had won the wood-chopping contest. The prize was a new ax, a gift that brought a lot of laughter from the onlookers.

"If you run out of wood to cut, you can come over to my woodshed this afternoon," Bishop Andy called. "Or the schoolhouse. They're always looking for firewood."

Micah rubbed the blisters on his hands and groaned. "I think I've had enough chopping for one day." That brought more laughter from the crowd.

"If I'd known he could cut wood that fast with an ax," Simeon shouted, "I wouldn't have bought that new saw."

Micah's friend Abram came over to slap Micah's back and congratulate him. "Don't forget there's a singing at the Rupps' tonight," he reminded. "You two are coming, aren't you?"

Micah looked at Ellen and grinned. "What do you say?"

"I don't know," she hedged. "Tomorrow's church."

"I promise I'll get you home early." Micah reached for the cup of cider she was drinking, and she laughed and held it out of his reach. In turn, he scooped up a handful of woodchips from the grass and threw them at her.

Ellen giggled as woodchips fell into her cup. "Now you can have it," she said.

"See how she treats me?" Micah grimaced, putting on an aggrieved expression for his friend. "What will she do once we're married?"

"*If* we're married," she answered saucily. "I haven't made up my mind about you yet." She picked the woodchips out of the cup and tossed them back at him. Several struck his shirt and rolled off, leaving apple-cider stains.

He reached for her hand. "Come to the singing with me," he said.

"I'll think about it." She was tempted. She loved the singings but if she didn't get enough sleep tonight, she'd be yawning through the next morning's sermons. And that definitely wouldn't set a good example for the younger girls.

"Cutting wood is thirsty work." Micah indicated the barn where the men were still making cider. "Shall we walk over there and get some more before I collapse and die of thirst?"

They walked down the lane through the apple trees. On either side, young people were climbing ladders to reach the ripe fruit. Girls were holding out their aprons to catch apples tossed from boys in the trees and children ran under the branches snatching up fallen apples and taking bites. It was a wonderful day, a day of laughter and fun and combined work that would provide delicious cider and apple butter in the snowy days of winter.

As they walked, Micah's hand closed around hers. "Have you had as much fun today as I have?" he asked. "I hope so. Because anytime I'm with you is the best time."

She tried to pull her hand free, but he held it tightly. "We shouldn't—" she began and then broke off when she spotted Neziah standing a few yards away, watching them. Surprised, Micah released her, and she tucked her hand behind her back like a guilty child caught with her fingers in cake icing.

There was something in Neziah's eyes that worried Ellen. Was he upset that she and Micah had been holding hands? She met Neziah's gaze. No, she sensed it was something else.

"I need to tell you both something," Neziah said as he walked toward them. His features were solemn, his eyes dark with swirling emotion.

Ellen and Micah exchanged glances as they approached his brother.

Neziah cleared his throat when they were standing in front of him. "I've been watching the two of you together and…" His voice was deep and raspy. "I see how happy the two of you are together. And I realized that…" He looked away and then back at them, making eye contact with first Micah, then Ellen. "I realized you belong together."

Micah frowned. "Brother—"

Neziah held up his hand. "Let me speak my piece while I have the nerve for it. I've been thinking on this all week. Praying on it. What I'm trying to say is that I'm stepping out of the…whatever this is we've been doing." He motioned to all three of them. "Micah, you and Ellen belong together. And I wish you… happiness." He straightened to his full height, and his lips thinned as he swallowed. "There's no need for you to wait. Ask Bishop Andy to cry your banns."

"You're sure?" Micah asked. "You're all right with this? Giving Ellen up?"

Neziah shook his head and smiled faintly. "Do you not know her any better than that? Ellen isn't mine to give." A look of resignation passed over his face. "Congratulations, brother. Ellen, I wish you all the best."

She stared at Neziah, feeling as if the wind had been knocked out of her. She was shocked by his words and if she admitted it to herself, a little angry with him. "You've changed your mind? Now you don't want to marry me?" She exhaled. "After everything you said about—"

"It's best this way," Neziah interrupted. "As you said a long time ago, we're too different." He grasped Micah's hand and shook it. "You and Ellen have more in common. You'll make the best match."

Micah broke into a grin. "You're serious, aren't you?"

"*Jah.* Make her happy, Micah. I know you can. Just don't ever give me reason to think I made the wrong decision."

"I won't," Micah assured him, pumping his hand.

Ellen suddenly felt as though all the strength had gone out of her legs. She had the strangest desire to sink down on the grass and lean against the trunk of an apple tree. She couldn't think of what to say to Neziah and so she said nothing as he strode away. Then it occurred to her that she should be relieved. Her decision had been made for her. Now she didn't have to choose between the brothers. She would marry Micah. He would accept baptism, and they would wed with the full approval of their families and the church. Micah would be the father of her children, and they would live as best they could in their faith and grow old together.

"You heard him!" Micah caught her by the waist and swung her in a circle. "You're mine! Let's go to Bishop Andy right now! Neziah's right. There's no need to wait another day! We can start planning our wedding! Isn't it wonderful?" He lowered her to the ground. "We can be married in November," he went on. "I'll ask to join the church immediately and get them to cry the banns as soon—"

"Nay," Ellen managed, pressing her hand to her forehead. She felt dizzy, from Micah spinning her around, no doubt. "Not yet."

"What do you mean, *not yet*?" He looked at her, his eyes crinkling at the corners. "You heard Neziah. He's taking back his offer of marriage. I've won you. You're mine, Ellen. Finally, really mine." He laughed and clapped his hands together. "This is the best day of my life. Of course, I know you'd have picked me in the end, but having Neziah's blessing makes it easier, doesn't it?"

Ellen pressed her lips together, only half hearing what Micah was saying. "We'll not make the announcement yet. Our agreement was for a month. To announce sooner would be inappropriate."

He scowled and opened his arms. "There's nothing inappropriate. We've known each other our whole lives. Neither of us is a kid. No one will think poorly of you for such a fast engagement."

It wasn't herself she was thinking about. It was Neziah. She didn't want to hurt him, not for anything. And it would hurt him, wouldn't it? For her to announce the engagement so quickly. Or was that what he wanted? To be done with her. To be over with it. "My father gave me a month," she said stubbornly. "We'll wait until the full month has passed. Then we'll tell everyone. Until then…" She nodded. "Until then, it will be our secret."

Chapter Fifteen

On Wednesday morning Gail stopped by the craft shop. She came in by the front door and waited, looking at the merchandise until Ellen rang up purchases for two customers and they left the store. "Good morning," Ellen said.

Gail smiled shyly. "Good morning." She looked as if she wanted to say something, but she just stood there.

"Is everything okay upstairs?" Ellen asked finally. "Bathroom working? You have enough hot water? The hot water heater is getting finicky."

Gail smiled again. "It's all wonderful. I love it up there. Did you know that through the west window you can see all the way to the farms on the far side of Lincoln Road?"

Ellen could hear Dinah rattling around in

the kitchen, making an early lunch. Ellen had to take over the customers at two, while Dinah did her weekly grocery shopping. Dinah's sister always shopped on Wednesdays, too, and the two would enjoy coffee and a visit afterward.

When Gail didn't say anything, Ellen smiled at her. "Is there something I can help you with?"

"*Nay*, it's you I wanted to..." Gail caught the hem of her T-shirt between her fingers and twisted it nervously. "I was wondering if you'd like to come to lunch with me today. My treat," she added quickly. "I wanted to thank you."

"Gail," Ellen began. "That's not necessary. I'm glad you're staying here. It's company for Dinah, just knowing someone else is in the building at night. You don't need to spend your money on me."

"Please. Please come," Gail said all in a rush. "And it isn't costing me a penny. Except for the tip," she added. "Margaret allots us so many meals, and I saved one for you. We can have anything, so long as our bill doesn't go over ten dollars each. I know you always take off early for lunch on Wednesday, and it would make me happy if you'd have lunch with me."

"All right," Ellen agreed. It was clear that it meant a lot to Gail, and wasn't she always telling her mother that she had to learn to accept help from other people? What had she said to her just this morning? "You have to learn to be a gracious receiver as well as a giver." And besides, she would welcome the opportunity to get to know Gail better. Even if they'd gotten off to a poor start, Ellen felt that Gail was someone that she'd like to have as a friend.

Half an hour later Dinah was behind the counter at the store, and Gail and Ellen were seated in a quiet corner at the Mennonite Family Restaurant. To Ellen's delight, she was enjoying her time with her new tenant. There on neutral ground, Gail was more relaxed, even friendly. She didn't talk a lot, but what she said was sensible and interesting.

"Today's one of my days off," Gail explained after they'd ordered. She spooned sugar into a tall glass of iced tea. "Wednesday is meatloaf and mac and cheese day. It's one of their lunch specials, but you can have whatever you like. The meatloaf is so good that I asked the cook for the recipe."

"Did she give it to you?" Ellen asked.

Gail shook her head. "Not yet, but she will.

She likes me. She even asked me to come to one of their church services."

"Do you think you'll go? To Mennonite worship?"

Gail stirred her tea. "I don't know. Not yet, but maybe one day. It's all sort of confusing. I've always gone…" She sighed and glanced up at Ellen. "I've never gone to any other church service but Amish. It's hard to think of worshipping with another faith."

"The Lord is still with you, Gail, wherever you are."

She nodded. "I pray. A lot. But there's a lot of stuff that I haven't figured out yet."

"Can I ask if you were baptized?" Ellen kept her voice low. "It's none of my business, but—"

"You think I've been shunned?" Gail shook her head. "No. I wasn't baptized so I wasn't shunned by the church. Probably by my family, though. My father would…" She broke off and looked away.

Ellen waited and was rewarded when Gail went on.

"My father doesn't forgive easily. I love him, but I can't live with him. Not ever again." She met Ellen's gaze. "He's not a bad man, but I think he's troubled…in his head." She sighed again. "When he was a child, he went into the barn and found his father dead by his own hand. *Mutter* says it preys on his mind. He was only seven years old. Too young to see such a thing."

"I'm sorry," Ellen said, seeing that Gail was near to tears. "I shouldn't have asked."

"Nay." Gail gave her a half smile. "I should have told you that I hadn't been shunned. I would never do anything to get you or anyone in trouble." She took a sip of her iced tea. "I guess you could say that I'm *rumspringa*. I never joined the church. *Vadder* wanted me to. Said I shamed him by not being baptized with my younger sister. That's why I left when I did. It has to be my decision to accept the Plain life, doesn't it?"

"It does," Ellen agreed. "Let's talk about something else. I'm sorry if I've upset you."

"Jah." Gail forced a smile. "It is your treat and my pleasure to have you. At home, I had friends. And my sisters and brothers. I was close to them. It hurts to think I might not see them again."

"Because you don't think you can go home?"

"Jah."

"Life changes, Gail. It may not be as bad as

you think. As they grow up, they can choose to visit you if they like."

"I suppose, the ones that *Vadder* hasn't convinced that I'm *schlecht*." Wicked.

"I don't think you're bad," Ellen assured her. "I think you're a kindhearted person."

Gail lowered her hands to her lap. "I try to be. But sometimes I have resentful thoughts about my father. It is a failing of mine, to always question and not accept my father's rule. Honor your mother and father, the Bible tells us. *Mutter* said I should just obey him, and everything would be all right. That was her way, but not mine."

Ellen listened without saying anything.

"Usually I honor *Vadder* with my actions, but not always in my thoughts." She crumbled her napkin and laid it beside her plate. "Here I am still talking about my troubles when I should be congratulating you. I hear that you and Micah Shetler are going to marry. That's wonderful." Her eyes took on a sparkle. "I've seen your Micah. He's very tall and very handsome."

"*Jah*, he is, isn't he?" Ellen agreed. "We've been talking, spending time together for the last few weeks, trying to decide if we want to walk out together. It's a big decision, who you will marry. Someday, you'll have to choose a husband. Is there anyone you left behind? In your community?"

"Me?" Gail chuckled. "*Nay*. There is no one special." She glanced around to see if anyone was close enough to hear and said, "I've seen you with the other one, too. Micah's brother?"

"My *vadder* and his *vadder* wanted me to marry one of them," Ellen admitted. "I just didn't know which one."

"The older one looks nice, too, but very serious. And he has *kinner*. How many?"

"Two boys. One is four and one almost six. The oldest just started school."

"Ah, the chunky one. He's cute. They are both cute children. Well behaved."

"Not always. They need a mother. It was one of the things that I considered—if it was God's plan for me that I should nurture these motherless children."

Gail nodded. "But you're happy with your choice of Micah?"

"Very happy. We're perfectly matched." Ellen paused as the waitress brought their lunches, thanked her and then continued after she left the table. "The last few weeks have been so busy I haven't had time to sew a single piece for my trousseau. Micah took me to

Hershey Park, bowling and to the apple butter frolic on Saturday."

Gail bowed her head, and Ellen clasped her hand and did the same. Steam rose from Ellen's soup as she offered a silent grace. And when she opened her eyes, Gail was studying her intently.

"What? What is it?" Ellen asked.

"Nothing." Gail poured catsup on her meatloaf. "I just wondered …" She shook her head. "It's nothing."

"It must be something," Ellen said.

"Forgive me. I speak when I should hold my tongue. It's another of my faults."

"What?" Ellen looked at her across the table. "Tell me."

Gail sighed. "You say you're happy, but your eyes are sad, and there's no shine to you. Usually, you bustle about and everyone can feel the joy shining out of you. But when you speak of the man you will marry, you don't look happy."

"Nonsense," Ellen protested. "Of course I'm happy. Micah and I are perfect for each other. We're so much alike. He likes to laugh and have a good time and so do I."

"Pay no heed to me." Gail gave a wave. "I talk when I shouldn't. You know your own affairs best. I wish you happiness in your marriage." She flushed pink. "And…and I hope you will invite me to the wedding."

Although she'd thoroughly enjoyed her lunch with Gail, something about their conversation troubled Ellen, and she kept going over and over it in her head as Micah drove her home that evening. Gail's statement about her not *looking happy* lingered in her mind all evening. The next morning, as she was cleaning away the breakfast dishes, she couldn't resist mentioning her uneasiness to her mother. Her *dat* had already gone outside, and Ellen and her mother were alone. Her mother seemed fine this morning, cheerful and energetic, and it eased Ellen's heart to see her old self.

"*Mam*, are you pleased that I've decided to marry Micah?" she asked as she carried the milk and butter back to the refrigerator. Her mother was standing at the big farm sink, scrubbing away at the already spotless surface.

Her mother turned and smiled at her. "Of course I am. He is a *goot* boy. With Micah you will always have laughter at your table. And you always were one who loved to laugh. Like your *dat*." She dried her hands on her apron, went to the cupboard and retrieved the sugar bowl that she'd just put away. Removing the lid, she sprinkled sugar liberally into the sink and started scrubbing again.

Ellen suddenly felt uneasy. "*Mam?* Did you just pour sugar in the sink?"

"*Jah*. I'm cleaning. I always use *tzooker*. Didn't I teach you that? And to clean out the drains, mix it with vinegar. Better than the stuff in the can from the store it is."

"Drains? *Ach*, you mean baking soda, don't you? Not sugar, baking soda."

"*Nay*, you have the wrong of it, girl. *Tzooker*. Would you teach a hen to lay eggs? Who taught you all you know about cleaning and cooking?"

Ellen nodded. Once her mother got a thing in her head, it was best not to argue with her. And what harm would it do, to wash the sink with sugar? Other than to attract a few ants? And empty the sugar bowl.

"So," her mother went on. "It worries you. That you chose Micah over the other one. What's his name?"

"Neziah." Surely her mother hadn't forgotten Neziah's name. "Neziah is the oldest. But I didn't say I was worried."

"The one with the two sweet children. So sweet, those *kinner*. Like little *fett fastnachts*. You ask the Shetlers to supper tomorrow night. I will make gingerbread for them. Your Micah, he likes gingerbread, too. When he was a boy, he used to steal it off my windowsill when it was cooling." She laughed. "He didn't know I left it for him on purpose."

"Micah stole gingerbread?"

"*Jah*. His mother, you remember her." She wouldn't mention Irma's name if she could help it. It was a habit of the older generation. Dead was dead. In heaven. In a better place. And best not to linger and grieve too long. At least not in theory. Or in public. "A *goot* woman, she was. A kind heart. But a terrible cook. I tasted her gingerbread once." Mam grimaced. "Fit for *hink el fress a*." Chicken feed. She emptied the remaining sugar into the sink. "So you think maybe you have made a mistake?"

"I didn't say I made a mistake." Ellen crossed the kitchen to stand within an arm's length. Her mother turned from the sink, dried her hands on her apron and hugged her. It was such an unusual gesture that Ellen's throat constricted. Her arms tightened around her mother and for long seconds they stood there, content in their embrace.

"You will be a bride," her mother said softly. "You should be happy. It's one thing to be nervous, but you should be thinking about Micah all the time. His face is the last one that should come to you before you fall asleep and the first when you open your eyes in the morning." A rosy flush tinted her cheeks. "I was like that with your *vadder.* That I do not forget. Some things I do. I know that. But the time before we married..." Her smile lit up her eyes. "Just seeing him walk down the road toward me was as sweet as molasses candy. And if Micah doesn't make you feel that way..." She shrugged and gestured with her hands. "Then maybe you should think some more."

"But...but you like Micah best. You said—"

"Pfff." Her mother shook her head. "What I like is nothing. What's not to like about a pleasant young man from a *goot* family with a face like his?" She raised a warning finger. "Always you were the logical one. Even as a child. Thinking. Sensible. But maybe for this picking of a husband, you are too sensible."

"I don't understand," Ellen protested. "You always said that marriage was a great responsibility, that a woman had to choose carefully because it would dictate the rest of her life."

"*Jah.* True, true," her mother agreed. "But it is not that simple. For me…well, you know that I came from a family…" She struggled for the words. "Not rich, but comfortable. Very comfortable, with rich land and big barns full of fat cattle. So many horses to work the land we had to have a separate stable for them. There was another young man who came courting me, and my *mutter* and *vadder* liked him best because his family had even more land than we did. He was a preacher's son with his own dairy farm, while your *vadder* was poor, without a cow to his name. No disrespect to your *vadder.* They wanted only that I, their daughter, should be well cared for."

"But you loved *Dat* and so you chose him."

"*Jah.* Sometimes a woman must follow her heart. Logic said marry the man with the farm, but your *vadder* warmed my heart."

"And you never doubted your choice?"

"*Nay,* never once. We have been happy together. Our greatest trouble was that I could not give him a houseful of sons and daughters. But he never blamed me. And he does not blame me now that my tongue says the wrong word and that I forget—"

A loud knock at the door interrupted her *mam*. "Ellen!"

"Coming, Micah," she answered. Ellen leaned close and kissed her mother's cheek. "Thank you," she murmured.

"Is that Micah?" her *mutter* asked. "Is he looking for gingerbread? Tell him I'll bake gingerbread tomorrow."

"He's taking me to work. To the shop."

"Is your *vadder* going to the shop?"

Ellen shook her head. "He's staying here with you. I'll be late this evening."

"Micah's taking you?"

"Jah." Ellen removed her work apron and donned the starched one she wore at the store. "Just a second, Micah." She hurried out onto the porch. "Just let me get my scooter."

"Don't bother," Micah said. "I'm coming back for you."

"But…we always take my scooter."

"No need for it," he said firmly. "I'm looking out for you now."

As Micah guided Samson out of Ellen's lane and onto the blacktop, she looked back toward the house. Micah was right. He was picking her up after work; she didn't need her scooter. But not having it made her uneasy.

They always took the scooter in the back of the buggy so that she'd have it if she wanted it. It wasn't about needing the scooter so much as knowing it was there if she did need it. Or want it. It was silly of her, but the farther she got from home, the more the absence of the green scooter became like a thorn in her heel that she couldn't pluck out. It was a dull ache she couldn't dismiss.

If she was unusually quiet on the ride to Honeysuckle, Micah didn't seem to notice. He was as entertaining as always, relating a story about an Amish farmer he'd met at the sawmill. There was no traffic on the road, and Samson was moving along at a good clip when raindrops began splattering on the horse's back.

"See, it's starting to rain." Micah gestured toward the sky. "Wouldn't you have been a fine sight riding home after dark in the rain on that scooter of yours?"

Ellen squirmed on the seat. Her distress was making her more uncomfortable by the moment. She didn't want to be warm and dry and safe in the buggy with Micah; she wanted to be on her scooter. It made no sense. She didn't know why she felt she'd been wronged when all Micah was doing was trying to take care of her, but that was exactly how she felt.

She'd heard other girls talk about wedding jitters. This must be what they meant. It was probably just the excitement of their pending announcement that was making her feel like she didn't fit in her own skin. She hadn't been herself since Saturday. She nibbled at her bottom lip, thinking about how excited she had been that morning, how eager she'd been to go to the apple frolic. She'd had a wonderful time, and the day had ended with the problem of her husband solved.

She should be relieved, she told herself. She should be elated that Neziah had made the decision of which brother to choose for her.

But then she thought about what her mother had said to her in the kitchen. Her words reverberated in Ellen's head. *If Micah doesn't make you feel that way, then maybe you'd better think some more.*

Did Micah make her feel *that way*? Was his face the last thing that came to mind before she fell asleep and the first thing she imagined when she opened her eyes in the morning?

She squeezed her eyes shut, not caring if she looked silly.

She loved Micah. She *did.*

But did she love him as a husband or a friend? And was part of the excitement having handsome, popular Micah court her? Had she been influenced by what everyone else thought? She loved him, but was she *in love* with him? Would she ever be?

The thought of her scooter sitting in the shed came to mind again and she opened her eyes. Suddenly, she realized it wasn't the scooter she cared about, it was the fact that Micah didn't understand how important her scooter was to her. How important her independence was to her. "Stop," she said abruptly. "Micah, stop the buggy."

"What?" He looked down the road and then glanced in the mirror. "What's wrong? Did I miss something?"

"Please, Micah." She bunched her skirt in both her hands and stared straight ahead at the wet pavement. This was crazy, but she couldn't help herself. She couldn't ride another moment in the buggy. "Stop the horse. I have to get out."

"What do you mean you have to get out? In the rain?"

She gripped the dashboard and got to her feet, even though the buggy was still rolling.

"I mean it, Micah. Stop the horse or I'm jumping out."

Micah reined in Samson and turned to her, his face flushed. "What's wrong? Did I say something to upset you? Did I do something?"

"*Nay*, Micah, you didn't. This isn't your fault. Please know that. It's mine. It's me." She reached out and gripped his upper arm and made herself meet his gaze. "I'm sorry, Micah, but I need to think. I have to be alone."

"Is this about your scooter?" He was upset now. She could tell that he was fighting to control his annoyance. "If you want the scooter that bad, I'll go back and—"

"It's not the scooter. Not really." Suddenly, her heart was pounding. "Oh, Micah, I think I've made a terrible mistake," she murmured as much to herself as to him.

"What do you mean, a *mistake*?" His shocked blue gaze locked with hers. "About what?" he asked suspiciously.

He knew.

"I can't marry you, Micah," she blurted, tears filling her eyes. She didn't want to hurt him, but to marry him would hurt him more someday. "I love you, but we're not right for each other. I'm just so sorry I didn't see it sooner."

"What...what do you mean you can't marry me? We're perfect for each other."

"*Nay*, we're not."

He looked away. "But I've told everyone we're going to be married. I'll look like a fool. What will I say to them?"

"That's what matters to you? What others will say?" she asked him.

He looked at her. Blinked. "What?"

She shook her head. Now she was even surer of herself than she had been a minute before. "You can tell people the truth. Tell them that we decided that we were better friends than husband and wife." She climbed down out of the buggy.

"Ellen, you can't be serious," he called down to her. "You can't break up with me."

"I'm sorry," she said once more. Then, straightening her shoulders, she started walking the way they had come. Raindrops wet her face and cheeks and arms, but she didn't stop. And she didn't look back.

Chapter Sixteen

By the time Ellen reached the end of her parents' lane, the spits of rain had turned to full-fledged raindrops, but if she squinted she was certain that it looked brighter to the west. The way the clouds were scudding overhead and the way the air smelled, it seemed to her that serious rain might miss them and the sun might come out. Either way, she'd made up her mind to go to the shop. If it cleared, she'd take her scooter. If it was going to rain, maybe she'd just take the buggy.

It was funny how it was Micah's insistence that she leave her scooter behind that had brought her to the realization that she couldn't marry Micah. She felt bad about the way she had broken the news to him; she knew she'd hurt him. But better to endure short-term pain than one that would stretch through years of marriage. Now Micah would be free to marry the woman God truly intended for him.

As she walked up her driveway she was surprised that thoughts of Neziah drifted through her head. She loved him. And not the way she had loved him as a young girl. She loved him for who he was now: a mature man, a father, a son, a brother.

Ellen fought back tears. What had she done? She'd made a mess of things, that was what. How could she have been so blind not to see it? She'd never stopped loving him and wondering how their courtship had gone wrong. It was Neziah whose plain face rose in her dreams… Neziah, whose fathomless, dark eyes touched a chord in her heart. But loving someone didn't mean that you couldn't live without him. Marriage had to be the coming together of *two* hearts and *two* minds.

But Neziah had been the one to reject her, she reminded herself. *Neziah* had decided she wasn't the one for him.

So now she would have neither of the Shetlers. Maybe God's plan for her had always been to remain unwed. This way, she could devote her life to caring for her parents. She wasn't unhappy. It was a life full of joy. She had friends, her faith, her family and a job that she looked forward to going to. If she didn't marry, she wouldn't have children of her own, but that wouldn't keep her from caring for other children. She could still help raise his little boys; she could volunteer to help other young mothers in her church. She could be content with the many blessings the Lord had bestowed on her.

Ellen continued trudging up the steep driveway, feeling older than thirty-three, wishing she'd been wiser, kinder. Micah hadn't deserved the way she'd sprung her decision on him. She hoped he would forgive her and that they would continue to remain friends. She hoped Simeon wouldn't be too disappointed with her. She didn't know how she would explain things to her parents. But somehow, she would make them understand that she just couldn't do it. It would be unfair to become Micah's wife if her heart longed for Neziah. Of course, she couldn't admit that to anyone, not even to her mother and father. That was too personal. They'd just have to accept her explanation that she'd decided not to marry. And they would accept it. They loved her unconditionally. No matter how they might wish she'd make another choice, they would support her decision.

What she'd done to Micah was awful, but going through with the courtship and wedding would have been worse. Marriage was forever. "God forgive me," she murmured. She only hoped that whatever gossip their parting caused in the community, it would be directed at her and not him. Micah had done nothing wrong. And neither had Neziah, honestly. He had the right to say she wasn't the wife for him, the same way she had the right to say Micah wasn't for her.

As Ellen walked into the yard, headed for the shed where she kept her scooter, her mother came bustling toward her. "What are you doing?" She'd thrown an old apron over her head to protect against the rain and peered out from beneath it at Ellen.

"*Mam*, it's raining. You shouldn't be out in the rain," Ellen admonished.

"Nonsense. Do you think I'll melt? I'm not a sugar cake." Her mother pulled the apron off her head and tugged her blue scarf in place over her gray hair. As always, her bun was secure and not a pin was out of place, a skill Ellen had never learned. "Didn't I see you ride away in Micah's buggy? I thought he was driving you to church service."

"Nay," Ellen replied gently. "It's not the Sabbath. Micah came to drive me to the craft shop."

Her mother's eyes narrowed suspiciously. "So why are you here? What's wrong? Did you and Micah quarrel?"

Ellen shook her head. "We didn't quarrel. But I've broken off with him. I can't marry him, *Mam*." She let her hands fall to her sides. "I'm sorry. I just can't."

"And what's wrong with Micah, I ask? Such a *goot*-looking boy. Such a hard worker. But naughty to make you late for church. Shame on him."

"It isn't Sunday, *Mam*," she repeated. "And, it's not Micah's fault that I refused him. Nothing like that. It's me. I don't love him—not in that way. In the way you talked about this morning." Rain ran off the shed's tin roof, dripping down the back of her dress. "Can we talk about this later? I need to get my scooter and go to work."

"On a Sunday? *Nay.* You'll not go to work on the Sabbath." Her mother pushed her firmly back into the shed and followed, stepping around the scooter that blocked part of the door. "Best you tell me all of it," her mother said.

Ellen felt like she had the time she was fourteen and had played hooky from school to spend the afternoon fishing with friends. Her mother had found out, and she'd been more concerned that Ellen didn't consider the gravity of her offense than angry. But the intensity of that concern had stung more than harsh words. Ellen hadn't repeated the mischief. And after that, she'd applied herself to her studies. Mam had never told her father, saying that it would disappoint him too much. That kindness had endeared her to Ellen and strengthened the bond between them.

"There's nothing to tell," Ellen hedged. "I made a mistake. I thought that I could marry Micah, that those feelings would come with marriage, that being his friend was enough. But it isn't."

Her mother folded her arms. "So? You feel the same about Neziah? You turned him down, too?"

"Neziah turned *me* down. He doesn't want to marry me." She'd told her mother that when it had happened, told both her parents when she'd announced that she'd be courting Micah only. Ellen didn't want to remind her that they'd already gone over this, especially since her mother had seemed so lucid earlier that morning. She'd given her good advice, advice that might have caused a problem today but would prove to be wise in the years to come.

"Neziah decided that I wasn't the right woman for him, remember?" Ellen explained softly. "Isn't that what courtship is for, so that both parties will have the opportunity to get to know each other?"

"*Jah*, that is true," her mother agreed. She tilted her head to one side and tapped the side of her nose in the way she did when she was thinking hard. "But why did Neziah decide not to marry you? Was he thinking of his happiness or yours?"

"His," Ellen replied quickly. "I'm sure…at least…" She hesitated. "I think…"

To her surprise, her mother did an unusual thing. She put her arms around Ellen and whispered, "You are sure you know Neziah's mind, or you *think* you know his mind?" She peered into Ellen's eyes. "There's a difference."

Ellen's throat constricted. "I…I'm sure," she answered. She returned her mother's embrace, amazed that she'd showed so much emotion twice in the same day. Ellen was almost overcome with love for her. She'd never doubted it, but their relationship had been reversed for so long. Oftentimes she felt like the mother instead of the daughter. But at this instant, everything was as it should be. She hugged her mother tightly.

"Doesn't sound like you're sure to me. Best find out. You must go to him," her mother said firmly as she let go of her. "To Neziah."

"To Neziah? I can't do that. What would I say to him?"

Her mother released her and stepped away. "You must go to him and tell him that you've broken off with his brother. That you made a mistake and that he's the one you should have chosen."

Ellen stared at her mother. "I didn't...didn't say that."

Her *mam* smiled. "I'm old, and sometimes I'm confused, but I'm not blind. Go to him, daughter. Tell Neziah the truth."

"And then what? What good will it do?" Ellen asked. "It's too late."

"Nay." Her mother chuckled. "When you're in the grave, only then is it too late to right wrongs. I'm not saying you telling him how you feel will change anything. It probably won't, but you'll have done the right thing.

You'll say your prayers tonight with a clear conscience. Now, gather your courage and go to him. Now."

"Now?" Ellen's eyes widened. "I…I can't go now. I have to open the shop. Customers may—"

"Horse feathers. Dinah is there."

She shook her head. "No, she has a doctor's appointment this morning."

"Then your father can hitch up the horse and we can go to the store ourselves. All day he putters around the house spying on me, fussing like a broody hen. You go and make right what you have made wrong with your Neziah." She stepped back to the open shed door and called. "*Vadder!* Where are you?"

Ellen tried in vain to think of a reason not to do as her mother ordered.

Her mother glanced back at her and made a shooing motion. "What are you standing there for? It's stopped raining. Take your silly green scooter and go find Neziah."

Ellen was halfway up the Shetler lane when she realized that there was no reason to believe that Neziah would be at the house at that time of the morning. He would be at the sawmill. She hadn't heard the grinding of the big saw, but if Neziah wasn't there, he could be away from the farm buying or surveying uncut timber. Joel would be at school, and Asa would be with Simeon. Ellen hoped she wouldn't meet Simeon before she found Neziah; she was unprepared to explain her decision not to marry Micah.

It hadn't stopped raining as her mother had said, but it was more of a drizzle than a downpour. Much of the lane passed under trees, and they dripped an unending series of drops on her head and clothing. The dirt road was hard-packed and not so steep as her own driveway, but the rain had made the surface slick. When she reached the fork that led to the sawmill, it became easier to walk than to use her scooter. She propped it up against a fence post and hurried on toward the mill.

A movement at the wood line caught her attention. Just coming out of the trees was a team of oxen pulling a massive log. Two men walked beside the animals, one tall, and the other shorter and stockier. It was too far to be certain, but from the way he carried himself, Ellen guessed that the taller man was Neziah and the other, one of his employees. She waved and shouted.

On her second attempt, Neziah saw her

and waved back. He left the plodding team and cut across the field toward her. Ellen's heart sank as warm needles of rain pattered against her face and arms. Wet grass under her shoes squished with every step she took, and tendrils of her wet hair clung to her face. She wished she hadn't come. What was she thinking? Now, not only would she embarrass herself in front of Neziah, but they'd have a witness.

"Ellen!" Neziah called. "What are you doing out in this rain?" He tugged off his raw-hide gloves and banged them against his trousers to knock off the mud. "Is everything all right?"

She walked toward him. His shirt was soaked through, and it clung to his broad chest and shoulders. His boots were muddy and the bottom of his trousers caked with bits of leaves and dirt. His straw hat was dark with moisture and bore bits of twigs.

Ellen swallowed hard as they met half-way. She wondered how she could have ever thought his features plain. A flush of heat washed over her throat and crept up to scald her cheeks. Looking at Neziah here in the fields, his callused hands scarred and blis-tered from the heavy work of cutting timber and handling logs, his stride so confident and graceful. He didn't need the beard to identify him as a mature man. That was evident in his gaze and in his bearing. Next to him, she realized, handsome Micah was still a boy.

"I need to talk to you," she said, her voice sounding oddly vulnerable to her ears. "I've broken off the betrothal with Micah."

He stared down at her. His features revealed nothing of what he was thinking. "This is no place to talk. You'll catch your death of cold." He motioned toward the sawmill's main building. "Let's get inside, out of the rain."

Numbly, she followed him. This was worse than she'd thought it would be. Why had she let her mother convince her to talk to Neziah today, while she was still reeling from the implications of what she'd done? As they walked quickly toward shelter, it began to rain harder, and she started to shiver.

When they reached the overhang that ran around the side of the building Neziah said, "Let me find you something to put on. Wait here." Seconds later he was back with an old denim jacket. She stood stock-still as he draped it around her shoulders.

It smelled like sawdust, the forest and Neziah. She huddled inside the coat, wishing she could disappear. “I…I told your brother I can’t marry him,” she said.

“And why would you do that?” He was standing very close. His dark gaze held hers.

She sucked in a breath. “Because…because I don’t love him.”

“But you had told him that you *would* marry him?” Neziah’s tone was matter-of-fact, not accusing. Calm.

“I did, but it was a mistake, a terrible mistake.”

“I see.”

She sneezed, and to her shame, her nose was beginning to run. Neziah pulled a clean handkerchief from his back pocket and handed it to her. Gratefully, she took it.

“And now you’ve come to tell me.”

She nodded.

“In the rain. You rode your scooter here in the rain to tell me?” He offered her the hint of a smile.

“I don’t love Micah,” she repeated. “I can’t marry him.” She wiped her nose with his handkerchief again.

He clasped the leather gloves in his hands, twisting them as he spoke, his eyes watching her. “And you won’t change your mind about Micah?”

Ellen shook her head. "*Nay*. I won't."

"Is there someone else?" he asked.

She averted her gaze. Why was he making this so hard for her? "I shouldn't have come here," she said. "I just…I didn't want you to think…" She trailed off. Why *had* she come? "I'm sorry. I guess I just wanted to tell you."

"But there is someone else?" he pressed. "Another man you'd rather have?"

She nodded dumbly. "But it's impossible. He doesn't feel that way about me."

"He doesn't?"

"Nay."

"And you're certain of that?" He took a step toward her.

Her shivering had become shaking. She wanted to run. "He told me so." She lifted her gaze to meet his, afraid she would burst into tears at any moment. "You…you told me in the orchard."

"I told you that I didn't want to marry you?" He smiled. "*Nay*, Ellen, I didn't say that. I said that I thought you and Micah would be happier together. It was *your* happiness that I was thinking of. But if you don't want him, then there's no reason why I can't marry you. Is there?"

She stood there for a moment, staring up at

him, him staring down at her. "You *do* want to marry me? After the way I've behaved? The trouble I've caused your family?"

"You can be trouble," he agreed. "But then, I think most things worth having can be." He hesitated and then went on. "Don't you see? I've never stopped loving you, Ellen." His smile widened. "So if you've behaved unwisely, you are no worse than me." He chuckled. "Of course, if we are to consider marriage, I have conditions."

She didn't know if she wanted to laugh or cry. Neziah wanted to marry her! He wanted to marry her. "What conditions?" she asked suspiciously.

"I've had some time to think this over, and I'll warn you, it's take it or leave it."

She waited, unconsciously holding her breath.

"First, I don't believe I would be comfortable having you and Micah under the same roof. It would make things too awkward when he starts courting again and later brings home a wife. And my boys are mischief enough without my father adding salt to our butter, so we'll have to live with your parents." He grinned at her. "Until I can build you your own house, of course. Or a *grossdaddi* house for them, whichever you'd prefer."

She nodded. "*Jah*, I would like that. I would like to be close to my mother and father, so I can look after them. And my mother would love to have Asa and Joel at her table."

"*Goot.* That's settled." He reached for her hand. "And two, building a house costs money, so I think it would be best if you kept working at the shop. At least as long as you want to."

Tears clouded her eyes. "You mean it? You don't care if I work?"

"So long as I can hire a girl to help with the housework and tend to the boys. You can hardly be in two places at one time, can you?"

She shook her head.

"And one more thing."

"*Jah*, Neziah?" Her eyes were so clouded with tears that she could hardly make out his sweet, strong face, but she could feel the warmth of his coat around her.

"I think it would be a *goot* idea for you to continue to ride your scooter to work in the morning so you have a few minutes to yourself each day. The boys and I will pick you up in the afternoon. Does that sound right?"

"It sounds exactly right," she said.

"So you agree to my terms?"

She smiled at him through her tears. “I agree, Neziah. But…I have one requirement of my own.”

“Do you?”

She nodded. “November is the traditional time for weddings, and I’d like ours to be the first in the community this fall. We’ve wasted too much time already.”

“Agreed.” He pulled her into his arms and looked down into her face. He was so close that she could feel his warm breath. Her heart was pounding so hard she was certain that he must feel it through the thickness of the denim jacket and their clothing. “So, will you do me the honor of becoming my wife and the mother of my children?”

“I will, Neziah. With all my heart.”

Smiling, he bent and kissed her, and the kiss was every bit as wonderful as she had always imagined it would be. And in that instant, the tenderness of that caress washed away all her doubts. Her mind and her heart filled with joy. In spite of all her missteps and stumbles and the twists and turns of her journey, this was the path the Lord had laid out for her. And she intended to walk every step of the way with her hand in Neziah’s.

Epilogue

Chincoteague National Wildlife Refuge, Virginia
September, one year later

"There. Just as they told us at the Visitor's Center. We can see the whole Snow Goose Pool from the observation platform." Neziah propped his black push scooter against a post at the end of the walkway, and Ellen did the same with her green one.

They climbed the steps to the viewing platform, and Ellen raised her binoculars to scan the large, brackish pond. There were so many geese, ducks and waterbirds swimming and diving over the surface of the blue-green water that she didn't know where to aim her binoculars. It was early morning, and few visitors were out yet. This was fall migration for a multitude of bird species, but the only other birders they could see were far away. The closest, a man in fatigues wearing a cowboy hat, was sighting in a large telescope near the shore, several hundred yards away.

"Look, black-tipped skimmers." Neziah pointed out a line of gangly, black-and-white waterbirds with distinctive black-tipped red beaks swooping over the surface of the pond.

Ellen turned in the direction he indicated and watched the skimmers scooping up small fish until they swooped in perfect formation and soared out of sight along the edge of the marsh. "Be sure and write them down," she reminded him. Neziah was keeping a tally of species and numbers of each kind of bird that they sighted each day.

Their vacation, actually a belated honeymoon, was to be a week long, and this was their third day at the refuge. Neziah had asked her where she wanted to go, and she'd chosen Chincoteague for bird-watching during the fall migration. They'd saved all year so that they could hire a driver to take them to and from Virginia, stay in a motel, eat in restaurants and have enough money for admission to the refuge.

Although they had taken accommodations

on Chincoteague, the refuge was actually on Assateague Island, across the channel. There were over fourteen thousand acres of beach, marsh, dunes and maritime forest teeming with birds and other wildlife, including sitka deer, wild ponies and the elusive fox squirrels.

For Ellen, this was a dream come true. Neziah shared her fascination with bird-watching, and the trip was a welcome escape from their everyday life at home. If the sight of two Old Order Amish pushing their scooters along the Wildlife Loop or parking them outside the Tom's Cover Visitor Center did attract a little attention from the tourists, Ellen didn't care. She'd seen her first oystercatcher that morning, and the day before they'd sighted a merlin, a flock of piping plovers and six brown pelicans.

Neziah pointed to a broad-winged bird circling high over the pool. "Eagle," he said. "Must be a young one. Has the white tail but not much white on the head yet." He studied the bird through the binoculars she'd given him for his birthday, identical to the ones he'd presented her with as a wedding gift the previous November.

Ellen sighed with pleasure. This trip was everything she'd imagined it might be when they'd spent hours going over the maps and brochures describing the refuge and the restaurants and lodging available on Chincoteague. Neziah had wanted to bring her in May for the spring migration, but her mother had fallen and broken her wrist. Ellen hadn't felt able to leave her at that time. The six of them were still living in her parents' home, but the *grossdaddi* house would be ready for her mother and father to move into by the end of the month. When her father had opted for downsizing to a smaller space, Neziah had started planning for the cottage addition to the house. It had a separate entrance and another off the parlor so that there would be easy access for any of them to move back and forth between the two homes.

The children had settled into their new home easily. Asa continued to spend much of his day with Simeon while Joel was in school. Sometimes, Ellen took Asa to the shop with her, and other days he accompanied his father to the woods or his uncle Micah to the sawmill. Micah was courting a sweet girl from the next town over and seemed to have completely gotten over Ellen, with no hard feelings. Slowly Joel and Asa had come to think of Ellen as their mother, and she had come to love them both. She was still concerned about Joel's tendency to fill up on sweets when he was with Simeon, but she was gradually bringing order into both boys' lives. As she'd expected, her mother had gathered them into her arms and heart. Joel was surprisingly protective of his new *grossmama* and gave little trouble to Maddie, the girl they had hired to keep an eye on both of them. Her father, likewise, adored Asa and Joel, often spending hours making them wooden toys and teaching them how to care for the chickens and how to coax the largest and sweetest tomatoes from the garden.

Neziah stepped back from the railing and slipped an arm around Ellen's shoulders. She smiled up at him, and her heart leaped as she remembered the sweetness of their time together in the hotel room, with its private balcony and view of the water and marshland. The previous night had been a full moon, and the shadowy outline of the Assateague Lighthouse had loomed over the treetops.

"We should do this every year," he said. "Get away for a few days, just the two of us. I like having you all to myself."

She smiled up at him. She was content with life at home in Lancaster County. Her friends, her family, her community, their church and their children were there. Married life suited her, fitting as easily as a worn leather glove that was soft and warm and protective. She'd loved Neziah on the day they'd made their marriage vows, but that feeling had grown with each day that passed. They did not always agree, and some problems required patience and wisdom to solve, but they solved them together, cementing their bonds with love and respect and caring. Like his driving animal, Neziah had substance. There was no doubt in her mind that she had picked exactly the right man. Or perhaps… She smiled. Perhaps he had been chosen for her.

"We should come next May," Neziah suggested, pulling her back into the moment. "For the spring migration."

"Maybe," she answered. "That's a long way off to make definite plans." She had her own reason for thinking next May might not be possible, but she wasn't ready to share that hope with him yet. They had been praying for a child and though it was early yet, she suspected that that prayer had been answered.

"Hungry?" he asked.

She laughed. "Starving." They'd had coffee and a donut before they'd come out to the refuge, but he'd promised her a full breakfast with eggs and pancakes and sausage. There was a good restaurant with reasonable prices on the main street of town. It was a real treat to eat meals that she didn't have to cook or wash up after. In fact, she was ravenous. She was hungry enough to eat one of those snow geese if it came close enough. That was another reason she suspected that she might be with child. No morning sickness for her. She slept like a rock and woke wanting to eat everything in sight.

"A good thing you made me buy that scooter," Neziah said. "Otherwise, we'd have a long walk back across the bridge and into Chincoteague. And we need to have a good breakfast. We have that boat tour at two this afternoon." Neziah had reserved places for them weeks ago.

"Maybe I'll have the fisherman's breakfast," she told him, her mouth practically watering at the thought. "The one with two eggs, sausage, fried potatoes and bacon."

"Keep on like this and you'll get as plump as Maddie."

"Would you mind?" she teased. "If I did?"

"More to squeeze." Playfully he encircled her with both arms and backed her against the railing. “Have I told you this morning how beautiful you are?”

“Only once,” she replied. She stood on tiptoe and brushed his lips with hers, as bold as any English girl kissing her husband in full view of the world. “But I liked it very much.”

“And I like you very much,” he answered, looking full into her eyes. “There’s just one thing I’d like to get straight between us. A small pebble in my shoe that keeps rubbing.”

“With me?” She tried to think what she might have done lately that might not have met his approval.

“It’s your scooter,” he said, straight-faced, his eyes serious.

“My scooter? What’s wrong with my scooter?” She folded her arms, ready to make a stand. “You said that you wanted me to keep my scooter. To ride it to work. And now you’ve bought one of your own. And you just said how useful it is.”

Neziah grimaced. “It’s the color.”

“It’s green. It’s always been green.”

He nodded. “It is. As green as a lime popsicle. A very bright green. I was thinking, maybe we could buy a can of spray paint. And paint both scooters a nice shade of forest-green. So as not to scare the birds.”

She could hardly hold back a chuckle. "Not to scare the birds," she repeated.

"Jah." He grinned. "To blend in with the trees so we could sneak up on the warblers."

"Maybe," she said. "It would be more Plain. Not so worldly."

Neziah chuckled, and she laughed with him. He clasped her hand and they walked back together toward their scooters and all the years of peace and happiness that stretched out ahead of them.

* * * * *

Dear Reader,

I'm delighted to invite you to travel from Seven Poplars, Delaware, to the Old Order Amish community of Honeysuckle in Lancaster County, Pennsylvania for a special Love Inspired series, Lancaster Courtships.

In *The Amish Bride*, Ellen Beachey, unmarried and past thirty with aging parents and a fulfilling life, is startled to receive a shocking proposal from her father's closest friend and neighbor. Urged to accept the challenge by her family and still hoping to be a wife, Ellen finds herself swept into courtship by not one, but two suitors. She wants to follow God's plan for her, but how can she choose between two very different brothers? And which man will give her the forever love of her dreams without destroying both families?

And I hope you'll return to Seven Poplars in Delaware in February 2016 to meet Mari, the next prospective bride in the Amish Matchmaker series. Mari has wandered away from her Amish roots, but comes home to find love and acceptance with the Yoders and their friends.

Come join us for more laughter and friendship. There's always room at my table for one more; I keep the kettle on and warm scones on the back of the woodstove. Until we meet again, dear friend, be well and God bless.

Sincerely yours,
Emma Miller